A RAIN OF BLOOD

A RAIN OF BLOOD

Andrew
Go for it !
I'm here to help
Rick

Rick Lee

Paperback: 978-1-63767-409-3
eBook: 978-1-63767-410-9
Library of Congress Control Number: 2021916881

The author has his own website: www.crimewritingfiction.com

Ordering Information:

BookTrail Agency
8838 Sleepy Hollow Rd.
Kansas City, MO 64114

Printed in the United States of America

Contents

Acknowledgements

Thanks once again to my readers
Shura Price, Bruce Paterson and Nadine Venn.

Thanks to David H Wallace
at The Gallery Melrose
for 'the confession on the back of a painting' idea

MAY DAY

AD 1200

Silence fills the space.

The surrounding beeches flutter a few times and then are still. In the middle is a huge yew tree, its trunk all gnarled and twisted.

The horse's ears are pricking. The rider can feel the ripples in her muscles and her restrained breathing. Sweat cools and dribbles down her shining neck and haunches.

The rider is also restless, his eyes darting hither and thither, trying to catch any sly movement. His ears strain to pick up the soft fracture of a branch or a shuffle in the dry leaves.

But nothing. Just a slight zephyr not even strong enough to move another leaf.

He waits. Hand on his sword.

He can see the abbey across the river.

The sun has gone behind the clouds. The air fills with the scent of rain.

Lord Mercadier is dead.

Easter Sunday. There were six of them. Brandin's men, but at King John's bidding. He almost certainly killed one and maimed two others, but they prevailed. Hacked him to death. Butchered him like he was a malevolent bull.

He bade me go as he saw them coming out of the shadows.

I said no, but the sting of his hand knocked me against the wall.

I ran, tears spitting from my face.

The shame of the traitor, a coward, will haunt me till mine own death, which I fear is not long away.

The journey was long, the weather worse. I thought I was going to die in the raging sea. But now his will is done.

The treasure is safe in the care of my father. My promise is fulfilled. I pray he will now forgive me.

Something tells me something's coming.

    An arrow?   Or a whisper?

      Or just rain?

The moment lasts for ever.

JULY
2014

CHAPTER 1
BLO⊙D

LA CREUSE, FRANCE

It wasn't the blood.

Cécile Coquelin had been born on a farm. As a child she'd seen the twitching chickens on the washing line splattering their ruby guts all over the courtyard. And the Toussaint pig as it slathered itself in its own gore. And the gush of brightness spraying from the neck of a calf as its legs inexplicably splayed beneath its astonished body.

And she was a nurse. Not in the first flush of goodwill, checking a shallow pulse or redoing an ill-made bed. She'd done her training and her first five years in Montpellier and had seen enough blood spewing out of knife and gunshot wounds to harden any heart.

And even though she'd not seen much blood in the last few years as an *infirmière*, she had become accustomed to finding old people dead on her arrival.

It wasn't even the amount of blood.

It was whose blood that shocked her.

Made her gasp, hand over her mouth.

She staggered back out to the car and leant against it, telling herself to take deep breaths as she fumbled in her pocket for her mobile.

And when the calm voice answered, she couldn't find the right words, although some came anyway.

'Blood. So much blood. Everywhere.'

She didn't remember much after that. The *pompiers* found her sitting in the mud with her back to the wheel arch, her car door still open. One of them knelt beside her.

'Cécile?' he said.

Without looking she raised her arm and pointed desultorily at the house and the open door as though she couldn't be bothered to give them any more help.

The other two *pompiers* approached warily. The older one led the way. He took one look inside and then put his hand on his younger companion's chest and pushed him back. After taking a deep breath he whispered urgently to him, and the younger man's eyes went wide. He nodded, pulled away and spoke rapidly into his radio mike.

The first man indicated he should change places, so the younger man went and held Cécile's hand and watched as his older colleagues, faces grim with determination, nodded at each other and walked through the door into the dark interior.

Like Cécile, they had seen terrible things. Severed limbs, crushed bodies, burnt carcasses, but nothing like what was in that house.

When – and it wasn't often – they were asked to describe that horror, they said they couldn't. Meaning they'd nothing to compare it to, nothing to give the interrogator an idea of what they saw and smelt. The words *abattoir* and *bloodbath* crossed their lips, but they didn't seem enough somehow.

And it was the same for them as it was for Cécile. They just couldn't take in that this act of carnage had been inflicted upon the particular occupants of that house.

They knew not to disturb anything. But, in all honesty, they wouldn't have wanted to. They stepped outside and stared at their footprints on the stone flags. They were still standing there when the police arrived. The first officer unwisely ignored the shaking heads and walked briskly past them. In the circumstances it seemed a long time before he reappeared, staggering backwards, until he turned. And, fighting his body's urgent need to express its revulsion, he stumbled across the road into some bushes and noisily ejected the entire contents of his stomach.

The other officers were more circumspect, but most of them fared little better.

It was only the scene of crime officers, with their gallows humour and cast-iron constitutions, who were able to manage any lengthy exposure to the interior.

Picat, the pathologist, took less than ten minutes on his initial examination. But he had little to say to the prosecutor, who had arrived to find a grim and silent crew who couldn't maintain eye contact for long with him or anyone else.

Cécile was driven home.

It was many weeks before she returned to work. And, from then on, she would always call out her client's name before entering a house, even the old folk she'd known for years.

Her nightmares never stopped.

~

'Bugger.'

Ex-Detective Inspector Fletcher looked down at the little white ball that sat disdainfully in the long grass by his feet.

He glanced forward to see the backs of his three companions as they walked away. Had they seen his air shot? He gripped the club and hacked at the ball as hard as he could.

In disbelief he saw the bloody thing fly effortlessly towards the left of the fairway and heard the crack of wood as it hit one of the big beeches.

Geoff shouted back at him as he pointed towards the green.

'You jammy sod.'

Fletcher couldn't see his ball, but he grinned to himself. About time he had a bit of luck. Stupid bloody game.

As it turned out, the ball was three feet from the edge of the green, and although it took him two more shots, with his two-shot handicap he was still the best ball for the hole.

Geoff filled in the card and they walked to the next tee.

The foursome in front of them were searching for someone's ball, so they sat on the bench and relaxed.

Fletcher contemplated the scene. What the hell was he doing there?

'The rest of your family here yet, Fletch?' asked Tom.

Fletcher nodded.

'They arrived on Saturday. It'll be utter chaos.'

The others laughed.

'How many did you say there were?'

Fletcher looked at Steve. How could you talk seriously to a man who drove a Jaguar S-type and wore a pink jumper with green trousers?

'Er... We're now...' He had to stop and count. 'Eighteen.'

'Bloody hell,' said Steve. 'A horde of rabbits.'

Fletcher sighed. Steve wasn't far off. They are the huge tribe he'd inadvertently inherited through Laura's daughter Grace.

She'd married Quill – Sunday name Torquill de Camville – who had three brothers. They all had children, and so it was like living in a tribe.

Before anyone could comment any further about this, Geoff pointed away towards the clubhouse.

'Is that Julie running over there?' he asked.

They watched as the young woman approached the four men further up the fairway. One of them pointed in their direction and she set off towards them.

She wasn't overweight or anything, but by the time she reached them she was fighting for breath.

Fletcher and his three friends stared at her as she gathered herself, all of them thinking the worst.

But it was his name she spoke when she could.

He had arrived in the Dordogne a fortnight ago. One of the houses the de Camvilles had inherited was a pleasantly dilapidated mid nineteenth-century bourgeois house on the outskirts of a small town west of Limoges. Quill's mother had inherited it from her parents, but it had long been the family's escape hole. Now it was her grandchildren who were enjoying that freedom that they didn't experience in England.

On this occasion Fletcher had ended up being the token adult until the arrival of the rest of the family at the end of July. Quill's two nieces, Tillie and Jo, had started their holidays earlier and were trying hard not to kill each other while waiting for their cousins to arrive.

Fletcher was helped in the daily peacekeeping activities by a young au pair, Elise, a local girl, who was hoping that the summer would improve her English. Fletcher had no such linguistic hopes. His French was terrible.

He was also missing Laura, who had stayed at home to look after her ailing mother, who was hanging on to life with a doggedness that filled Fletcher with dread. She was barely conscious most of the time. And, when she was, she hadn't a clue who they were. So it was decided that he was to put on the blue uniform of the UN while Laura took on the Red Cross role. They hadn't spent so long apart for years, and Fletcher was missing her – although he'd never admit it.

Anyway, things had looked up ever since he was re-acquainted with a group of ex-pats who dragged him off for rounds of excruciatingly dreadful golf followed by cards and pool in the local bars.

This teenage lifestyle was exacerbated by numerous drinking bouts and long slow evenings round the dinner table. The one thing that Fletcher could do was cook. He and Laura had come to this agreement when they'd taken up running the pub back in Todmorden. He supervised the cooking and she ran the bar, which probably saved his life! The food side had become more and more successful and he had less and less time to drink the profits.

Now that was all in the past and they were used to being part of the troupe of grandparents that came with Quill's family. It took Fletcher some time to control the chip on his shoulder about people with a 'heritage', but gradually he'd slipped effortlessly into the role of old 'grumpston' and was surprised to find this was a big hit with the grandchildren, no matter how hard he tried to fend them off. Even though he was in his sixties, he was still a big kid and enjoyed the rough and tumble of the kick-abouts and had introduced them to various other games he'd played as a kid. He was happy.

His days of being a cop seemed long, long ago and he had no intention of revisiting them. Apart from anything else he couldn't cope with the technology. Computers and mobiles, emails and texting – his only defence was a resolute contempt. He'd only agreed to a mobile as a safety precaution, but rarely used it. He got involved in a fraud case with the son he didn't know he had a couple of years ago, but that only served to remind him of what he hated about the whole business and confirmed his long-held belief that the real villains were becoming more and more untouchable.

Best of all was the absence of a television, a decision made by the parents, which the kids moaned about for a bit and then forgot all about it and being so far from any mobile coverage meant no access to all their twittering.

The golfers also had a non-Brexit talk rule, so all that had receded into the ether as well.

Eventually, and perhaps just in time, the rest of the family, apart from Laura, began to arrive. Fletcher set off to the airport to pick up one lot, whilst another battalion arrived under their own steam. Later in the day, Laura phoned to say she was on her way as the Macmillan nurses had told her to get out from under their feet. And so it was one perfect late July afternoon the whole family was lounging about in the garden, tables groaning with food and drinks to hand; Quill had been to fetch his Aunt Marie-Thérèse and Uncle Pascal and they were now seated centre stage telling the English their local news. Fletcher was finding this difficult, as Quill, his three brothers and many of the wives and children could all speak French. So he sat a few feet away, a cold beer in his hand, and let the incomprehensible chatter flow over him.

Through his half-closed eyes he watched as this gregarious but cantankerous family reassembled themselves into their accustomed roles. He couldn't imagine being like Quill. He only had one much older sister, who he hadn't seen for at least five years.

The four de Camville brothers could be told apart, but they were undeniably from the same gene pool. Yellowy-red hair and bright blue eyes were the instantly recognisable signature, although Fletcher reflected on how much each one's individual hairstyle belied their different characters. Quill, with his no-nonsense clinical number two; Rollo, the jazz musician, who had long, flowing locks and a Cavalier moustache; William, the unreconstructed hippie with his unbrushed hair tied back in a loose ponytail and Geoffrey, the bad apple, the only one to sport the floppy-haired Brideshead look and the superior smirk to go with it – all chattering away in a second language as though they'd lived here all their lives.

Their other halves were a different matter. Grace had still not adopted the longer hairstyle her mother favoured. Fletcher smiled as she turned to look at him while he studied her slim form weaving from one group to the next. She smiled back and brushed her hands through the short dark bob cut she'd had since he first met her. Gwyneth was picking beans, looking like one of Van Gogh's farm workers, with her muscled bronzed arms and shoulders, billowing Moroccan trousers and long brown hair coiled up in a loose chignon. The children all gravitated to her, coming and going, as she suggested jobs they could be doing or games they could be playing.

And Harriet, sitting to one side in the shade in a black dress, her face serious, a book balanced on her knee, watching. Like Fletcher. She returned his look. A slight arch of her left eyebrow and twitch of a smile on her lips. Glossy black hair severely tied back in a tight bun. Dark red lips. Self-composed and difficult to read. Didn't say much. Didn't drink. Went to bed early … but he knew that this belied a vicious sexual appetite that he was determined to avoid.

He escaped her transfixing gaze and looked for Tina. Christina Lucca was Rollo's latest. Tillie and Jo weren't her children. She was much younger than the rest of the women and was slightly embarrassed by her peripheral position. Rollo had that effortless, thoughtless ability to move from one beautiful woman to another, but once he'd acquired them he seemed to forget they were there. She stood uncertainly under the cherry tree, trying to feel her way in.

Inevitably it was Grace who took her arm and took her over to meet Marie-Thérèse. Fletcher couldn't hear what was being said, but knew that the old lady was speaking to Tina in Italian. Within minutes the young woman became much more animated. Her eyes shone and her shy laughter drifted across to him as she relaxed in the old woman's company.

Fletcher sighed and closed his eyes.

Later, as the twilight descended and Elise lit the yellow mosquito-repellent candles, William and Geoffrey set light to the wood of the bonfire they'd collected. Fletcher watched out of the corner of his eye as these two surreptitiously passed round the dope. One or two of them glanced over to where he was sitting, even though they knew he'd never said a word about it. He smiled to himself as he remembered his own brief dalliance with drugs, which led him back to the ongoing mystery of how on earth had he ended up with this lot.

The answer to this question squeezed his hand and whispered in his ear.

And so to bed.

⤙

'Fletch? Will you take William and the kids?'

Fletcher looked round to see which kids that might mean to find Ellie, Tillie and Alys grinning at him. A few yards away he could see Angharad looking a little downcast.

'Angie?' he said. 'Do you want to come as well?'

He ignored the face that Ellie was pulling at him as Angharad ran over with a big smile on her face.

'All aboard,' he shouted, and the girls ran to the car and sorted themselves out – meaning Ellie decided who sat where.

William got in beside him and they set off.

'How's the forest?' asked Fletcher.

William glanced across to see how serious this question was.

'It grows, lives and dies,' he replied, his eyes back on the road ahead as Fletcher accelerated onto the autoroute.

'Aye, well. It's no use me asking you anything more about that. You know I can't tell an oak from an ash,' laughed Fletcher.

William sighed.

'If something isn't done soon, you won't be able to see any ash,' he said disconsolately.

Fletcher patiently listened to the latest assault perpetrated on the UK countryside by the landowning classes. He wondered how William reconciled his passion for rural life with his own heritage.

'But you must exercise some control over the environment you work in, mustn't you?' he asked when there was a pause in the anti-establishment diatribe.

'Only through natural methods,' came the quick reply.

Fletcher thought he was already way out of his depth, so he changed the subject. William could always be relied upon to give you chapter and verse about the local history, so by the time they got to Terrasson Fletcher was back up to speed on the twenty-first century retaking of Aquitaine by the Little Englanders.

They arrived just after ten and found the market in full swing. Fletcher tagged on to the group heading straight for the bar via the boulangerie.

Ten minutes later they were looking out over the river at the tide of market-goers wading back and forth across the old humpbacked bridge. The river was low, revealing sandbanks and vegetation in the slow-moving water glinting in the bright sunlight.

'So how long will the Italian job last?' asked Geoffrey with a sneer, his hand elegantly holding his cigarette in the air as he lounged back on the chair.

'Eff off, you pompous bastard,' said Rollo. 'If you were any more jealous you'd turn into a bloody frog.'

'Ooh,' breathed Geoffrey. 'That's a bit raw.'

'Leave it,' said Quill.

'Yes, my lord,' laughed Geoffrey.

'And where's Cruella this morning?' asked Rollo.

Geoffrey glared at him and looked away.

Quill raised his eyebrows at Fletcher, who shrugged his shoulders. The four of them watched the world – or rather, if they were honest, the girls – go by.

Gradually the rest of the party arrived, carrying a variety of useful and not so useful items they'd bought or persuaded an adult to buy. Fruit and balloons. Vegetables and ice lollies. A couple of *fermier* chickens, still with their heads and feet, and a set of hula hoops.

The girls sang all the way back, and an hour later everyone was tucking into lunch.

This had been much the same pattern for the last fortnight: outing in the morning, swimming in the afternoon, long lead-in to food, followed by noisy cards or charades late into the night.

Laura made a phone call every day and managed to dry her eyes before she came back to the table. The girls practised their never-ending plays, while the two older boys went fishing and exploring the woods. The four brothers argued and made up. The women sighed and chattered away. Fletcher did a lot of watching and listening – enjoying a family life he'd never had before.

The days passed. Blue skies were replaced by blue skies. All the de Camville men went red and then crispy. Fletcher and the women went brown. Harriet stayed white. This is how it normally proceeded, although this time there seemed to be fewer rows – if you didn't count the bad losers at cards. But there were no hard feelings the next morning. Time melted one day into the next. Nobody watched the news or read a paper.

The battle lines of Brexit were forgotten – a relief to them all, even though it hadn't been that difficult – with only Geoffrey sticking up for the Leavers, and everyone knowing it was just to wind up his eldest brother.

Fletcher couldn't remember much of what happened after he drove back to the house. In fact he couldn't think how he had managed to drive at all.

At first, he couldn't get Laura to make any sense on the phone, but then Geoffrey took over and told him bluntly.

'Tonton and Tata have been murdered. You need to get back here.'

He found a house, which was usually ringing with laughter and chatter, eerily quiet. The adults sat in twos and threes, hugging each other.

None of them could take it in. It had even shaken Geoffrey out of his sarcastic, cynical view of life. And how could they explain this to the children?

Gwyneth took it upon herself to gather them all together in the old salon and talked to them for a good half hour.

'What did you say to them?' mumbled Quill, as the children came out and went off in twos and threes.

'A mixture of truth and half-truth,' she said, her eyes red with crying.

'So what do they know?' asked Harriet. Gwyneth looked at the woman she could never fathom. Harriet stared back her with a blank face. 'So that I don't confuse Alys, when she asks me,' she added, her dark eyes boring into Gwyneth's.

Gwyneth sat down.

'I said that Tata and Tonton had been attacked by burglars and had died from their injuries because they were old. I said they'd been very brave.'

'But you didn't say what injuries?' asked Harriet.

Gwyneth shook her head.

'Would you?' asked Quill.

Harriet turned her gaze on her brother-in-law.

14

'I think it's best if we all stick to the same story, don't you?' she replied.

Quill regarded this strange woman, whose relationship with Geoffrey had always puzzled him. He nodded.

'You're right,' he agreed.

All the other adults agreed as well.

~

The period between the attack and the funeral passed in a haze. If asked, many of the family would have been hard put to tell you what they'd done or where they'd been. Each one of them had been interviewed several times. They had nothing to tell the police. Although Marie-Thérèse and Pascal had come to the house, the family rarely went to their home. In fact the only regular visitors had been the three eldest girls, who would wander through the lanes to Tata's house and return with stories of cooking and Tonton's 'terrible tales'.

Quill and Grace had sat in while a woman sergeant gently probed at the girls' memories, but they had little to tell of any significance.

As the eldest member of the family, it was Quill who went to see the notaire. Maître Georges Virondeau had been retired for many years and was nearly as old as the Maladrys. But he'd insisted on dealing with the matter – which they could tell was of considerable relief to his son, who'd taken over his father's business.

'As they died childless, the issues are simple,' he said. 'As their only surviving relatives, you and your three brothers will receive a quarter of the estate each and will need to agree a similar proportion of their possessions.'

Quill shook his head.

'We're not in any state to deal with that yet,' he said.

'Of course not,' replied Virondeau. 'I'll wait until you tell me you're ready.'

The clock ticked on the wall as Quill stared unseeingly through the window at the sun-baked lawn. The old notaire cleared his throat.

'However, there is one other thing you need to know,' he said.

Quill slowly dragged his thoughts back into the room. 'What?' he asked.

'Your daughter, Eleanor. How old is she now?'

Quill frowned.

'Ellie? She's – er – twelve. Why?'

Virondeau leant back and pulled out the drawer in his desk. Carefully, he lifted a small box from the drawer and placed it on the table.

Quill stared at it. It was old, he could tell that. Looked like it belonged in a museum. He could even smell its mustiness.

'What's that?' he asked.

'I've no idea what it contains,' said Virondeau. 'And Marie-Thérèse only gave it to me a few weeks ago…'

Quill shook his head in puzzlement.

The box sat squatly on the desk. For some reason he didn't like it. In fact he shivered.

'Why Ellie?'

'Your aunt didn't say. Just that if anything happened to her, Eleanor was to receive this box, and *only* she should open it. Marie-Thérèse was most insistent, in that quiet way she had.'

The two of them sat in silence for some time.

Quill looked at the old man, whose face was set in a stern expression.

'Perhaps after the funeral might be a good time,' he suggested.

Quill nodded and watched as the box was returned to the drawer.

He shook hands with the old man and allowed himself to be shepherded back out into the sunshine. He walked all the way home, forgetting that he'd come in the car.

Later he told Grace, and the two of them pondered over what might be in the old box. Neither of them was keen to share the myriad products of their imaginations, but the matter niggled away at them because they knew they'd have to deal with it as soon as the funeral was over.

∼

Fletcher was at a loss. He felt all their pain, but he'd hardly known the old couple. Pascal spoke a few words of English but it hadn't got them very far. He suspected that the old lady understood far more than she let on, but most of his stumbling attempts at bridging the language gap were met with a knowing smile and a cold hand laid gently on his wrist.

The only use he could make of himself was to ferry people here and there as most of them seemed to have lost the ability to concentrate, apart from the stern-faced Harriet. The two of them ended up doing most of the shopping. He and Laura did the cooking, while Gwyneth managed as a sort of washer-up and bedtime storyteller on autopilot.

It was an odd relationship. Harriet didn't seem to have any small talk at the best of times. In the current situation this was even further curtailed to nodding and pointing in the *Super Marche* or at the market stall. Like the rest of the family she spoke excellent French, but never engaged in the relentless banter the others had with the shopkeepers and bar staff. Nor did she speak the local argot, which Grace had informed him was Limousin Occitan.

Not that she went in bars anyway.

This arrangement lasted until people decided to go home. Rollo was the first to leave, citing work. He had gigs in Edinburgh and some recording to do. Tillie and Jo begged him to let them stay and were granted their wish.

The children kept out of the way, finding it difficult to deal with weeping or indifferent adults who seemed to have lost all sense of purpose.

The day of the funeral was hard. Lots of crying and standing around, not knowing what to do or say. They were not too astonished at the number of people who assembled in the small church. There had been a constant stream of sorrowful well-wishers knocking on their door since the day of the tragedy.

The old priest looked at them through rheumy eyes and delivered a mercifully short service, which included his own heartfelt memories of two of his oldest parishioners.

The police mingled with the crowd and could be seen questioning numerous people who they hadn't already interviewed.

Later that evening the adults sat round the dinner table and waited until Gwyneth reappeared from her storytelling round. No one had said there would be such a gathering, but even Tina had realised this wasn't the time to avoid an inevitable conversation.

As Gwyneth took her seat, Quill cleared his throat and reached for his glass. No words were said, but they all held their glasses aloft and remembered the old couple.

'I've nothing much to say,' said Quill. 'I don't begin to understand what has happened to us. But I intend to do my utmost to help the police apprehend the killers and see them punished for this … this terrible…'

Words failed him, and he bit back a heart-breaking cry. Grace reached out and held his hand. Some of them looked at one another. Others looked away. The room was silent, apart from a few suppressed sobs.

Suddenly a laconic voice broke the silence.

'While agreeing with your sentiment, dear brother, I can't for the life of me think what any of us can do.'

Geoffrey was sitting with his leg over the arm of the old chair he favoured. The company focused back on Quill, who looked at his younger brother in despair. But before he could reply, another voice cut through the growing sense of confrontation.

'I've got a few questions.'

They all turned to where Fletcher was sitting next to Grace.

He leant forward onto the table so that the light caught his face.

They waited.

'You might not like my questions or the implications, but I think there a few things you need to face up to – if you're serious about helping the police with their enquiries.'

One or two looked at each other with frowns on their faces.

'OK, Fletcher. You're an ex-copper. What is it? Thirteen, foureen years away from the front line? And that was back in the UK. You don't speak any French. How are you going to help?'

Fletcher smiled at Rollo.

'You're right. It's seventeen years, actually, if you don't count my intervention in a certain fraud case four years ago – where, I assure you, I wasn't at all welcome, even though I helped them get a result. But...'

Rollo took a swig of his drink.

'Some things never change. No matter where you are or the language you speak. And I'm pretty certain the police involved in this case are doing what I would have done all those years ago. The only difference is they've got more information.'

'How do you mean?' asked William.

'Computer records, CCTV, DNA and international cooperation for starters,' he said.

'Which you or we don't have access to,' said Rollo.

'You're right,' said Fletcher. 'And do you know why?'

There was a collective shaking of heads. Apart from Harriet, who now spoke.

'Because we are the prime suspects.'

Another collective sigh gathered. This time it was a collection of gasps, eye-widening and a rapid shift of focus.

'What?' said Rollo, momentarily knocked out of his 'We can't do anything' stride.

'She's right,' said Fletcher. 'That's why we've all been asked a lot of questions, but they haven't told us very much.'

Before any of them could respond to this he continued.

'It's the classic response. The first suspects are the people who find the victims. Considering in this case that it was everyone's favourite district nurse and a bunch of highly trusted firemen, I think we can assume that they were quickly eliminated from the enquiry. Second on the list are family and friends, who just happened to be readily to hand and who might have both access and motive.'

'Motive,' exclaimed Quill, pushing himself to his feet and knocking over his drink. 'What are you suggesting, Fletcher?'

'I'm just telling you the most probable train of thought the police would have followed, all right?'

Grace pulled Quill back into his seat, her lips set in a fierce line.

'Let him go on, Quill. Sensitivity has never been one of his strong points. But he does know what he's talking about. Bear with him.'

Fletcher smiled at her, but she didn't smile back.

'OK, Fletch. Tell us,' said Rollo.

'Well, as I was saying … we're within walking distance of the house. I'd be surprised if any of us could act as a reliable witness to each other's whereabouts that night. I for one can't even remember if I won or not.'

This brought a few half-grins to one or two faces.

'Can any of you for certain know where everyone else was that night?'

'OK. But, as Quill said, "Motive?"'

'Well. I don't know. The usual ones are money, money and … money.'

There was a deathly silence, broken only by the shuffling of awkward limbs and a few frowns and glances at each other.

Rollo managed a wry laugh.

'I can see your point, Fletch. We may look the part, but we've not a decent income between the lot of us. We might have inherited a few tumbledown ancient piles in some very desirable places, but none of us can afford the repairs and none of us are prepared to part with what we've got. I bet there isn't one of us who hasn't had an argument with their bank in the last six months, and as for savings… Well, it's not in the DNA, I'm afraid.'

This produced some more uncomfortable shuffling and the odd cough or two.

'I'm assuming you're only referring to the masculine DNA,' said Harriet with a brittle smile.

'Of course, Harriet, darling. Everyone knows it's your salary that keeps Geoffrey from the wolves … and that Gwyneth doesn't believe in money and that Quill and Grace are as poor as church mice.'

Harriet gave him a blank look and glanced at Tina, who was busy examining her nails. She had no intention of getting involved.

'So, as I was saying … money?' said Fletcher.

'Rollo's right,' said Quill with a sigh, 'but you're missing the point, Fletcher. Tata and Tonton had nothing. The house is old and would cost more to renovate than it would be worth. What little sticks of furniture they had have been smashed or ruined. None of us will walk away with much. In fact it could turn out to be a burden and a constant reminder of what happened to them. If it were up to me I'd burn it to the ground and sell the land. We could be lucky to walk away with a few hundred euros each.'

Everyone considered this for a while.

'All right. It's not for the money,' said Fletcher quietly.

They all waited, dreading the next possibility.

'Family secrets? Skeletons in the cupboard?' asked Fletcher.

Not surprisingly, this produced a lot of sly glances and the odd knowing smile.

'Aye, well. You've got us there,' said Rollo with a hollow laugh. 'We've plenty of them. Going back centuries.'

There were a lot more nods and glances.

'But none of them would have motivated any one of us to kill Tata and Tonton,' said William quietly.

The room was serious again.

'So who's next on the list?' asked Harriet.

They all looked at her. She didn't normally have so much to say.

Fletcher stood up and reached across for one of the wine bottles.

'Well, that's why they're stumped,' he said.

'How do you mean?' she said.

He filled his glass and poured some for one or two others.

'Misguided burglars thinking the old couple might have a stash under the bed?'

The assembly waited.

'Young thugs from the city high on something or other?'

He could see they were unconvinced.

'Do you know what the crime rate around here is?' asked Quill.

Fletcher waited, although he'd a fairly good idea.

'Non-existent,' said Quill. 'And as for drug gangs, I think we can discount them. We're not anywhere near the *autoroute*.'

'So? What do you think, Fletcher?' asked Harriet again.

He sighed.

'Well, I think we can now see why the police haven't got anywhere.'

The atmosphere sank. It was as if people had hoped he might have an answer.

'However, I do have another question,' he added.

'What?' pursued Harriet.

'Not a pleasant thought, but why have none of us been asked to identify them?'

Quill looked up. His forehead furrowed.

'I offered,' he said. 'But they said it was unnecessary. Cécile and the pompiers knew them as well as any of us.'

Fletcher shrugged his shoulders.

'I'm not inclined to think that the French police are any kinder than ours, but I suspect that their reason for not asking you was that … it would have been too upsetting.'

'How do you mean?' asked Grace.

Fletcher reached across the table and squeezed her hand.

'Because it was unusually violent or obscene,' he said.

There was more than one intake of breath and a gasp of surprise.

No one spoke for a long time. Their thoughts ran hither and thither into the dark alleys and terrible cul-de-sacs they'd avoided until now.

'So what can we do?' asked Harriet, like someone picking at a scab.

'Think the unthinkable,' came the swift reply.

This produced looks of consternation and puzzlement.

'Such as?' asked Geoffrey, who'd been drawn into the moment and was leaning forward from his chair.

'That one or both of them had something or knew something worth killing them for.'

Geoffrey's eyebrows rose up.

'How about revenge?'

'What do you mean?' asked Quill.

'How about the war?' suggested Geoffrey. 'There was a lot of Resistance activity here. The Nazi massacre at Oradour happened only twenty-five kilometres away.'

'Tonton was down south in the Cevennes most of the time,' said Quill.

'And Tata was in England with Mother,' added William.

'OK. Maybe Tonton was having loads of affairs,' said Geoffrey.

They all laughed at the idea of Tonton daring to even look at another woman, but the memory of the couple's undoubted love for each other brought a tear to quite a few eyes. They shook their heads at the very idea.

'So, what else?' asked Harriet.

Some of them were tiring of this insistent voice and Rollo glared at her, but she continued to stare at Fletcher and waited.

'There is one thing,' muttered Quill.

They all looked at him.

He reached out and held Grace's hand. She looked at him fearfully.

'I'm sorry,' he said. 'I've not told anyone else.'

'Tell them now,' she said, gripping his hand with her own.

'You remember I went to see old Maître Virondeau?' Everyone held their breath.

'Tata left something with him.'

No one spoke.

'For Ellie.'

'Ellie?' Harriet asked.

'Only Ellie. He said Tata had insisted.'

'Why Ellie?'

'I've no idea, and I don't think he has either.'

They all looked at one another.

CHAPTER 2

PERFUME

Inspector Jean Leveque stared at the boards. It was late. He should go home. His wife Nicole had tired of scolding and pleading with him. Neither approach had worked. Even when he was at home he wasn't really there. He would sit there, gazing off into the distance with a frown on his face. She'd given in and planned meals she could cook at the last minute.

Various theories were concocted and considered, but the truth was that no one had the slightest idea as to why anyone would want to hurt Marie-Thérèse and Pascal Maladry, let alone butcher them in such a savage manner.

'*Mon dieu*,' he whispered to himself, as he stared at the horrific images and recalled the moment when Picat, the pathologist, had shared his conclusions once he'd finished his autopsy. That this elderly and infirm couple – the old man could hardly walk and the old lady was nearly blind – had been hacked to death by not one but four weapons, which in his opinion could only have been swords. Large swords with heavy, sharpened blades, which caused both the slashing, blood-spurting wounds but also the bludgeoning bone-breaking wreckage of their mangled bodies. It had been a sustained attack, carried out by four people intent on completely annihilating their prey. His only comforting suggestion was that this meant that the victims would have not suffered for more than a few seconds.

These appalling facts had only been disclosed to a small coterie of experts and senior officers … and Leveque and his sergeant, but only because they had seen the mutilated bodies with their own eyes.

'You should go home, Jean.'

He looked towards the doorway, where Sergeant Dominique Sanchez stood with her bag over her shoulder.

He nodded but didn't get up. She came over to stand beside him and looked at the collection of photos and reports with the arrows and lines, squiggles and crossings-out. They'd got nowhere on day one, and hadn't moved forward since.

'How can at least four people slash and cut two old people to bits and then disappear?' she repeated. It was the question that had been haunting them ever since they'd walked into that bloody chamber.

'Covered in blood,' repeated Leveque desultorily, as though saying his line in an existential play.

'No footprints.'

'Only a few specks of blood outside the house – by the door.'

They'd done this scene twenty times plus, but it didn't get them anywhere.

They both lapsed into silence.

'I'm going,' said Sanchez.

Leveque nodded, but continued to stare at the boards. She walked to the door, gave him one last look and set off down the corridor, her heels clicking on the tiles. There was a time before this when he would have watched her go, her hips swaying and her shiny black ponytail bouncing with the rhythm of every step.

He was still there as the sun left the room and shadows invaded the corners.

Finally, when it was nearly eight o'clock, he grabbed his jacket and set off home, knowing full well that he would follow the unnecessary diversion so that he could go past the house.

Tonight, he stopped and got out of the car. The house was shuttered. There was just the one streetlight about thirty metres away out on the road, so most of the yard was in darkness. He went and stood looking at the house, scanning the walls and the ground, knowing full well that every inch had been microscopically searched and photographed.

He turned to go and froze. He listened, his heart thumping.

Yes, there it was again. The unmistakeable sound of a shutter squeaking on it hinges.

He walked slowly towards the corner of the house and looked round. One of the shutters was hanging open. He walked towards it.

Not only was the shutter open, but inside the window was open too.

His mobile was in the car.

He stood uncertain what to do, before suddenly turning on his heel to walk back to the car. This probably saved his life.

The strike caught him a glancing blow on the side of his head. He fell to his knees and then face forward into the dust. He was vaguely aware of his pockets being searched and a voice whispering close by. As he drifted into unconsciousness, he heard some words. They were English, he thought, just as the blackness closed in on him.

～

He came round the next day. His wife was holding his hand. As he focused on her he realised that her eyes were red-rimmed. Why was she crying?

She saw that his eyes had fluttered open. Her eyes lit up. She reached forward to hug him and almost suffocated

27

him. A nurse appeared and ushered her out. Doctors appeared, and he was prodded and poked around until eventually an older man came in and stood looking at his progress report.

'Lucky escape, Inspector,' said the doctor as he held his wrist.

'Uh-huh,' was all Leveque could manage.

'Your wife's outside, but I think your superior wants a word first,' he said. 'I've told him he can have five minutes. You need to rest. Head injuries are difficult to monitor.'

Superintendent Boucheron's large frame filled the room.

'*Très stupide*, Jean,' he muttered.

Leveque didn't think that needed to be discussed or argued with.

The superintendent loomed over him.

'What were you doing?'

Leveque shrugged and grimaced as his head swam.

His superior stepped back.

'You could have been killed. They've shown they're animals. What were you thinking of?'

Leveque said nothing.

'Anyway. I've sent the techniciens down there again. Maybe this time they might have slipped up and left us a clue or two. They must have thought whatever they were looking for was worth the risk.'

Leveque managed a frown.

'They've turned the place upside down. Ripped the cupboards out, lifted the floorboards upstairs. Even poked up the chimneys. We can't be sure they haven't found what they were looking for or not.'

Normally Boucheron preferred it if his officers didn't interrupt him, but Leveque hadn't said a word. With one final shrug of his massive shoulders, he put his hand on Leveque's shoulder and then strode out of the room.

When his wife flitted back in, Leveque was struck by how slim and petite she was in comparison. She fussed around him, clucking away about this and that, trying hard to hold back her tears, until he stopped her with a touch on her arm.

'They're English,' he whispered.

She stared at him and shook her head.

'How do you know?' she asked.

His forehead furrowed.

'She said, "Leave him, Fitz."'

'She?' asked his wife.

⁓

'She?' asked Sanchez.

'I'm certain. There was perfume as well,' he added.

Sanchez walked over to the boards.

'Have you spoken to Picat?' she asked.

Leveque nodded.

'Yes.'

'But he was drunk?'

Leveque gave her a sad look.

Sanchez pulled a face and looked out of the window.

Nothing was said, but the room filled with the stink of a cover-up.

'He says it's possible, but we'd need to look for an Amazon,' said Leveque.

'An Amazon?'

Leveque shook his head and smiled.

'Nothing like you, Sergeant. A giant female warrior.'

She frowned.

'Greek mythology?'

She nodded without understanding.

'And she said, "Leave it, Fitz."?'

He nodded again, recalling the huskiness of the voice.

'And I'll bet she's a smoker.'

29

'That narrows it down a bit. A giant female English smoker.'

'I'd recognise her perfume again.'

Sanchez looked unconvinced.

'I don't know many men who could do that,' she murmured.

He joined her in front of the boards.

'I'll go down to Sylvie's later,' he said with a pout.

She sat on the edge of his desk, her skirt riding up to reveal that the suntan went all the way.

He frowned at her.

She shrugged.

Leveque rubbed his chin. He played the sound of that voice over and over in his head. It was confident, certain, even sarcastic.

He began pacing the floor.

'We've been looking at this completely wrong. They're not animals, they're game-players. That's why we can't find anything. They'd worked it all out beforehand. They knew they were going to be covered in blood, so they figured out a way to get out without being seen and without leaving any evidence. That's what we've got to do. Think like them.'

Sanchez stared at him. He stopped and swung round to face her.

'Who is the most competitive person you know?' he asked.

She looked at him in astonishment, shaking her head in bewilderment.

Before she could say anything, he grabbed her by the arm and whisked her down the corridor.

'You drive. I don't trust myself,' he yelled.

She got into the car and inserted the key.

'Where are we going?' she asked.

'Where do you think? Tex. Who else?'

She shook her head. She knew who he meant, but still had no idea why Leveque could think that computer nut could be any use – assuming he wasn't asleep.

As it happened, he wasn't. They found Gilles Teixeira in his upstairs office, surrounded by bits of computers piled on every available surface. The man himself was squirming about in one corner of the room, shouting and screaming at a screen and flinging himself this way and that with a control monitor in his hand. Even as they got to the top of the stairs, he yelled '*Merde*,' at the top of his voice and threw the control across the room, narrowly missing Sanchez as she ducked at the last second.

They all froze for a minute, until Tex put his hand to his mouth and giggled.

'*Ouf*,' he whispered. 'Sorry, Dom.'

Sanchez glared at him.

'Lucky for you that I saw that coming,' she said sternly.

'There was a time when I would have caught all three,' he said in a bad American accent.

'What?' she said.

'Robert Vaughn in *The Magnificent Seven*,' he explained. 'He was talking about flies, but he was a gambler,' he added, to mystify Sanchez even further. She looked at Leveque in despair.

Leveque picked up a tangled collection of computer innards and considered them.

'Our problem, Tex, is that like me and this bit of ... of ... computer? I don't know what I'm looking at or what to do with it.'

Tex frowned.

'What?'

'More like "How?" and "Why?" actually,' said Leveque.

Tex walked across the computer graveyard and clicked the switch on the coffee machine.

'If you're going to talk in riddles, that's fine, but I'll need coffee. You too?' he asked.

The police officers nodded. Sanchez found a corner of a battered old settee to perch on. She was thinking they'd be better employed by going to see what the scene of crime techniciens had come up with.

Tex turned, leant with his back against the table and folded his arms.

'So what did someone throw at you?' he asked.

Leveque reached up to feel the bandage which he'd been told he had to wear.

'I've no idea,' he sighed.

'Was it Nicole?'

Leveque gave him a sharp look. Sanchez knew there was history between these two men going back to their schooldays. Not that she'd been there. She was from Hérault.

Instead of rising to the bait, Leveque chose to throw Tex the line.

'Leave it, Fitz.'

Tex stared at him and then closed his eyes.

'Is that all you've got?' he asked.

'Yes.'

'In English?'

Tex opened his eyes and turned to the coffee machine, which had started to splutter. He didn't say any more as he found three cups and poured them all a drink, which he brought to them. He took a small sip and wiped his mouth.

'Well … your best way in would be to find where the moniker comes from.'

'The what?' asked Sanchez.

'It could be just a nickname. But whatever it is, it'll have an origin.'

'Origin?'

'You know, like I'm called Tex. Two originating factors. One it's an abbreviation of my name and two because I'm nuts about all things American.'

'Which is why I have to put up with Pancho,' said Sanchez, with a sigh.

'*Exactement.*'

'So the chances are that it's short for a name beginning with or including "Fitz".'

Tex shakes his head.

'And do you know what 'Fitz' means at the beginning of someone's name,' he asks.

They both frown as after all it's an English thing.

'The illegitimate son or daughter of royalty,' said Tex, like he's an old fashioned history teacher.

'No, I don't think so,' said Leveque, laughing. 'And, in any case, it was a woman's voice.'

'You sure?' asked Tex.

'Pretty certain.'

'Is there anything else you haven't told me?'

Leveque stood up and headed for the door.

'How long do you think it'll take?'

Tex shrugged. He'd little respect for most people's preoccupation with time or deadlines.

Sanchez got up, straightened her skirt and followed the inspector, who was stuck at the top of the stairs.

He looked at Sanchez and then at Tex.

'If you repeat what I'm about to tell you, my feet won't touch the ground. Understand?'

Tex nodded.

'Whoever Fitz is … his and his accomplices' weapon of choice is a sword. A large, flat-bladed sword. Like knights of old used to use.'

Tex's eyes went wide.

'Ah…' he whispered.

'Ah, indeed,' said Leveque, and put his index finger to his lips.

He gave Tex another long look before he and Sanchez went down the stairs and left him standing there.

Tex heard the door close behind them and stood in the silence of the room. His mind was leaping in all directions, but he kept coming back to the idea of the swords. Large, flat-bladed swords. He shuddered. He could think of lots of possibilities, and most of them were worrying. He knew plenty of gamers who wielded swords of all sorts. But 'large, flat-bladed' meant only one thing. Medieval. Which was fine in a computer game, but in real life? He shuddered again.

Was that really what had happened to that old couple?

He scuttled round the room, switching on his computers. He had any number of programmes that could do this research in minutes. He sat at one of the screens and rapidly typed in the instructions. Very soon all the monitors were beeping their finds and he went round and round until he stopped and stared at the first screen.

He sat there for some time weighing up the odds before reaching out and pressing the key.

∽

Quill and Grace took Ellie to the notaire's. It had also been agreed by everyone that they should be accompanied by Fletcher and, following Rollo's surprising suggestion, Harriet.

Quill had rung up to say that there would be five of them, and so Maître Virondeau had arranged for them to meet in a different room. His secretary, Isobel, ushered them straight in and they took their places as she indicated the name cards.

Ellie had a chair on its own at one end of the long oak table, with all the other five at the other end. Grace insisted on standing next to Ellie's chair until the notaire entered though another door carrying the small box which he placed in front of Ellie.

He politely asked Grace to go and take her seat and then pulled up another chair next to Ellie.

They could hear what he was saying but were surprised to hear that he was speaking to her in slow, heavily accented

Occitan. This immediately excluded Grace, Fletcher, and Harriet, and, although he concentrated really hard, Quill found it difficult to keep up. What surprised them all was that it didn't faze Ellie at all. She listened intently and nodded her understanding.

Maître Virondeau made his way down the room and sat at the far end facing the young girl.

'I have done exactly as I was instructed to do by Marie-Thérèse,' he explained to the adults in his perfect if old-fashioned English.

'I have told Eleanor that she is to open the box on her own and that she need not speak to us until she wishes. She may ask us to leave her alone and we must obey if that is the case. She doesn't have to tell any of us what is in the box and can decide what she wishes to let us see.'

He paused.

'These are the instructions, which you can read on the copy in front of you.'

The adults had already glanced at the paper and saw that what the notaire had just said was written in three languages: English, French and what Fletcher assumed to be Occitan.

The five of them looked down the long table at the solemn young girl.

Eleanor de Camville stared back at them. Her long auburn hair was tied back in a braid, which Gwyneth had willingly agreed to plait for her. She was wearing her favourite emerald-green dress and her feet were bare.

The adults became aware of a strange shift in the atmosphere.

'Tata told me about this,' said the girl, without the slightest hint of trepidation. 'I would like you all to leave now.'

Maître Virondeau stood and stepped towards the door. Without considering any form of resistance the other four adults stood and dutifully left the room. Only Grace looked back to meet the steadfast gaze of her firstborn. A look that sent a chill into her heart.

In the corridor outside the five of them stood in silence, unable to meet each other's eyes. Quill's hand sought his wife's, and they held each other in an iron grip.

It was less than four minutes, but for them it was an eternity.

Not a word was spoken.

The door slowly opened, and Ellie beckoned them in. She went back to her seat, and the adults felt compelled to return to those previously designated to them. Ellie waited until everyone was seated. She looked at each one of them in turn, until finally she fixed her father with a fierce gaze.

'Tata has asked me to tell you some things and not others,' she began. 'For your own safety.'

She paused and glanced at her mother before returning to her father's face.

She began to speak.

Later they were all to reflect on the gravity that this young girl brought to these incomprehensible riddles. Not once did her voice falter, nor did her resolve waver from sharing her recently acquired knowledge with these uncomprehending adults.

The first words were in a harsh language none of them understood.

There was a pause, and then quietly they were repeated in Occitan.

Her audience was transfixed, even the three who were unable to understand what was being said.

Ellie paused again, and a slight frown briefly darkened her face as though she was trying to remember something. But then the frown disappeared and her voice continued, now stronger and in French.

'Life is but the flight of an arrow. If it be true or if it be wayward, it will be brief.'

'But … if the blood sings the heart will beat, and the body will stir. The time is crooked, yet precise. The sun will eclipse the moon and the sky will bleed, and the world will drown in a crimson sea.'

The old notaire and her father stared at her. Grace clutched onto Quill's sleeve, not knowing but fearing the worst. What was happening to their daughter?

Ellie had one more thing to say. Her voice grew softer until the final words were whispered.

'The she-wolf will have the scent and she will not rest.'

No one moved. No one spoke. A tear welled up in Ellie's right eye, overflowed and slowly trickled down her cheek.

Grace pushed back her chair, rushed over to her daughter and held her close. She turned to look at the others, a fierce expression on her face despite the free-flowing tears.

'Take us home,' she said through gritted teeth, her eyes burning into Quill's dumbfounded face.

The four other adults stirred. Words were mumbled. Maître Virondeau was thanked. He shook his head and ushered them out. As they drove away they saw him standing at his door. He looked older, more stooped. His bloodshot eyes sunk into a tired face.

Fletcher drove the car steadily. No one spoke. Grace held Ellie tight, but was aware that the girl had stopped shuddering and a stillness had replaced the tension in her body.

She pulled back to look at her. Ellie looked out of the window. The tearstains were dry, and her eyes were staring, staring … and Grace knew that she was looking somewhere far away.

Back at the house the four adults tried to explain what had happened to the others.

Ellie sat in the garden on the swing. She refused all offers of drinks or food.

She said she wanted to be alone. And that everyone should stop fussing and let her think. Grace reluctantly walked away but watched her from the kitchen window. Quill knew better than to speak or question her. A kiss was all he could manage.

Grace had remembered every word that Ellie said, apart from the first line. She repeated it in a dull, quiet voice, as though she was reciting a poem she didn't like or understand.

The others frowned at the riddles. Geoffrey shook his head and would have made a dismissive comment if he'd not felt Quill's fierce look upon him. He shrugged and slouched back in his chair.

Rollo took a deep breath and asked Grace to repeat the words, but before she could do so Harriet handed him a sheet of paper on which she'd written them down.

Rollo looked at the elegant green handwriting and up at Harriet's stern face.

'Read it out,' she said. 'I may have misheard or got something wrong.'

He sighed and reached for his glasses.

He spoke the words with his singer's voice, which made them sonorous and heavy.

When he'd finished he let the paper fall on the table. Grace nodded her assent.

'Anybody have any ideas?' he asked, looking round at the serious faces.

He could see that Geoffrey thought 'Gibberish,' but wasn't going to say it. The others looked vacant or puzzled, but no one seemed to have any bright ideas.

'Should we tell the police?' asked Quill, although he knew he was in the company of a family who had little faith in the police for all sorts of reasons. Except, of course, for his father-in-law, who he now turned to.

'What do you think?' he asked him.

Fletcher was standing at a different window from Grace, but he was also watching Ellie.

He grunted and glanced back into the room to see a horde of eyes looking at him with a dull expectancy. He looked back out of the window.

'I think she's our best chance, actually,' he said.

Grace looked his way. He knew that look. He'd seen it in her mother's eyes a long time ago when he'd first been invited to her house. It said,

'Be very careful. That's my daughter.'

'But we can't rush her,' he added. 'She's out there now. Working it out. We've all seen her do that. Let's be patient.'

No one could offer any other suggestion, so they dispersed with an unspoken agreement to reassemble when Ellie had had time to think.

Fletcher stayed at the window. The other kids had instinctively kept away until then, but as he watched he saw Tillie and Alys slowly making their way across the garden. They approached Ellie and he could see that they were talking to her.

Eventually Tillie sat on the swing next to her while Alys leant against the tree. The three of them didn't make many movements. Alys was twisting the stalks of a few flowers she'd picked into a necklace. Tillie fiddled with her long hair. Ellie didn't move. Didn't seem to be speaking.

He turned to look at Grace, to find she was already looking at him. She looked sad.

'Why Ellie, Fletcher?' she asked.

He shook his head.

'I've no idea,' he replied.

'I know she loved Tata, but so did all the others. So did everyone. And Tata loved us.'

'She is the eldest,' he offered.

Grace nodded.

He hesitated and knew she wouldn't like to hear his second thoughts.

'I know she hasn't had any of her "visions" lately, but…'

Grace glared at him. They'd all agreed to not talk about them, and Ellie hadn't told them of any more since the missing girl had turned up. He looked out through the window.

'And let's be honest … as far as the kids are concerned, she's the boss.'

He turned to look back at her and smiled.

Grace gave him a watery smile.

'I know … but she's only twelve, Fletcher.'

He smiled again.

'But did you see and hear her in that room?'

Grace looked at him. Her smile had gone.

'She's wise for her age, Grace,' he said. 'I think we have to trust her. Trust Marie-Thérèse.'

Before Grace could reply, they both became aware of the movement in the garden. The three girls were making their way back to the house.

Two minutes later they sidled into the kitchen.

'Are you alright?' asked Grace.

'Um,' said Ellie. 'Can we have something to eat now?'

'Yeah, of course,' said Grace, glad to have something to do.

She quickly raided the fridge and the cupboards, and with help of the other two girls assembled some lunch. Without any questions the five of them sat at the table and began to eat. No one had thought of going for anyone else. It just felt right.

Words had been spoken, but it was as if everyone was waiting for the moment when Ellie would speak. They all kept glancing her way, but she would meet their eyes with a blankness that forbade questions.

Eventually they were all done. The plates were put in the dishwasher and things were tidied away. This had all happened around Ellie – who continued to sit with a cup in her hands, staring into space. Grace sat down again and reached out to hold her hand. Ellie looked at the hand and then up at her mother.

'I need to go to Tata's house,' she said.

Grace looked across at Fletcher.

'Er… I'm not sure, darling… It's all closed up. The police…' She faltered and stopped, looked across at Fletcher for help.

'Why?' asked Fletcher.

Ellie looked at him severely.

'There's something I need to look for,' she said.

'What?'

She hesitated, her eyes burning with indignation.

'It's something important. Something Tata is trying to tell me.'

Fletcher leant forward.

'You know what Gwyneth told you?'

Ellie nodded.

'It won't be … nice.'

'I know. But I need to go.'

Fletcher looked at his 'granddaughter'. Where did that determination come from? That straight-lined mouth? He knew damn well where it came from. He looked over at Grace and then back into those green eyes. Ellie was just waiting. He knew she'd go anyway, and he didn't want that.

'All right,' he said. 'But on one condition.' He hesitated and looked again at Grace. 'You let me and your mother come with you.'

Ellie shrugged her shoulders and nodded. He thought for one second that there was the glint of a mischievous smile, but it disappeared. She stood up.

'Now,' she said.

Grace's eyes went big.

'We need to tell your father,' she said.

Ellie nodded and made for the door.

'I'll wait for you at the bottom of the garden,' she said, and set off. The two other girls followed. Fletcher let out his breath and looked at Grace. She came to him and he held her.

This was how Quill found them when he came to see what was going on.

It took some time before Grace and Fletcher could persuade Quill and the rest of the adults that they should go ahead with Ellie's demand, but eventually they joined Ellie at the garden gate and set off along the grassy track that led to Tata and Tonton's house.

⌒

'Pigs? What pigs?' said Sergeant Raynaud.

He was from Orléans, and still had trouble with the local accent. The voice at the other end of the line was gruff and the accent strong. He listened again, holding the phone away from his ear as the voice was raised in anger.

'*Attendez*,' he said. '*Ne quittez pas.*'

He quickly got through to Sanchez and asked her to take the call, transferred it and went back to his comic.

'Bloody Catalans,' he muttered under his breath.

Upstairs, Sanchez listened with increasing alarm as the voice on the phone berated her. Her attempts to interrupt were ignored, so in the end she just listened. Eventually the gruffness descended into a hacking cough, which allowed her to assure the caller that someone would be on their way immediately and he was to stay exactly where he was.

She couldn't be sure that he'd either heard this or would obey her instructions, so walked quickly down the corridor to Inspector Leveque's office and told him the story.

42

He stared at her in disbelief as the implications of what she was telling him expanded exponentially. He shook his head in dismay.

He grabbed his coat and told Sanchez to get the car.

As he reached the door he hesitated. If it was true, he ought to tell Boucheron straight away. But if not, he'd look a fool. What was that American phrase? Catch 22?

He closed the door and ran down the stairs.

It only took them ten minutes to get to the village, but another twenty before they found the shed in the woods. It was less than a kilometre from the house.

Why had no one told them about it? Why had it taken so long for someone to realise?

The smell was horrendous and the flies more furious the closer they got.

Standing to one side, apparently unbothered by the flies, was the old man. Leveque offered his hand and wished he hadn't – even the sleeve of the coat he was offered made him gag.

'Monsieur Chassignol? Did you tell my sergeant they were the Maladry's pigs?' he asked.

The old man nodded but made no effort to approach the shed.

'So why didn't you come forward with this information before?' he said sharply.

'I've got plenty other things to do, and your men were all over the place. Wouldn't let me through.'

'So what's this about blood?'

'They've been bled, and it's gone.'

'What do you mean by 'gone'?'

Chassignol gave him a look of contempt.

'There's no sign of any.'

Leveque frowned at him.

The old man sighed.

'There are the two pigs hanging from the beam, but the blood bucket's gone.'

Leveque was trying not to think of a terrible possibility taking shape in his head. He shook it away.

'So someone has slaughtered the pigs and taken the blood?'

The old man turned spat into the mud again.

'It'd be about eight litres,' he muttered.

'*Merde*,' whispered Leveque.

Chassignol gave him a toothless grin.

'A feast of boudin,' he said.

Leveque gave him a fierce look, turned on his heel and walked away.

Chassignol looked at Sanchez, who shrugged.

'You'd better come with me,' she said. 'You'll need to make a statement.'

By the time she'd got him back to the car, Leveque had made his call and was staring grimly through the windscreen.

'Drop me off at the hospital, Sergeant,' he said, without looking at either of them.

Things could only get worse.

⌒

They did.

Picat wasn't at the hospital. He'd phoned in sick.

Leveque made a phone call to Boucheron. It wasn't a pleasant exchange, but the superintendent agreed to the inspector's suggestion.

He found the pathologist's assistant, a young woman called Yvette Lavignac.

She was at her bench in the lab, leaning over a microscope. She looked up and gave him a delightful smile.

'Can I help you?'

Ten minutes later the smile had gone. She had confirmed Leveque's worst nightmare.

The test results from the laboratory in Limoges confirmed it. The blood samples that Picat had sent them were mainly pig's blood. All ten samples. He just hadn't read the report.

Leveque rang Boucheron again. The rage at the other end of the line was apoplectic.

But his orders to Leveque were crystal clear.

'Not a word to anyone. Get round to Picat and arrest the drunken bastard.'

Which is when it went from bad to worse.

There was no answer when Leveque knocked loudly on the door. He went round the back and found a window open. He knew Picat lived alone. His wife had left him three or four years ago.

Leveque stood in the silence of the empty house and knew the worst. He climbed the stairs with a heavy heart and went straight to the bathroom.

As he had feared, Picat's face stared up at him from the rim of the bath.

Leveque leant his head against the door and looked down at the pathetic sight. It struck him that there was a certain cruel irony in the fact that Picat, lying there in the crimson water, had bled himself to death.

The inspector went back downstairs and called the station.

While he waited for the techniciens to arrive, he stared out at Picat's untended garden.

He was still there when Sanchez arrived with the rest of them. She suggested they got out of the way. They went and sat in the car.

Neither of them could think of anything to say, but both of them could sense the other's brain whirling away with a variety of possible scenarios. Neither of them wanted to see Boucheron, but knew he'd expect them to wait for him.

Sanchez coughed and risked a quick glance at the inspector. His face was set in a frozen block of grim, grey granite.

'What are you thinking?' she asked.

He looked her as though he'd forgotten she was sitting next to him. He sighed and put his hands on the wheel.

'I'm thinking that I was right about game-playing, but what I thought was disgustingly brutal and vicious now turns out to be sick … *incroyable*,' he said in a quiet monotone.

She nodded but thought it best not to interrupt.

'To think that these people have planned this obscenity and then carried it out like some kind of game. To tease us with a riddle.'

He banged his hands on the wheel.

'Boucheron was wrong. They're not animals. They're worse than that.'

On cue, a silver Citroën C5 pulled up in a cloud of dust and the superintendent stepped out onto the road. He looked across at their car and marched towards them. They got out to meet him.

'Tell me it's not true, Leveque,' he said.

Leveque shook his head.

Boucheron exploded.

'*Mon Dieu*,' he said. 'How am I going to explain this to the prosecutor?'

Leveque had no answer for him.

Boucheron spun round and clenched his fists. The other two watched as he fought to regain his composure. He turned to face them, his face worryingly purple with rage.

Leveque decided it was best to be factual.

'At this stage we still don't know what actually happened. All we do know is that the murderers planned this meticulously. They must have spent time here, finding the Maladry's two pigs, slaughtering them and catching the blood, which they then transferred to the house and...' Words failed him.

Boucheron had calmed down.

'So are we thinking that the Maladrys were already dead before the blood was...' He fumbled for the right expression.

'Before it was thrown on their bodies?'

Leveque hesitated.

'I don't know. In fact, we can't even be sure at this stage how or when they were killed.'

'There will have to be another autopsy and another coroner's court,' said Boucheron, his eyes bulging at the thought of how this would be reported in the press.

And again on cue two cars came racing along the road.

Boucheron glared at the men who tumbled out of the cars. They looked round and spotted him. They rushed across. Boucheron growled at Leveque and the two officers got back in their car and drove away.

Sanchez didn't ask. She wasn't stupid. She drove them straight to the hospital.

Twenty minutes later they were back in the pathology lab.

Picat's assistant looked up at their stern faces. She wasn't stupid either. She had found the reports and was studying them with mounting alarm.

'Tell us the worst, Doctor,' said Leveque.

She looked up and stared at him.

'I didn't know he was so bad,' she began.

Leveque sat down.

'None of us did. Don't blame yourself,' he offered.

She shook her head and held out a sheaf of documents at them.

'But the results are clear,' she said in exasperation.

'Tell us,' said Leveque.

She looked at him, then shuffled through the papers and picked out one.

'Blood samples,' she said.

'We know,' said Leveque. 'Pig's blood. Or, to be precise, the blood of two pigs.'

She looked at them in horror.

'But why?' she asked.

Leveque sighed.

'At this moment, I'm more interested in how,' he said.

She stared at him.

Leveque indicated the reports lying on the table.

'Can you tell me how the victims died?'

She shook her head again.

'It's not clear. But I'm pretty certain they were dead before the wounds were inflicted. There's little of their blood.'

She looked up from the papers. 'You don't bleed when the heart's stopped pumping,' she added unnecessarily.

'So what was the cause of death?' repeated Leveque.

'I'm not sure,' she said. 'I think there'll have to be another autopsy.'

'How soon can you do that?'

This startled her, even though she knew it would have to happen.

'What? It can't be me,' she said.

'So who do I have to contact?' he asked.

Later he felt bad about the way he'd remorselessly questioned her, but in the event the bureaucrats were efficient for once and a pathologist from Bordeaux was on his way within the hour.

To say he didn't want to do this was an understatement. But nevertheless that was what happened. Leveque declined to be part of the team overseeing the disinterment of the bodies and left Sanchez to deal with the relatives.

He went off to find Tex. He needed answers.

Chapter 3
Tata's House

Fletcher has only been to Tata's house once before. Must be three years ago now.

All he can remember was how dark and claustrophobic it seemed. So he isn't looking forward to going now, especially considering what has happened.

Ellie leads the way.

It isn't a route that either he or even Grace has taken before and the path becomes less and less obvious as they progress, although Ellie has no doubt where she's going.

What they aren't expecting is the crowd of police officers, mostly gathered near the lane from the house to the main road.

Ellie is then disconcerted to find that the last few yards are barred by a six-foot-high fence.

Before they can get any further one of the officers spots them and shouts at them. Within seconds they are rounded up and taken to the senior officer in one of the cars.

None of these men recognise the three of them and it takes some time before Grace is able to convince them who they are, and this is only because one of local officers happens to turn up.

'I'm afraid it's not possible, *madame*,' she is told.

Grace looks at Ellie's stern face, takes a deep breath and explains as best she can what happened at the notaire's.

The senior officer listens attentively, occasionally frowning when he can't understand, but eventually he nods and asks her to wait while he contacts Inspector Leveque.

In the event he's already on his way, and he arrives five minutes later.

Grace repeats what she said to the other officer, despite being a bit disconcerted by the bandage swathing the inspector's head.

When she's finished he turns to look at Ellie, who stares back at him with her intensely resolute gaze.

'Can you tell me what you think you might find in there?' he asks.

She doesn't hesitate.

'*Un message de ma grand-tante.*'

Leveque stares at her.

He wants to ask,

'What kind of message?' But something in her expression tells him she won't tell him.

He looks at Grace and at the man he knows is a retired detective.

'Can I speak to your mother and…?'

'Grandfather,' mutters Fletcher.

Ellie remains stony-faced, so Leveque gestures for the two adults to follow him towards the gateway.

He looks them both in the eyes.

'If I am to allow this, my superiors will be incredibly angry with me,' he says, in good enough English for Fletcher to understand. 'So I need an extraordinarily strong reason to let this happen.'

Grace and Fletcher share a conspiratorial look.

'She was close to my aunt,' says Grace, 'and the message she left in her will is very direct.'

Leveque looks at Fletcher, who begins to think he might sense a like-minded copper behind the weird moustache.

'I think you might have the best witness you're likely to find. They were very close,' he begins. But then he hesitates, knowing full well that Ellie is no way guaranteed to share whatever she discovers.

Leveque looks back at Grace.

'Do you have any idea what it's like in there?'

Grace fights back her tears and manages a shrug.

Leveque stares at her for a long time.

He is thinking,

'No, you don't. No one could imagine that level of horror.'

He looks over at Ellie, who is staring straight at him.

Unable to meet that gaze, he looks away. He knows all the other officers are waiting on his decision and knows they know he is risking all sorts of trouble and recrimination if he allows this.

He turns to look at her again. The gaze never falters.

He walks over to her.

'Do you know what you're looking for?'

This is in French and too soft for anyone else to hear.

Her eyes bore into his.

The nod is imperceptible, but the eyes become even harder.

He holds her gaze and then looks down at the gravel.

'*Veux-tu me dire ce que tu vois?*'

'*Peut-être,*' comes the immediate whispered response.

He continues to hold her gaze for a second, then looks back at her mother and the old detective.

'You must let me come with you,' he says.

She agrees, but the eyes are still hard.

The pause is what Fletcher remembers most.

Afterwards, when Ellie reappears, Grace has managed to stop her tears, but the paleness of her daughter's face and the haunted look in her eyes are too much.

She runs to her and, sobbing helplessly again, folds her in her arms.

All Fletcher can see is those green eyes staring at him … through him.

Ellie pushes herself away from her mother and turns to the inspector.

'Can I go into the barn?'

Leveque looks across to where she's pointing. They've not found anything to suggest the killers have been there, so he nods.

Ellie marches straight over and pushes the door ajar.

Thirty or so pairs of eyes exchange puzzled glances, but she reappears only a few moments later … clutching a startled black-and-white cat, which is blinking in the sunshine.

No one says a word, although there are a few half-smiles among those officers who were brought up in the countryside.

Ellie doesn't have a smile, but her mother puts her arm around her and strokes the cat's head.

Fletcher nods and the two of them set off.

He waits until they've gone and then turns to talk to the inspector.

Leveque indicates his car and the two of them go to sit inside.

The other officers have gathered into small groups until a sergeant tells them to take up their positions, as they've been ordered to do.

In the car both men wait for the other to begin.

Neither of them wants to talk immediately. The one is afraid of what the other will tell him and the other is trying to find the words to say it.

'*La louve ne craint rien.*'

Fletcher waits. He has no idea what the words mean, but somehow knows it's something about Ellie's courage.

'Your granddaughter is very brave,' Leveque translates.

Fletcher nods.

'Initially it was the smell,' Leveque continues. 'Like metal in your mouth ... but in the end it was the small things. A severed finger was the worst for me...'

Fletcher has seen enough murdered bodies to know this is true, but he also knows that sharing that knowledge won't help either of them.

There was another long pause, with both men staring out of the car windscreen at the house, which gives off a sullen wariness.

'I don't suppose she told you anything,' mutters Fletcher.

Leveque slowly shakes his head.

'Did she find anything?'

Another pause.

'I'll tell you what I saw... Maybe something will make sense to you or another member of your family... I understand that Eleanor's sisters often went with her, didn't they.'

Fletcher nods.

'At first, she just stood in the doorway and ...' – he gives a scanning motion – 'looked around like the light on a lighthouse.'

'Then she walked to the fireplace ... and touched the remaining objects very carefully ... one at a time, like they were ... *objets religieux*.'

Leveque stops and looks hard at Fletcher.

'You realise of course that most of their possessions were scattered all over the room ... like a whirlwind had visited. We moved as little as possible, and so I was really interested in what she was looking for.'

'And did she find anything?'

Again, Leveque hesitates. Then he frowns.

'I'm not sure, because suddenly she went into the ... *cellier*, where you keep food cool.'

Fletcher nods, remembering seeing the rabbits and birds hanging there.

'I followed, but I think I was too slow... She had her back to me. I think she possibly found something or saw something.'

Fletcher knows well about the secrecy of Ellie and her siblings: their secret language, hiding places and signals.

Leveque continues.

'I asked if she'd seen something but she didn't answer … and then she turned round and walked straight to the door. Never looked back.'

They are both quiet again.

'I can't promise anything. And, in any case, I think everyone wants to go home... But if I can I'll let you know,' is all Fletcher can think of to say.

Leveque nods and gives him his card.

Back at the house, Gwyneth has chivvied Christina into helping her make a meal and people are trying to be normal, except of course the de Camvilles are never as quiet as this.

Ellie isn't there.

He frowns at Grace, who indicates upstairs.

He grabs a sandwich and a brew and goes to look for her.

The girls always commandeered the large attic room for their holidays, and the boys had learnt the hard way to leave them alone.

Fletcher hesitates at the door and then knocks.

No reply.

He waits a few seconds and then slowly pushes the door open.

Ellie is sitting on the window seat, the cat on her lap, who is looking straight at him with the same green eyes as her.

She doesn't turn to look at him.

He walks slowly over and sits on the edge of one of the beds.

He can see the tracks of her tears, which she's allowed to flow down her cheeks.

He finds and offers her his handkerchief … and is both surprised and cheered to see a slight smile caress her face.

They sit like this for some time, the late afternoon sun catching the fluttering beech leaves outside.

'When I was young, I was really frightened of Tata… I thought she was a witch.'

Fletcher smiles. He'd thought the same.

'But when I was eleven, she told me she had visions like me and that I'd probably inherited it from her.'

Fletcher doesn't believe in witches, but he's come to respect Ellie's 'dreams' – or what the psychiatrist described as 'foreshadowings'.

He waits. The sun goes behind a cloud. The wind drops. The room settles.

He shivers.

'What?' he whispers.

She shakes her head.

'If I show you, you mustn't tell anyone, not even my mother…'

The green eyes turn on him.

He nods.

She stares at him.

He looks at his hands.

When he looks up again, she shows him a key.

'Tata showed me where it was years ago. It opens the box she gave to Maître Virondeau.'

Fletcher frowns.

'But…'

She produces the box from behind the cushion at her side.

He watches as she put the key into the only keyhole and opens the lid as she did at the notaire's … without the key.

She can't stop herself from smiling at his confusion, but then turns the key again and a slim drawer slides out from one end.

Fletcher's eyes widen as he sees her take a folded brown piece of paper from this secret compartment and offers it to him.

It's old. Not paper, but parchment.

He unfolds it carefully.

Something like a coat of arms. Spidery but elegant handwriting. Unintelligible words. A signature and a blob of something he assumes is a seal.

He looks up at Ellie, her eyes are shining.

'It's Occitan, I think, but I can't read it. I think it's really old.'

He nods, the only word he thinks he can make out is *Deu*, which he assumes means *God*.

He looks up at her, but she's turned her face to the window. He hears her sob.

He wants to reach out and hold her, but something tells him not to.

He waits.

It's a long five minutes.

In the end he has to shuffle his old limbs and stand up.

The sun has gone from the garden and the breeze has strengthened again.

He reaches out and touches her arm, which makes her flinch.

He whispers 'Sorry,' but the look she gives him is 'scarifying'.

He looks away, unable to meet the naked anger.

As he looks down, he hears her get to her feet and stand up.

She has her back to him. The cat arches its back on the seat and drops down to floor, where it begins to lick itself, apparently indifferent to the tension in the space.

'We must give it to the police,' he says.

Ellie shakes her head.

'No. I must have it. *C'est mon obligation morale.*'

Fletcher looks down at his hands. What can he do?

Before he can come up with a solution, she turns to look at him.

Her anger transcends her tears. He can't face her, so he looks away.

Before he can think of anything to say, she slips past him and leaves the room, banging the door shut behind her.

By the time he gets downstairs, she's gone.

The others are all looking at him.

Grace comes back in from the kitchen, looking worried.

'What's happened? Where's Ellie?'

Fletcher can't speak. The others all look at each other.

Alys points through the window.

'She's in the garden under the 'jigsaw' tree.'

Grace goes to the window, her eyes searching in fear, but then she sees Ellie and her shoulders relax. It's where she always goes when there's been an upset or an argument … anything she's finding difficult to deal with.

She turns to Fletcher – who's sitting at the table, his head in his hands.

She goes over to him and puts her hand on his shoulder. He shudders.

'What did she say?' she asks.

He shakes his head and looks up at her.

'Tata has given her a … mission.'

'A what?'

'A mission.'

Grace looks round at the others. Most of the family are now assembled in the room.

Alys looks back at them from the window.

'She often did that. Sometimes it was just going to the garden or the shed for something, but sometimes it would be weird.'

'How do you mean, "weird"?' asks Grace.

'Oh, you know. Find some special flowers or plants … or a beetle … something witchy.'

Grace steps toward Alys.

'Why? What did she do with these things?'

Alys shrugs her shoulders.

'Dunno. Make potions? She always had something if you fell and hurt yourself, or if you had a cold or a sting from a bee.'

Grace frowns again and looks back at Fletcher again, who is now standing at the other window.

'Did she say what this mission was?'

Fletcher manages a rueful smile.

'No, and it's written in very old French, so I've no idea.'

Grace is insistent.

'What do you mean?'

'She found a key, in the *cellier*, probably, that opens a secret drawer in the box the notaire gave her. There was a paper, very old, in the drawer, which she thinks is asking her to do something or go somewhere… I don't know. And I haven't told you this… She won't give it up.'

Grace looks from him to Alys, who is looking guilty now.

Grace goes to the window. Quill comes to her and puts his hand on her shoulder.

'Give her time. She'll come back. She always does.'

No one moves or speaks. Even Geoffrey is still, standing by the kitchen door with an empty glass in his hand.

JULY
2019

CHAPTER 4
Πoms De Guerre

Olivia is furious.

Instead of being asked to work on the terrace – from where, if he were on the bridge, she could wave to Edouard or see him busy at his father's vegetable stall – that bitch Greta has assigned her to the private party in the indoor room.

The aircon is full on to cool the parboiled Brits, two of who look as if their skins will burst any moment to release the suppurating pulp from inside their ugly faces.

So she's going back and forth from this ice-cold room, along the hot, clammy corridor to the infernal heat of the kitchen and back, taking food to them – which they just play with, like spoilt children, before she has to take it all back again.

What they don't know is that she can understand most of what they're saying as she achieved her highest grade in her exams in English, mainly because she'd spent three Easter holidays with her exchange family in Leicester. By their accents and conversation she's figured out they're public schoolboys, who pepper everything they say with insults and sarcasm.

Two of the men have blatantly leered and talked about what they'd like to do with her. And one has tried to touch her bottom. But she slapped it away, producing a roar of laughter and silly giggling.

She knows it's no use complaining to Greta, but she is conjuring up a tirade of English expletives that she might say if it gets any worse … although she knows she really won't do that. So instead thinks she'll write it up as a piece of sarcastic repartee in a murder mystery spoof.

Apart from the two sunburnt men – one thin, one fat – one of others has the good sense to be wearing a jaunty large-brimmed straw hat that matches his cream linen suit, and is now lounging in that way that English upper-class chaps do.

The fourth has obviously avoided the sun altogether and seems unable to take his eyes off his laptop. Probably stays indoors most of the time, anyway. Although this hasn't stopped him constantly glancing at the rest of them, like a weasel checking for a suitable rabbit to savage.

The only person who seems at home here is the suntanned lady with the gleaming black hair tied back from her face. She's sitting at the end of the table so that her long sunburnt legs can catch a touch of a river breeze as the waitresses come in and out of the terrace.

The other waitresses have already given them rude names.

They've managed to mangle three courses already, even though this is a two-star Michelin restaurant where most people eat all the food, as the portions are never overfacingly large anyway. Apart from the woman and the man in the cream suit, the other three have picked at a few bits and then left the rest.

The man in the cream suit seems disappointed about this.

'I can recommend the *île flottante*,' he says. 'It's heavenly.'

The thin man stares at him blankly.

'It's a dessert,' says the woman, with a smirk on her face. 'What you'd call *afters*.'

'A fragile meringue floating in a lake of crème anglaise, with a dark secret lodged in the depths,' intones the bon viveur.

The thin man shakes his head and pretends to be reading the menu.

The woman puts out her hand.

'I'll translate it for you if you like,' she offers.

'I'll have ice cream,' he mutters, like some sulky teenager.

This idle, unpleasant banter continues for the rest of the meal, although, as with the main courses, much of the food is merely pushed around on three of the plates.

As three of them have drunk far too much wine, they stagger off to their rooms. The woman says she's going for a swim, while the laptop man sidles out without a word.

To Olivia and the other guests this group of rich English overgrown public schoolboys are the worst sort of self-important examples of their nationality and class, with their silly nicknames and unpleasant banter.

But this is precisely what they want her and other people to see and hear.

Actually, they are far worse than that.

Their nicknames are part of the cover, but are also arrogant crossword clues to their purpose.

Hollis, the man with the laptop fetish, is the one responsible for persuading them to accept these game-playing online monikers. He's chosen 'Morton' for himself, given that it alludes to the most likely link to the buried treasure that the whole enterprise is intent on retrieving – Hugh de Morville.

He chose 'Fitz' for the thin man, a shortened version of Reginald Fitzurse, or 'Arse', as the others call him behind his back, who met a particularly miserable and painful death in the Holy Land – which, as he has promised himself, will happen to him too, although probably not in the Holy Land. And 'Bret', aka Richard de Brito, is a perfect soubriquet for the man in the cream suit. 'Trax' is short for William Tracy, the fat man, who he allows to think he's the leader.

Despite her disdain for this silly charade the woman has accepted the title 'Nora' as a shortened version of Eleanora d'Aquitaine, Henry the Second's errant wife and Richard the Lionheart's doting mother. It was Henry who demanded that someone should rid him of the troublesome priest, Thomas a' Becket and the afore mentioned soubriquets were the clowns who did the job. The nonsense about what bits of Richard can now be found is the quest they're now on.

People glancing across at her generally frown and wonder what on earth she's doing with this dissolute band of posturing idiots. What they would be least likely to guess is that she's the wife of the miserable Fitz. Not that he's happy with that, or ignorant of that irony, but he's rich enough to cover her excessive gambling expenses and satisfy her and his penchant for sadomasochistic sex. Although, to be honest, she's more intrigued by the possibility of Morton's conjectures being true.

They're back here again in France, having heard that the annoyingly persistent De Camville girl is on the move again. Morton is certain she knows something, although he thinks it's better to follow her around rather than grab her and torture her to find out what she knows. The other three men are up for that in their various sadistic wet dreams, but he's pointed out that if she were certain, she'd have already gone looking elsewhere. At least he knows the three other items are secreted in other – as yet – unidentified sites.

He also knows that the retired gendarme has been on many of the same information sites he's investigated online. Some are obvious. But, even then, it isn't clear how that helps. Most of the actual physical sites have been damaged or emptied of any of the relics they seek, except for the remains in Rouen cathedral, some of which he's managed to 'acquire', but even that is dubious. He doubts whether a few crumbly flakes of a petrified 'Lion' heart are scientifically useful, but it keeps the fat oaf on board. As long as his ill-gotten coffers keep the others interested, it's worth bearing the excruciating unpleasantness of their company.

Sometimes he also thinks that the whole enterprise is a waste of time.

The Brits are already so deluded with Brexit suicide that producing a couple of battered old relics out of a bag might not be so earth-shattering as they previously thought. Still, it isn't as if this is his only iron in the fire. He has plenty more projects simmering along nicely. What a pleasure it is to feed off their ever-giving herd stupidity.

As it happens, the bad news for Fitz is that he's going to continue shadowing the de Camville girl, assisted by Nora – mainly to irritate the pair of them, but also because Nora speaks excellent French.

The other two are going back to Blighty and to their ongoing skulduggery, which involves manipulating various Tory halfwits, to keep up with the exhilarating bonfires of regulatory irritations.

He's told Fitz that he's going too, but he's going to shadow their every movement and will be ready to pounce if necessary.

He's not entirely sure of Nora, as he knows she is clever enough to have a plan of her own, but again – in good time – he's plotting a particularly unpleasant exodus for her as well.

He's the only one who realises that the waitress is paying attention to their conversation and that she can probably understand what they're saying. So it's just as well that the loudest two are departing tomorrow.

But that doesn't mean he should do nothing about her.

A brief 'encounter' might be fun.

I watch as that idiot Hollis aka 'Fitz' follows the waitress with his eyes.

You might ask why I continue to associate myself with this pathetic gang of immature boors.

Well, as you might expect, money is the first thing. I was born and brought up in poverty: single mum, council estate, three violent brothers ... and the rest. My mum died when I was seventeen from an overdose. Two of my brothers have spent most of their lives in prison and the third only avoided it because he's the nastiest, vilest human being I know, who learnt early to get other people to do the bad things on his behalf and be far too afraid to ever betray him.

So finding a man who will do what I want, just for the occasional pathetic fumble, seemed a damn sight easier life than the one I was used to.

Now, of course, running three businesses – all legit, if you don't count his financial input into the first one, which, I've clarified with the taxman anyway, to his everlasting annoyance – is how I fuel my independence.

And one day, soon, I'll dump him.

And he knows it.

And he knows what secrets I might divulge, if he doesn't agree to the crippling settlement he's going to pay me.

Secondly, I am genuinely intrigued by the wilful Machiavellian intentions of the other three, and what the weasel's dark plans are that they are financing.

I know he doesn't trust me, especially after that brief encounter when I marked his card. Pathetically, he fell for my come-on at some debauched grand estate weekend, and only realised his mistake as I was strangling the breath out of his weedy little throat.

I explained how I knew where the bodies were buried and told him about the insurance I'd taken out to make sure he would certainly go to jail for a very long time, where he was likely to encounter one of my brothers or, even worse, come to the notice of my eldest sibling.

So here we are.

Or rather here I am, the sweat on my naked body starting to cool, as the nice young waiter is whistling to himself in the shower. Just the right sort of no-strings encounter. The best sort of room service. Half an hour later I'm in the bath. I'm considering what we're doing here right now. I'm still not sure why the weasel is so sure there's something useful – something 'old' – that is here somewhere.

I still can't believe what happened back then. What is it? Seven years ago now? I was, of course, only holding the horses. Literally.

Having only arrived the previous night, I'd no idea what they were going to do in that run-down farmhouse. It was inferred that it was just another public-school prank, although the brightness in their eyes wasn't only the stuff they'd taken.

To be honest there wasn't a great amount of noise, apart from their yelling and the sound of breaking furniture and crockery.

It wasn't until they reappeared covered in 'blood' that it dawned on me this might be something far worse. The explanations were at best unsatisfactory. It was a prank, a local traditional activity, and at that time my French was so non-existent that I was unable to read the papers. And, in any case, we were on our way to Spain the next day.

So it must have been over a week before I saw something on the TV:

Old couple slaughtered in their home.

The weasel had already disappeared, but eventually I forced a confession of sorts from you-know-who. Typically, he descended into the pathetic wheedling, excuse-making – 'It wasn't my idea. They made me do it,' – pack of lies, which he invents when he's found out.

I put him straight.

I reminded him that he was the one who thought he'd lost his watch at the farmhouse and made me go back with him to try and find it.

Lucky for him the detective ducked out of the way, or he'd have killed him.

The buy-out price was doubled.

'Marital' sex was no longer a commodity he could afford.

His recorded misdemeanours, including the confession about this latest one, were safely stashed, and their whereabouts were only known to certain undisclosed legal persons.

And I never told him I found the watch under the bed a few days later.

So … why am I still on board?

There's no cure for curiosity.

SEPTEMBER
2020

CHAPTER 5

THE SINGER, NOT THE SONG

THE CITADELLE RAMPARTS, BLAYE, GIRONDE, FRANCE

A young woman is standing looking out over a shimmering estuary.

She's tall and slim. Her sun-blanched amber hair hangs loose, waves falling to her shoulders.

Behind her a few people sit at tables on a large terrace, where there's plenty of room for social distancing. The hotel and restaurant only reopened recently, and still isn't seeing many customers.

She glances over to another young woman standing a few yards away, listening intently to her phone, while now and then wiping tears from her cheek.

She has dark hair, also loose but more curls.

Eventually the call ends and she slips the phone back into her handbag.

There's an awkward stillness, but then she turns and manages a weak smile.

The two of them come together and embrace as lovers.

Other people smile or shake their heads, but then look away.

The two women walk arm in arm down towards the town.

In the car Mali tells Ellie what her mother has just told her. Her parents have to go to Beirut to help relatives and friends caught up in the terrible explosion.

They drive back to her family's summer house, which seems empty without Mali's mother's continuous chatter.

The only solution they can think of is to go to bed and make love.

Later Mali brings Ellie a drink and they sit looking at each other in the darkened room.

'Do you know what day it is?' asks Ellie.

Mali frowns and shakes her head.

'Thursday?'

'No. The date, you dummy.'

Mali gives her the trademark pout, which always works with her father.

Ellie stares at her.

Mali understands, blushes and reaches out to hold her hand … and starts to sing.

Ellie remembers the first time she heard Mali's voice in a bar in Edinburgh the previous October. She was singing the same song. The busy room had gone quiet. Her voice was strong, but piercingly tender. Ellie was certain that no one else there could understand or even know the language, but she did.

When the applause died down, she made her way over to her and put her hand on her shoulder.

'Your song was beautiful,' she said in Occitan.

Mali stared at her and then smiled.

They made love that night and have been inseparable ever since.

After Christmas Ellie went with her to Bordeaux for the new year celebrations and she told her family the terrible story of her Tata and Tonton… Was it nearly seven years ago? They even went to a snowy Creuse to see the old house, which was now an overgrown ruin. None of the de Camville family could bring themselves to either restore it or knock it down. Ellie herself had been the most vociferous in saying that it must be left alone, to gradually disappear into the woods.

When they had visited in the following years, she would always sneak off to clamber through the undergrowth and spend time in what was left of the main house. Most of the outhouses had collapsed by then.

What the rest of the family doesn't know is that she's made a shrine in what was the old kitchen. She's found broken pots and trinkets, which she's festooned with wild flowers and pieces of material she's bought from the local markets.

Fletcher thinks he's the only one who she's ever taken there. But he's not entirely sure, and she made him promise not to tell anyone anyway.

Mali was moved to tears as they sat there on the garden wall and shivered as the afternoon sun dropped behind the silent trees.

The de Camvilles' house was also cold, and so they retreated to a nearby hotel.

And it was there that Ellie showed her the secret drawer in the ancient box that Tata had left her, with its mysterious message.

Now she's staying with Mali's family, who have a summer house here in Blaye, overlooking the Gironde estuary, although because of the disaster in Beirut her mother and father have gone back again to help their family and are now trapped in the stricken city.

Next morning, early, Ellie insists on going again.

It's a good two and a half hour's journey. But there is hardly any traffic, despite the lifting of the lockdown.

Something is nagging at her as she goes straight back in through the kitchen door, which is clinging dangerously onto its hinges. Mali is sitting on what's left of the yard wall.

She's refused to go into the house itself, saying she thinks it's unsafe, but they both know it's because it frightens her.

She listens as Ellie fumbles about inside. More worried when she can't hear her.

Like just now.

She tells herself to count to ten.

Not a sound.

She gets up.

A couple of crows flutter up from the roof.

The stories her grandfather told her come like a cloud of blackbirds.

She calls out.

Not a sound.

Everything is still.

The hairs on the back of her neck prickle.

Was that a twig snapping?

She swings round.

There, not ten feet away, is Ellie, with a strange look on her face.

Mali's heart is thudding.

'*Salope*,' she gasps, standing up.

Ellie giggles and then puts up her hands.

'I'm sorry,' she says.

Mali shakes her head.

'How did you do that?'

Ellie comes towards her while pointing back at the small outhouse behind her.

The roof has collapsed and the whole structure is leaning at a dangerous angle.

Ellie nods back at the house.

'There's a trapdoor in the kitchen. It was underneath the cooker. Someone must have been here and found it. Tata never told me about it. Maybe even she didn't know.'

It was only now that Mali laughs and points at Ellie.

'You're turning into a witch,' she says.

Ellie reaches up to find cobwebs in her hair, which she hates. She shudders and tries to wipe them away. Mali laughs, and helps her.

They go to the car and find a torch.

Ellie goes back inside and is gone for a good five minutes.

Mali's nerves are fraying again until Ellie reappears from the house, shaking her head.

'I couldn't see anything else. It's just an escape route, I think.'

They sit on the wall again. It's nearly lunchtime and getting hot.

A tear runs down Ellie's face.

'I really miss Tata and Tonton,' she whispers.

Mali puts her arm round her and holds her close, but says nothing. She misses her grandma as well.

This sad scene is interrupted by the noise of an approaching vehicle. It's an old Citroën, creaking on its suspension as it navigates the ruts in the unused lane.

The two girls watch as it comes to a stop near the gates. The face of a man with a beard staring out at them.

He gets out. Stiffly. Stands looking at them.

Ellie frowns.

The man smiles.

'*Bonjour, Aliénor. Ça va?*' he says.

'*Bonjour, Inspecteur. Je suis bien. Et vous?*' she says with a smile.

He makes a face, but then nods.

'*Ça passe.*'

Leveque is quickly introduced to Mali and he suggests a drink back at the local village bar, which is just the same as it always was. The patron and his wife both recognise Ellie, but feel awkward because they are not able to do the usual hugging and kissing.

Coffee and croissants are brought out to the terrace.

There's lots of talk about lockdown and how the different countries have dealt with it, including how daft the English are, both here and back in the UK, until eventually the weight of their shared relationship intrudes.

Leveque explains that he's retired now. Earlier than he intended, but he doesn't want to talk about why. Ellie tells him about her grandmother dying and he shakes his head.

'*Une malédiction terrible,*' he says quietly.

Ellie nods. She doesn't want to go there either.

They're all silent for a while.

Leveque nods at Jean, who brings them all another coffee and a round of Izarras. Ellie frowns at him as he looks away. Has he something to tell her? She reaches out and puts her hand on his jacket sleeve.

He can't stop himself from flinching, but then turns and smiles at her. A sad smile.

'Your tonton and tata were well loved by everyone here,' he says, as though he hasn't said it many times before.

Ellie glances at Mali, who is frowning. Even she realises that this is just an introduction.

'I've never stopped thinking about it,' he continues, as he touches the scar on his forehead, 'although I only have to look in a mirror to be reminded about what happened.'

Ellie offers him what she hopes is an encouraging, sympathetic smile, although she knows Fletcher would be shaking his head and telling her to be careful who she stares at with her 'terrible emerald eyes'.

'The thing is… Now I'm on my own, I have the time to do some digging…'

He looks away again.

They wait.

'You may or may not know what Tonton did in the war.'

Ellie frowns.

'Wasn't he was down south somewhere? Near Lourdes?'

Leveque shakes his head.

'That's what he told everyone. But he was actually further east, near Montsegur.'

Ellie looks at Mali to see if she understands the significance of that, but her querying look seems to indicate that she doesn't.

Leveque looks from one to the other.

'She's the history student, not me,' says Mali, making a sly face at her.

Ellie laughs.

'Probably not my period,' she intones, offering the usual history student excuse.

Leveque shakes his head.

'Not my special subject either,' he says.

They two young women frown at each other.

'So I did some research,' he continues. 'It's famous for three reasons. One is the religious persecution in the thirteenth century, when hundreds of Cathars were killed. Another is the subsequent Nazi interest in Aryan mythology, which then became the subject of investigations by Holy Grail theorists.'

The two girls shared another look.

'So I know that Tata left you a mysterious box…'

Ellie stares at him.

'Who told you that?'

Leveque looks at his hands.

'Old Virondeau, the notaire, contracted the virus and died in April. His son brought me a letter only a few weeks ago. His father told him to give it to whoever I thought should know.'

Ellie stares at him.

He takes the letter out of his jacket pocket and offers it to her.

She takes it, hesitates, and then quickly reads it. Spidery French handwriting. She frowns, looks back at Leveque, who clears his throat.

'I did some more research. "Maladry" is a common name in the departments of Ariège and Aude. The story goes that the Cathars managed to secrete their treasures and gold away before the siege was ended and the survivors were all burnt to death.'

The two girls stare at him.

'Are you suggesting that Tonton knew something?'

Leveque gives her a weary smile.

'I very much doubt whatever secrets he knew he'd be able to keep from Marie-Thérèse.'

This makes Ellie smile and nod.

∽

TODMORDEN, CALDERDALE, WEST YORKSHIRE

Fletcher stands looking out over the valley.

If there was a sun it would be shining full at him, but the rain has only just stopped. Briefly, he suspects. Stoodley Pike is lost above the thick grey cloud as well, so all he can see is down into the valley, where traffic is moving slowly. Roadworks are holding up the morning traffic, as usual. No doubt they are part of the further underfunded attempts to ward off the now annual floods, which will cause yet more tired but hopeless outrage. The same people who have voted in a Tory MP three times already. The same man who blames Bradford for the spread of Covid.

He realises he's shaking his head.

As if he cares.

Tears come.

He lets them.

He could stump back down to the house.

Do some shopping.

But instead, he sits on a rock and closes his eyes.

A memory stirs.

It always does here.

One winter morning aeons ago.

He and Grace had been snow-sledging on empty compost bags. Falling off and giggling with excitement.

Then that moment when she turns to look at him and tells him straight.

'If you ever hurt my mother...'

He shakes his head.

Did he?

Maybe.

There were other enticements.

That young woman with the dark eyes. Sorcha. Whatever happened to her?

And, of course, Louisa ... but they'd come to an agreement. Hadn't they?

He shakes his head again.

'The dead can't suffer any more.'

That was Cassie, of course, stating the bleeding obvious, but making it sound like it was some gnomic truth.

So what now?

No birds sing.

Nothing. Just the wind.

Later, as he sits drinking a strong coffee, he wonders where Ellie is.

Finds his phone and tries to ring her.

No response. As usual.

Laboriously he taps in a brief message.

Where are you?

Thinks again.

I need cheering up...

He stares at the screen.

All those spelling tests you did at school. Didn't know then it was going to be a waste of time, eventually. All those reports he forced himself to write. With a pen.

Then a message flutters on to the screen.

Tata's + Mali. Wot u up2?

He frowns.

What is she doing there? All he can think of to say is,

Are you OK?

Then he sees,

Why not come? Pick u up at Limoges.

He shakes his head.

A gust of rain batters on the window.

Is that possible?

⁓

TATA'S HOUSE

Whenever Fletcher comes back to the scene of this terrible crime, it feels scarily different from all the others he'd attended in his long and 'illustrious' career.

It's the silence that gets to him.

He's now standing by what was once the gateway.

If he turns around he will see Mali, because he knows she will be still in the car. She's told him she's only once followed Ellie into the courtyard, but that was as far as she ever got. The only way she could explain it was to say how cold it was … even at the height of summer, when it was thirty-odd degrees everywhere else.

He watches Ellie go back into the house, fighting her way through the now luxuriant jungle of greenery. There are even some maturing trees shouldering their way up through the ruins now. The roofs are completely collapsed inwards and a couple of walls have followed them down. Just the chimney stack is still standing proud somehow.

The air is full of angry insects, noisily expressing their indignation at this disturbance of their Eden. A young deer stops briefly to figure out who they are, before coming to its senses and bolting through the gap in the courtyard wall.

Crows flap from the walls to the nearby trees and circle around, grumpily chattering to each other as they go.

As usual Ellie disappears, and silence descends.

The part that makes him twitchy involves recalling that moment when she suddenly appeared behind him.

The silence deepens, like the air is sinking into a void.

He glances back at Mali. Her suntanned face is looking pale and her eyes are wide and worried-looking, flickering from him to the house.

Ellie reappears.

A frown on her face.

She fights her way back through the undergrowth.

Shows them the thread of dark cloth in her fingers.

'Someone's been here,' she says, quietly.

Fletcher shrugs his shoulders.

'Someone just curious?' he suggests.

Ellie shakes her head.

'No one local ever comes anywhere near. They're all too scared. Even the kids. They know something evil happened here.'

He shrugs and tries a smile.

'Someone lost on a randonnée?'

Again, she shakes her head and hands him the cloth.

He fingers it and frowns.

'A jumper?' he asks.

She nods back.

'Cotton, I think.'

They both stare at each other.

Who would come here, other than the murderers?

Ellie looks at him.

'Let's go and find the inspector,' she says.

～

It's never hard to find Inspector Leveque.

He's usually either at the bar in the village or at home on his laptop.

He's all alone now. His wife left him not long after the terrible events seven years ago. She'd given him an ultimatum, which he couldn't agree to, so she packed her bags and left. Although the fact that she went straight out to Léon's car was a clear indication of what had been going on for some time.

He still misses her, but mostly he's lost in his searches. If his sister didn't bring him food two or three times every week he'd probably have starved to death by now.

There's rarely any small talk when he and Ellie meet. They both know what they're going to discuss to bring each other up to date with their separate investigations.

Leveque is following up the connections between Tonton and his time in the last war, when he was hiding in the same places as the Templars and the Cathars did all those years before … while Ellie has been investigating the riddles in the document that Tata entrusted to her.

She's finally found someone who could help with the translation, which is still hard because it's written in a code they can't crack.

'So,' she says, 'I'm pretty certain now that the *trésor* it refers to is what was found at Châlus.'

She shakes her head as Leveque pulls a face.

'I know that the historians have always said it was just some old Roman treasure. But of course that's what Mercadier and the others wanted people to think.'

Leveque shakes his head.

'Yes, but what's the connection between him and de Morville? There's no proof that he was even at Châlus.'

Ellie frowns.

'But we do know they were both close to Richard. Mercadier was his right-hand man, but it was de Morville who was his hostage at Dürnstein.'

Leveque shrugs.

'But that was six years earlier. There's no reference to de Morville after that.'

'Except that he went to Dryburgh after Mercadier was killed.'

Leveque shrugs.

'But you can't prove any connection other than coincidence.'

'Yes,' she rasps, 'it's a coincidence, but why on earth should he go there? He must have known he didn't have long to live. He may have been as much a threat to John as Mercadier was, so going back to England would have been suicidal.'

Leveque shrugs.

'Show me some proof.'

Ellie shakes her head.

'You know I can't, but I feel it's what he did.'

Leveque can only smile.

'But even if he did, why would Mercadier have entrusted it to him?'

'Maybe he already had the treasure.'

Fletcher can't contain himself.

'Hang on a minute. What treasure are you talking about?'

Both Leveque and Ellie stare at him and then look back at each other.

Ellie points to the translation of the document that was in the secret drawer of the box that she was given by Maître Virondeau.

'It's here,' she says.

Fletcher frowns.

She points.

Le sang du roi, son anel and son espaca…'

Fletcher stares at her. She knows he doesn't know what that means.

'The king's blood, his ring and his sword.'

He shrugs.

'Well, I can believe a ring might have survived, but a sword? Wouldn't it have rusted away by now? And blood? No way.'

She shakes her head.

'There are swords that have survived far longer than that. Not many, and none in pristine condition, but it's possible if it's been in a dry, airtight place.'

Leveque nods his agreement.

Fletcher shrugs.

She glances at Leveque, who gives Fletcher another weak smile.

'You probably didn't hear about Richard's coffin being opened and samples being examined a couple of years ago?' he murmurs.

Fletcher stares at him.

'No,' he admits.

'And you certainly won't have heard that there was a break-in at the lab where those remains were being examined.'

Fletcher looks at both of them in turn.

'And we haven't mentioned the fourth thing,' says Ellie.

Leveque rolls his eyes.

'There's a smudge on the parchment. It's eight hundred years old, but we think it might say *"grazal"*.'

'What's that?' asks Fletcher, but then he works it out.

'Grail'.

January
2021

CHAPTER 6
THE FAIR OPHELIA

TWEED VALLEY, SCOTTISH BORDERS

DI Magda Steil is up early.

Up here they are above the snow line, and across the valley she can see a slow tractor trundling along the lane.

The house is still, despite the number of occupants.

It has been a long time since it has heard and felt the galloping of young legs up and down the stairs and corridors. In and out the bedrooms into her lady's chamber.

She can't stop a smile.

Although it quickly fades.

This time last year this was a house slumbering before the great wave of deaths and lockdowns. Belated, as they proved to be. Time after time. Even now a UK government is running on an empty, continuous stream of lies, while the SNP leadership eyes up another referendum.

She sighs.

Nothing she can do about any of it.

Down in the kitchen she waits for the cafetière to burble.

Hengist and Raven are playing up and down the terrace like they are still pups.

She watches as Hengist tires of the game and stands looking out over the valley, his breath condensing in the air like a hairy dragon.

Searching for his master ... yet again.

Her brother Tomasz.

She knows he's back in the country, but is not sure where he is yet.

He's still wanted by the police for questioning, regarding the deaths of more than a couple of people.

Something tells her – some sibling sense – that he's nearby.

Was that a creak on the stairs?

Soft feet padding towards her.

An arm around her waist.

A murmuring kiss on her neck.

Amelia.

⁓

Later, while she's getting dressed, her mobile blinks.

It's Rico.

DS Gatti. Looks as Italian as his name. Dark hair, dark eyes. Soft-spoken. Married since he was still in his shorts. Still turns the girls' heads, although he wouldn't even dream of returning their looks.

'*Buongiorno,*' she tries.

'*Salve,*' he replies, but she knows he's just being polite.

'You don't want me to try our lane this early, do you? Not likely to be gritted yet.' she asks.

There's a pause. Weighing his options.

'Well ... not that urgent, I think, given that the death – or the disappearance – was a long time ago.'

She waits, letting him make the decision.

'A Mr Robinson, local art gallery owner, has been given a painting to reframe.'

He hesitates, waiting for some response, but she outwaits him again.

'When he removed the back covering there was a note...'

Magda frowns.

'Saying what?' she asks, now getting intrigued.

'Well, it's a confession: *I murdered Susan Kingston and buried her body in the woods.*'

Magda catches her breath.

She is immediately back in the moment.

She had been only a fresh-faced DC, just another body searching the undergrowth. It went on for days, until they were stood down. Must have been six years ago. No. Seven. It was in 2014.

'Is there a name?'

'No. Just a grid reference.'

'What?'

'But it's eight figures, so...'

She frowns and quickly figures out what she should do next, who to contact, et cetera.

Orders given, she stands staring out of the window.

A quick check on the map reveals that it's only a ten-minute drive, she'll go in the Landrover, and she's likely to be there before anyone else.

She recalls doing her stint standing guard at the poor family's door, watching the comings and goings of other detectives and the forensics team. The cold look on DCI Connaught's face. That never changed. He died in a car crash at fifty-six, driving home after midnight, two months after the girl went missing. Probably fell asleep at the wheel.

She goes to find her mother.

Twenty minutes later, she parks in the recently tidied car park near the Wallace statue.

'Who did that?' she wonders. Not the council, for sure. Must be local folk, although she can't imagine the nearest village being keen on it with their *Slow down: children and dogs* signs.

The morning is still crisp. Frost on the grass.

A shaft of sunlight comes through the silent wood, blinking off the white tree trunks.

She knows not to go trampling about, so just listens to the silence.

Except, of course, the birds are busy, flitting from one branch to another, unaware of the impending rude interruption to their winter wonderland.

She's been past this car park lots of times. People going to see the statue of Wallace perched on the hillside looking out at the Eildon Hills. The path veers away from where the burial site is indicated, further to the left. She's never seen it packed out. Often only one or two cars are there.

She glances back down the road. There's not been a passing car for the few minutes she's been there.

This is a well-chosen place, she admits. Somewhere that's either familiar or well researched. It probably confirms what she heard at the time: that Connaught was convinced it was someone local.

She checks the map again and figures that the site is a couple of hundred yards away, beyond a field, in another line of trees, although she can see from the contour lines that it must be just above the steep drop down towards the river.

She frowns and looks again, then realises that it must overlook the ruined abbey and the hotel.

Has that any significance?

Maybe, but what?

Any further thoughts are cut short as a flurry of vehicles arrives.

∽

In the end the identification is easy to confirm.

Dental records verify that it is the girl's remains.

Magda is relieved that the parents don't want to see her. They'd split up a couple of years after the disappearance, and the father is now remarried and living in Stornoway. The mother insists on visiting the burial site, where she leaves a bunch of flowers.

Now Magda is on her way to interview her.

Obviously it is not her favourite duty, but she can't help being curious. She'd not even spoken to the woman seven years ago. She can only remember her being shepherded in and out of the house while she was on doorstep duty. A small figure with eyes like a frightened bird peering out at the crowd of journalists, photographers and rubberneckers.

She's moved from the semi-detached modern house in Galashiels to a rented estate cottage on the outskirts of Kelso. Only one neighbour. Hidden away behind some trees up from the main road.

Magda had considered taking Gatti with her, but then decided that a one-to-one might work better and be safer. Not that he isn't good at interviewing women, but sometimes his dark good looks can be a distraction for some.

As it turns out, she needn't have worried.

Tina Kingston is holding it together. The dark eyes glaring at her from the doorway look like a home-made mask. She glances over her shoulder, maybe expecting to see a gaggle of microphones and cameras. Magda has managed to persuade the chief to keep it under wraps for another twenty-four hours at least, while they proceed with their initial investigations.

Magda finds herself surprised by the welcoming nature of the room. Real paintings on the walls and a fire burning brightly in the grate.

Tina offers her a coffee, which she declines while giving her a frown because of the current Covid regulations, but she doesn't admonish her. Tina shrugs and says she's just made one for herself and goes to get it from the kitchen.

The furniture isn't new, but it is all well-chosen and tasteful second-hand finds. This is someone who has an eye for colours and matching. Certainly not someone still mourning or downbeat.

Tina sits on one of the dining chairs next to the table.

Magda becomes aware of her intense, dark gaze. This is someone who has made herself strong, and so she will want answers.

She rejects an opening icebreaker complimenting her on her eye for a bargain and dives right in.

'How are you?' she ventures.

This stops Tina in her tracks.

She looks away.

'Not sure,' she eventually mutters.

There is a silence between them.

She gets up and goes to the window, leaving her coffee on the table.

Magda waits. She lets silence do the work.

'I've always thought I'd be more ... upset.'

Magda is quite prepared to see tears now, but they don't come.

'I think I expected to be overcome. And maybe ... a day or two later...'

She turns round and goes back to her seat.

Magda hesitates.

'It isn't a bad place to be buried,' she murmurs, and then looks straight at Magda. 'Was she...?'

Magda shakes her head.

'We don't know yet, but it's unlikely that she was killed there. Unless...'

Tina frowns, and then realises what the question might be.

'No, no. I… We've never been there. Although, of course, we've walked along the path to get to the statue.'

'It's not somewhere we searched. Can you think of any reason why she would have been near there?'

Tina shakes her head.

'No, although we did go for other walks nearby. Up the Eildons … and I used to meet friends at the cafe down by the river.'

Magda nods.

She allows a silence to descend.

'So what happens now?'

Magda is relieved that she's got this far. Never been good with people weeping.

'Well, there will be an intensive search of the area. Although seven years is a long time, there's always the possibility of something dropped or forgotten.'

Tina nods her understanding.

'But then our best lead is the painting.'

She takes out her phone and finds the photograph.

Tina shakes her head.

'Is it somewhere local?'

'We don't think so, and the gallery owner doesn't recognise either the artist or the location. It could be just the artist's imagination.'

'Who does it belong to?'

'A local man who bought it in an auction.'

Tina frowns.

'So you can find out who put the message there?'

'We're on to that, but it turns out to have been part of a job lot that the auction house picked up in a house sale in Galashiels. Not sure yet which lot it came from, but we will find out.'

Tina looks away.

The first signs of emotion?

She stands up and walks to the window again, this time crossing her arms around her chest.

Magda waits.

'But it means it's someone local?'

She turns round and stares at Magda. The dark eyes are now fierce.

Magda shrugs and nods.

'That's where we're starting from.'

'But, if it's ended up in an auction, he could be dead.'

Magda purses her lips.

'In my line of work you learn not to jump to conclusions. But yes, it's possible.'

Again, she can see Tina's mind fast-forwarding.

'Someone who liked original paintings?'

Magda nods.

'Is there someone … who comes to mind?'

Tina looks away.

'No, not really…'

But Magda knows she's thinking of someone.

'Well,' she says quietly, 'if you have any ideas, you must tell us.'

Tina nods, but Magda isn't convinced.

She offers her card.

'Anything…' she says again.

Tina gives her a faint smile.

'Don't worry. I'm not going to turn into an amateur sleuth.'

Magda smiles back and stands up.

'Good to hear it.'

Half an hour later she turns up the lane to the site. The tapes are in place and a gaggle of SOCOs are doing their searches and tests, but there is no sign of the press yet. The exhortations to stay at home will hopefully stop the usual crowd of weirdos and ghouls turning up and cluttering the scene.

She sets off back to the station, wondering if the post-mortem has started.

Fletcher pulls into the next lay-by.

Anyone close enough to see him would have been puzzled.

For a full minute or so he doesn't even turn off the engine, and when he does it is more an afterthought than actual awareness.

No movement then for a good few minutes.

Just an old man staring into nothingness.

Not seeing the view or registering the passing cars and lorries.

Admittedly, there aren't as many as usual on this stretch of the A1 north of Alnwick.

Finally, he focuses and turns to stare out of the side window.

He knows the sea is only a mile or so away.

Cliffs and rocky shores.

Lonely beaches.

Like him now.

So is that the only reason he's on his way up there?

The comfort of strangers?

Obviously not.

The woman he's going to stay with is no stranger, even if she is still sometimes unpredictable.

He's known her for forty years or more.

He recalls their first meeting.

A warm summer's night. A rock band blaring away up the hillside.

Knocking on the door of her tree-shrouded mansion, suspecting she's harbouring a potential murderer.

That ridiculous portrait.

He smiles to himself.
But then the tears come.
Not for her.
Not even for himself.
Five minutes later he starts the engine again.
Continues his journey.
Even though he's feeling lost.
Rudderless.
No reason to exist.

What can an old man do when there's no purpose in his life?

His car disappears over the rise, and the lay-by breathes a sigh of indifference.
At least he didn't leave any litter.

The nearby trees gently sway in the north-easterly, sensing the onslaught of the wintry weather to come and resisting the gathering urge to encourage the awakening buds.

It's only as he turns off the main road into Berwick to stock up on a few essentials that he switches the radio on.
'... *found buried near a lay-by not far from Melrose...*'
He shakes his head.
'Don't even think it,' he says to himself out loud, but his eyes are gleaming. This is what he misses most in this long, dreary exclusion. The thrill of the chase: the frustration, the confusion, and the sudden realisation of what must have happened and who did it.
To celebrate, he stops and goes into an off-licence and buys a crate of fizz. Goes for a quick trundle along the sea walls, which are still standing after all these centuries. If they can still do their job after all this time, then so can he. Whether he has the authority or not.

'Whenever did that stop me?' he shouts into the wind, to the astonishment of a young woman pushing her pram.

She turns to watch as the old man in the battered leather coat strides away.

After all, it's not even dinner time yet.

∼

Magda wasn't present at the post-mortem.

Partly it's down to her continuing squeamishness and telling herself that the SOCOs and the pathologist prefer to take their time and don't want to have to answer difficult questions straight away.

But now she is getting impatient.

The one thing she has been told is that the body is encased in a body bag. Not a real one, but a DIY version made from groundsheets is the current verdict. But more curious still are the remains of lots of leaves and flowers strewn about outside as well as inside the bag.

So now she's waiting for a call.

Although something is nagging at her. Something to do with the flowers. What is that image?

A painting?

Then it dawns on her.

Ophelia drowning in the stream.

Checks it out.

Millais.

So what does this all mean?

Philip Carstairs is the most unflappable person she knows. Thanks to a lifetime of looking death in the face, she supposes, but watching him through the window of the laboratory as he sits typing his report makes her shiver.

Calm and collected in the presence of death is obviously necessary in his profession, but still...

Feeling her eyes on him, he turns and beckons her to come in.

Thankfully, the woman's body, or what she imagines she must more accurately call her *remains*, is not in sight.

Carstairs sighs.

'You do seem to have a knack of bringing me singularly unique customers, Inspector.'

She makes a face.

'Believe me, it's certainly not deliberate.'

He grins.

'At least there is a body this time...'

She nods, remembering his disbelief when she could only give him Edith MacDonald's woolly hat, necklace and shoes.

'And ... it's definitely Susan Kingston.'

She waits.

He gathers himself.

'However, you've still managed to provide something unusual, to say the least. A first for me, anyway. Elsewhere there have been surprisingly numerous examples of what you might call 'arranged' burials. Victims who are treated with a certain respect and made to 'fit' some imaginary pose or configuration. This can be some weird sexual obsession. Or, in this case, I suspect a more devotional desire to preserve the person in a particular way.'

He indicates the screen on the wall.

She forces herself to look and immediately closes her eyes.

When she makes herself look again, she realises it isn't so bad.

She's seen much worse ... in the flesh.

'Given that this is seven years in the ground, he's done an excellent job,' Carstairs continues. 'If it hadn't been for the hole – probably some rodent getting into the bag – it would have been more complete.'

'He?' she murmurs, more to herself than questioning his assumption.

He shrugs his acceptance.

Magda forces herself to take another look but can't stop a shudder.

They're both silent for a moment.

'So … an Ophelia scenario, I would suggest,' he murmurs. 'Despite being atop a cliff overlooking "the stream" rather than putting her in it.'

She waits.

'She wouldn't have lasted long in the Tweed, would she?' he adds.

She shakes her head.

'Cause of death?'

'Ah, that's a lot more difficult.'

She frowns at him.

He goes to his desk and brings back his notes.

'No signs of pre-death physical damage. No residue of poison. I'm waiting for results on some tests. But, for now, I can't tell you cause of death.'

'But … she didn't drown?'

He smiles and shakes his head.

'Can't say … yet.'

Magda waits to see if there's anything else. There generally is, with forensic people. They like to keep their best bit to the end.

'Can you confirm when she disappeared?' he asks.

'March,' she says.

'Um … I thought so, but these leaves were autumnal when they were interred and there are chestnuts, beechnuts and late summer woodland flowering plants.'

'You mean she probably didn't die until seven or eight months after she disappeared?'

He nods.

'November?'

He shrugs. 'I'll check the weather records, but that's my best estimate.'

She stares at the photo again as the horror of what he is intimating starts to unfold.

'Could it be drowning?'

He nods.

'Difficult to tell, as I said. But, given all the other signs of a staged death, I'd say probably.'

She stands up.

But then looks back at the photograph.

'But what about her hair?'

Carstairs frowns.

'Didn't Ophelia have long Romantic curls in the painting?'

He nods.

'I think so.'

'But Susan didn't…' she says quietly. 'I've seen photos from the MisPer files.'

He frowns.

'Um, well, she did have when she died.'

'So … that's why … he waited?'

He frowns.

'No, hair doesn't grow that fast… I'll double-check the remains.'

Magda calls the mother.

'Just one question,' she says. 'How long was Susan's hair when she disappeared?'

'What?'

'In the photos you gave us it was tied back … not long?'

'Yeah, but that was on her birthday months before. I didn't have any later ones. She didn't really like having her photo taken. Not like the kids today.'

'So was she growing it longer?'

'Yes. I did say I didn't think it suited her, but…'

'But she didn't tell you about a new boyfriend, an admirer?'

There was a pause.

'No … not me, anyway, although…'

Magda waits.

'Give her time,' she said to herself.

'As I told the police at the time, we weren't speaking or seeing each other very much. She was at college, living with a friend. You know all this. You interviewed Jenny. Maybe you should talk to her.'

The call is ended.

Magda stares out of the window.

Was this in the reports?

She wasn't involved, but surely Connaught wouldn't have missed something like this, would he? But perhaps he would have without a body, given that she was still alive after he died.

⌐

Ellie and Mali have decided to go back to their flat in Marchmont, as they were going to have to pay for it anyway.

They're both getting support from their tutors via Zoom and emails. So, apart from missing the pleasures of group sessions and tutorials, it's pretty much as good as it gets.

Although this doesn't mean spending a lot of time out of bed.

It's Mali who insists they go a for a daily jog unless the weather's too bad, but then it's her who does all the cooking as well.

'You're just like my mother,' she says, as she stands at the kitchen table cutting up vegetables.

Ellie looks up from her screen.

'In what way?'

'She always complains that if she were back in Beirut, she'd have servants for everything ... but especially a cook.'

Ellie shakes her head and tries to concentrate on the site she's on.

Mali looks over at her.

In the pale afternoon sunlight her hair shines like golden waves falling across her face. Mali's eyes fill up with love, but it quickly transmutes into savage lust.

The vegetables are abandoned while their executioner turns into a brutal ravisher.

⁓

Her cooking duty resumed, Mali pops the casserole into the oven.

Ellie, her naked body gradually cooling, lies spreadeagled on the bed.

Her eyes are shut, but a smirk of pleasure rests there. She had in the end gained the upper hand, as usual, and had turned the ravisher into the victim.

As she opens her eyes she can see her lover silhouetted against the window, looking for all the world like a Vermeer painting. She watches until she shivers and pulls the blanket up, while propping herself up against the headboard. From there she can watch the deft movements of Mali's brown arms and delicate fingers. Can see the frowns of concentration and the frequent pushing aside of her dark tresses. Enough to encourage further waves of lust.

'Were any two people more blessed?' she thinks.

Later, after eating, Ellie finds the article she had been reading.

She frowns and gasps.

'Listen to this,' she says.

Mali does her weary face. Yet another amazing factoid?

'It's an article about Dryburgh Abbey,' says Ellie.

Mali pulls a face. Dead stones are of no interest to her.

'It says that as well as Walter Scott, Erskine and Douglas Haig, that Hugh de Morville is buried there.'

'Who?'

'One of the men who killed Becket.'

'Who?' she repeats, knowing this will infuriate Ellie.

But no, Ellie continues to read.

'No, hang on. Not the murderer. His father. Bloody annoying, always calling their sons the same name. The father died before Becket was murdered. And then his son, one of the assassins, lost the rights to the Scottish lands.'

Mali waits to see if there's any more. But Ellie's flipping from one site to another. And then she flings the bedclothes aside and starts hunting among the pile of books in her collection.

This goes on for quite some time.

Foraging in books and studying Internet sites until eventually she flops back exhausted.

'Beaten you, have they?' Mali dares to ask.

'Not yet, but I doubt there will be much else … and if there is, it'll be in Latin,' breathes Ellie with a pout.

Later, after they've been for a run, Ellie returns to the hunt.

But again, there's not much more to find.

'We could go there and look,' she says.

'Won't it be shut?' asks Mali.

'Well, it won't matter. There's only a low wall. I went there once when I was small. Maybe seven or eight. We stayed in the hotel next to it. I remember the big dining room, looking out over the river. Huge trees and … and … weird 'see-through' statues…'

'See-through? What do you mean?'

Ellie closes her eyes.

'Not sure. They were up on a little hill by a bridge over the river.'

Mali shakes her head.

'See-through?' She can't help giggling, even if Ellie is glaring at her.

'Anyway, I'm going to go and see,' she insists.

Mali goes silent.

'We can't,' she says. '"Unnecessary journey", I think they'd call it.'

Ellie snorts.

'You mean like going to Barnard Castle to get your eyes tested?'

Mali's eyes go big when she realises Ellie's got her determined face on.

'Well, not today, obviously,' she says, looking out of the window at the gathering dusk.

This doesn't have much effect on Ellie's face, but she turns back to the laptop.

These two rarely fall out, mainly because Mali always gives in. Can't stand Ellie's big freeze – or the 'green glare', as her father calls it.

So it's left lying there, like an unfinished argument – which Mali can't bear, knowing full well how strong Ellie's determination can be.

∽

OLD TOM'S FARM, MANOR WATER VALLEY, PEEBLESSHIRE

The snow has been falling for three days now.

No chance of getting down to the town. Even on the horses.

They've cleared the path to the wood store and spent most of the time in bed.

Normally this is their activity of choice, but this is just to keep warm.

The man seems more phlegmatic about this, but the woman is restless.

She needs people, conversation, busyness, shopping.

Anyone watching – and that's something they're both very wary of – would see them constantly scanning the hillsides and the single-track road going back to civilisation.

But there's been no sign of human life for some time. Although that isn't exactly abnormal, either, given that they're the last but one house up this valley. And the last one is abandoned, anyway.

It's the perfect place for a hideaway. But these two are social creatures, adept at weaving encounters and alliances while always looking out for number one first and foremost.

They're both on the run from various dalliances and darker histories.

The man stands looking up at the snowy hilltops, a big mug of coffee in his hand.

There is muscle under the jacket. His eyes are a cold blue, but it's his elegant fingers that hide his daunting skill. He's a highly decorated rifleman with one of the highest tallies of sniper kills in the world.

The woman who comes out to stand with him is a different kind of creature. Underneath the tartan shawl there's a body covered with tattoos. One or two can be seen escaping up her neck or out on to her wrists. Mainly snakes and devils and crawling creatures. Her eyes are dark and her movements quick, like the birds picking at the crusts they've been offered a few moments ago.

They stand apart, not looking at each other.

No words are spoken.

Just their breath condensing in the icy air.

A horse whinnies in the field behind them.

She turns to look.

Sets off to one of the outhouses and disappears inside.

The man watches and glances up the hillside again before walking back into the house.

The woman reappears, carrying a large bale of hay, which she carries round to the horses. Then she watches as they come to feed and strokes and pats their necks one by one.

Two minutes later the only sounds are the wind and the horses snaffling the straw.

A single large bird floats across, searching the ground for unwary creatures. But, seeing none, it flaps its wings and disappears down the valley.

Inside, Tomasz has found a book and is lounging on the old settee in front of the roaring fire.

Imelda goes into the kitchen and comes back with the coffee pot, tops his mug up and pours one for herself.

After putting it down on the stove she settles on the floor and leans back against an armchair.

No words have been spoken. Hardly more than a glance or two between them.

But there is a tension here.

One that is building minute by minute.

Sex and fear are not unusual bed mates, but with these two it's what keeps them together. They return to each other to scratch an itch that won't go away.

'So…' she says.

He doesn't stop looking at the page, but he's not reading.

The fire crackles and settles.

'Maybe tomorrow,' he says in a sing-song.

She grins.

⌐

Magda saw the smoke from White Cottage two days ago and she now goes down to see which of the previous occupants have returned.

No one answers at first. But she can see a light on, so she opens the door and calls out. There is still no reply, so she follows the sound of tapping and comes up behind the predictably hunched figure of the man she still doesn't really understand.

Sigismund Hook grunts and murmurs,

'Take a seat, Inspector,' without looking up.

She doesn't sit but stands behind him staring at the moving multiscreen jigsaw, which he both manipulates and presumably comprehends.

'Be with you in a sec,' he says. 'Coffee would be good: black, three sugars.'

She shakes her head and goes through to the kitchen.

It's all neat and tidy. Not down to him, obviously, but it's a sign that his 'companion' is there as well – although not at the moment, meaning that she'll be out walking along the river or up on the hillsides. An odd combination and a mystery to Magda, but it seems to be working for them.

However, before she can begin her task, she's aware of someone behind her.

Momentarily not recognising her, she stares at the masked face, trying to place her.

The woman smiles with her eyes.

'Freya,' she says.

'Ah, yes,' says Magda. 'You've cut your hair ... and brunette suits you.'

Freya grins.

'Needed to do something. People kept recognising me.'

Magda nods her understanding. She's experienced the focus of the media and the obsessive online attention after last summer's extraordinary events.

'So why come back?' she asks.

Freya shrugs her shoulders and comes in to sit at the kitchen table.

'Well, I can't go back to work, although they're still paying me, so…'

Magda nods.

'What about Ursula?'

Freya grins again.

'Out for a walk first thing. She'll be back shortly, I expect.'

'So the cyborg has two carers now?' asks Magda, with a smile.

'Aye, you could say that. But he's paying, and he orders all the food and stuff, so we can't complain.'

Magda fills the coffee pot.

'But why back here?'

Freya shrugs.

'Ziggy's choice. Apparently he just extended the booking last September, saying he knew there'd be another, longer lockdown.'

Magda nods.

'He wasn't the only one to foresee that.'

Freya smiles.

'We're all in the same boat, I'm afraid, even though we know it's sinking.'

Magda laughs.

'Yeah, I hadn't thought of the *Titanic* comparison, but as soon as you said it, I knew it was perfect. Captain Boris Smith at the helm.'

Freya shakes her head.

'And we're all "dancing in the dark", or "rearranging the deckchairs".'

Magda puts her hands up.

'No more. It's too ridiculous.'

'What iceberg?' says another voice, and there's Ursula leaning on the door frame.

Magda turns to her and adjusts her mask.

It's a bit awkward now there's three of them.

They take the coffee pot through to the sitting room, which has had to accommodate much of the furniture from the dining room – which Ziggy has converted into his office again, so no shortage of chairs.

The three of them sit in silence for a few minutes.

'So what's new on the crime front?' asks Freya.

CHAPTER 7

LOCKDOWN-BREAKERS

Fletcher knows he might get stopped, but Louisa told him to say she is his sister and they're both on their own.

This made him laugh.

How terrifying to have her as a sister. Although he was brought up by his much older sister after his mother died when he was only three, and it wasn't the gentlest of experiences. He knows he gets his hard edge from her, and that grudging reluctance to admit any sign of weakness.

Anyway, it's plain sailing. No one shows any interest at all.

It's just after he's cruised past the turning to Louisa's that his mobile chirps, so he pulls into the next lay-by.

Only because he can see it's Ellie calling him.

'Hi, beautiful,' he says, knowing that will make her grin and shake her head.

'Fletch,' she growls, never ever having called him 'Grandad', because if you were being dogmatic it's incorrect.

'What can I do for you?'

'Where are you?'

'Just missed the turning to the wicked witch's house.'

'No way. Really?'

'Uh-huh. Just thought I'd break the law one more time.'

'You're bad, you know. But guess what? I've just rung her, and we're on our way in half an hour.'

'Really? That's great. A meeting of villains and wicked ladies. Are we going to set up an assassination squad?'

'Nah. I'm more interested in one that happened a thousand years ago.'

Fletcher looks out of the window. He knows she's got his stubborn streak, but he worries that it's become an obsession. He doesn't know how to tell her to let it go.

'OK, but I don't think we can escape to France right now.'

'No, but then I've found a possible link to the Borders that's only twenty minutes from Louisa's.'

Again, he hesitates. Involving Louisa might be a good idea. What she doesn't know about the area and its history would be a very short conversation.

'Have you told her about the box?'

'Not yet, but I did mention the de Morvilles and she was interested in that.'

'Really?'

'You always said she knows everybody.'

He sighs.

'And where all the bodies are buried.'

Ellie laughs.

'Exactly. See you there.'

And then she's gone.

He sits in the car listening to the wind.

Who the hell are the de Morvilles? And what were they doing up here?

∽

Louisa Cunninghame looks in the mirror.

Her acceptance of going silver rather than staying blonde no longer makes her wince.

'Is wicked witch worse than femme fatale?' she asks the mirror.

Her doppelgänger merely smiles.

She sighs.

Given that she's now expecting three people for an unlimited period of time, she would normally call Joan Hetherington over to come and give the rooms and the kitchen a good clean. But that's not possible, so she does it herself.

To be honest, she's quite looking forward to the cooking. Although she knows that both Fletcher and Ellie's friend, Mali, are both enthusiastic but very different chefs. None of these arrivals have indicated any clear reasons for breaking the law, but then Ellie is his 'granddaughter', and the influence is clear to see. Ellie has muttered something about a possible lead at Dryburgh, whatever that might mean. Fletcher just admitted he was lonely.

'Aren't we all?' she mutters at her reflection. 'Flittering around this great pile of ancient stones like Miss Havisham,' she adds.

In the event she gets herself well wrapped up and goes for a brisk walk along the riverside and back.

Michael has said he'd be here for lunch, and it's now almost eleven thirty.

A thought comes to her, so she diverts into the library and quickly finds John Knox's collection of local history books. Not the long-dead Protestant firebrand, but her deceased third husband, the one who finally came good with both the grand house and the surprisingly large endowment in his will. She'd known he was rich but had not known he was so Croesan.

Her own family had fallen on hard times after the Second World War, when her father's death duties had wiped out both the funds and the big house. It's still there, of course, further downriver, but now owned by a monstrous upstart banker, who tried to lure her down for a bite to eat as if he were being avuncular, even though he was young enough to be her son.

She shivers in disgust. What a nightmare.

Anyway, she quickly finds three books that reference Dryburgh and places them on the table for Ellie.

As she passes back through the hall there's a knock on the door and it opens to reveal the old detective.

They embrace for a little longer than they used to. And they have no intention of obeying rules, given that neither of them has ever stuck to any throughout their lifetimes except their own.

And, given what happened during the first lockdown after Laura died, they're both wary and uncertain. They make brief eye contact. But she just smiles and he looks away.

As she leads him through to the conservatory, she's glad that Ellie and her friend are coming. It will make them all relax and maybe, just maybe…

In the event it's only a quarter of an hour of stilted catch-up before the sound of laughter heralds the arrival of the two young things.

After a hearty meal jointly created by Mali and Fletcher, they retire to the conservatory and Ellie brings them up to speed with her ongoing investigations into the riddles and puzzles left her by her *grand-tante* Tata.

The three of them listen as intently as they can as Ellie flits from one book to another, explaining the connections she's found.

'So you see there is a connection between Richard Coeur de Lion and Dryburgh. Hugh de Morville, one of the murderers of Thomas Becket, came to Dryburgh, probably in 1200. He might have been disowned by Henry II, but he was one of the people who was hostage for Richard when he was captured in 1192. His father is supposed to be buried there, even though there's no stone or anything, but there's also an indication in the rolls that his son went there only a year or so before he died.'

The class is silent. Not daring to look at one another.

'All conjecture, as Mr McDonald would say,' she adds, as she looks at their attentive faces.

Fletcher knows Louisa will be smiling at him.

'Are you suggesting we go to dig?' he asks.

Ellie glares at him.

'Of course not. Even if he were buried there, there'd be nothing to find. It's eight hundred years ago.'

'Oh, I don't know,' he replies. 'They're finding stuff now from the Stone Age and earlier in some digs. I saw it on the telly the other night.'

'Yeah, but Dryburgh's been through countless changes. Literally tens of different owners or guardians. Each one of them has added stuff, dug things up or altered them. Even Walter Scott and Erskine knocked things down to make it look more Romantic.'

Louisa and Fletcher are trying hard not to look at each other or even smile in the face of such ferocious earnestness, but Mali just sighs.

'Don't get drawn in,' she says wearily. 'She'll have you reading all sorts of dreary documents. They're all about who owned things or inherited them or how much they cost. The only history that survives is all about money.'

Ellie sighs.

'It's OK. I'll shut up about it.'

Now Louisa does glance at Fletcher.

'Well, you're welcome to broddle through all of John's collection. He was as obsessed with history as you seem to be. His family were here since before the Conquest, so you're likely to find something.'

Ellie frowns.

'Really? I didn't know that.'

Louisa stands up.

'Follow me, young lady.'

Ellie looks at the other two, who just wave her away.

'I'll take the other young lady for some fresh air,' says Fletcher, as he stands up and gathers some of the plates.

Later, when the walkers return, Louisa is sitting reading in the conservatory.

'Nice walk?' she asks.

'Four herons and a red kite,' says Fletcher.

Louisa nods.

'Yes, I heard they'd released a pair a few weeks ago, despite the farmers' objections.'

Mali goes off to find Ellie.

The older couple sit in silence for a while.

'Is she alright?' asks Louisa.

Fletcher frowns.

'Ellie, you mean?'

Louisa nods.

He grunts, takes his time.

'I'm biased, obviously, but … how can you criticise someone for being single-minded?'

Louisa can't suppress a smile.

Silence descends again.

Until Louisa stands up.

'It's over the yardarm, I think,' she says and goes across to the drinks cabinet.

Later, after dinner, Ellie sits fiddling with her uneaten dessert.

'I didn't find anything,' she mutters.

'In that crumble?' asks Louisa.

Ellie grins and pushes it away.

'No, but John's collection is amazing. I haven't touched even a third of it yet, so there may be something there.'

She rubs her eyes.

'Too tired to take on two blind mice at cards?' asks Fletcher.

Ellie grins.

'All right, but no cheating.'

Louisa and Fletcher both give each other a look of astonished incredulity.

'Heaven forfend,' says Louisa, as Fletcher gets up to find the cards.

～

URSULA

So here we are again.

Although we only just made it before White Cottage disappeared into the snow. White in White covered in white.

Quite the conundrum.

Just to remind you, for forty-five years I thought I was Rachel Henderson, but it turned out that my real name is Ursula White. My mother Fern is – or was – a Robinson … and she is suspected of killing at least five women and three men.

I know.

This revelation was only four years ago … and I still have to pinch myself some mornings and remind myself.

Last summer we were here during the first lockdown and ended up mired in the local shenanigans. Anyway, that seems to have worked out all right, with Amelia swapping a bully husband for a feisty detective inspector called Magda – although her mother Helena is the one who makes me shiver.

And, of course, Ziggy was coordinating all this from the front room in this little cottage, conjuring up other shady characters like Fletcher and Violet Cranthorne, the equally scary Janet Becket and her shadowy bodyguard, John.

Ah ... Ziggy. Where to begin? I used to be an accountant, when I was Rachel, but when I turned out to be Ursula, I thought I would try something a bit more ... exciting. Although, becoming Sigismund Hook's girl Friday, as I think it's called, was not on my list, and I'm still waiting for the job description. Don't hold your breath. As far as I can count it's already included making the coffee, aiding and abetting, breaking the law, hacking government sites, making the tea, spying on people, using false passports, breaking and entering and making the coffee again.

But this time it's just me and the mysterious Freya keeping the computer whizz well fed and watered ... so far. Although something tells me there are maybe more lockdown adventures to come.

Magda is sitting outside on the terrace with a cup of coffee in her hands.

The sunshine is trying hard to convince the plants that spring is on the way, but only the snowdrops are coming out to play.

She is impatiently waiting for the saleroom proprietor to get back to her with the name of the house clearance firm who seem to be the most likely collectors of the painting.

There is not much else she can do.

The pathologist has finished his further tests but has already said there is nothing more to tell her, other than the girl was probably drowned and that there was some evidence of starvation.

Tracking down the last hours of her life before she was kidnapped has also proved difficult. Nobody seems to have seen her or missed her for over a week before her mother reported her disappearance to the police.

Is that the house phone?

She turns to look.

Her mother is inside. It keeps ringing. Magda sighs. She thinks that she might be going a bit deaf.

But no.

There she is, standing on the doorstep, holding out the phone, tears running down her face.

Magda jumps up and spills her coffee.

Cursing, as the heat comes through her trousers, she drops the mug onto the nearest plants and rushes over to her mother, who hands her the phone.

Inevitably, it is, of course Tomasz, her errant brother … who is the only person who can make her mother cry.

'Where are you?' she asks, trying not to curse him.

'In the forest car park, wondering whether I can gate-crash,' he laughs.

Magda, shuffling a thousand alternative responses, shakes her head. But when she looks at her mother's face she can only say yes.

She goes to embrace her and waits till the shuddering stops … but it isn't long before Helena shakes herself and marches back indoors, no doubt to commence concocting the prodigal son's breakfast.

He arrives five minutes later. Alone, she is relieved to see.

They embrace and hug each other.

She pulls away to consider a much-changed appearance.

As he'd got out of an old red Land Rover she's not seen before, her first thought was it was someone else.

'I know,' he grins. 'What a terrible beauty is born.'

She laughs.

'Well, I wouldn't say beautiful, but definitely terrible. How can you bear a beard like that?'

He shrugs his shoulders.

'Needs must, I'm afraid, given that my erstwhile appearance is almost certainly on every police and town noticeboard in the Borders.'

'I doubt it,' she says, shaking her head. 'You're yesterday's news, I'm afraid. Gone and forgotten.'

'No, he's not,' comes a quiet voice from behind her.

This is only seconds before a bundle of excited fur comes hurtling out of the barn.

Later, as they sit at the kitchen table, where the demolished remains of a Polish sausage breakfast clearly demonstrate that Tomasz's appetite hasn't diminished, Magda gives him another questioning glare.

He shrugs his shoulders.

'I can tell you that being on the run is not the most exciting activity you might think,' he mutters. 'In fact it's extremely tedious, and probably explains why most people give themselves up.'

The three of them are silent for a few moments as they ponder the possibilities, while Hengist's head is still glued to Tomasz's knee.

'Actually,' Magda sighs, 'I think that if you came with me to the police station you'd find the verdict is that you're no longer on the wanted list … mainly because the men in black would rather forget what happened last summer, as they've far more work trying to keep up with the ongoing cover-ups stacking up one after another.'

Tomasz pulls a face and shakes his head.

'I don't want to risk it.'

Magda glares at him again.

'And what about … what's her name?'

Tomasz shrugs his shoulders again.

'Aye … for some reason she's still putting up with me, but it's a long story.'

Magda pulls a face. The memory of the strange woman covered in crawling tattoos is not a pleasant one.

It's at this moment that Amelia arrives back from the early morning shopping expedition, trailing her four-strong brood, which inevitably results in a mass kickabout, followed by horse riding antics, which go on until lunchtime.

⁓

Keeping up with this determined young lady has been difficult, to say the least, but Covid is actually helping.

At least the decision to ditch the silly nom de plumes makes life a whole lot easier, and in any case the search for the old couple's killers is now presumably consigned to some suitably dusty underground storage facility in Périgueux.

The erstwhile bankers Marchant aka Trax and Sudeley aka Bret have moved on to the richer pickings afforded by the Tory outsourcing of government Covid projects. So it's only Hollis/Morton and Barnum/Fitz who continue to monitor the young woman's investigations, as it's clear she hasn't given up.

Fortunately they can carry out a minimal surveillance, as everyone's movements are still so circumscribed.

Barnum is still smarting from being stitched up by that vicious witch and having to fork out impossible sums of money every month as she lounges in ostentation in a mansion outside Newcastle.

So now they're intrigued to see that the girls are on their way out of town. It was easy enough to put a trace on Ellie's girlfriend's car.

They quickly realise that this wasn't just a shopping trip.

'Where the hell are they going?' wonders Barnum.

'Just keep an eye on it,' says Hollis, who is as usual lost in some gaming warren.

Barnum shrugs and goes off to make a coffee.

It's only an hour or so later that that Hollis's mobile bleeps at him and he switches to the tracker, which is stuck in the middle of nowhere in the Borders, east of Kelso.

He homes in.

On a single building on the banks of the Tweed.

Quite a large house. A mansion. Outbuildings. Extensive gardens.

Who the hell does she know who has a house like that? It's not one of her uncles, who have a trio of dilapidated old houses of the same size, because they're way down south. He switches to another programme, which tells him that this mansion is called Haverstoun House. Checks it out on the council records. A Mrs Louisa Knox-Cunninghame.

He checks her out.

Only to find that she was previously married to an ex-Tory politician in Rochdale who ended up in prison for fraud back in the nineteen eighties. He died five years ago.

He tells Barnum.

'Uh-huh,' is all he says, but agrees he'll have a look.

Nada is the result, which makes him far more suspicious.

'Only the rich can hide,' he murmurs, 'so let me dig a little deeper.'

This means tax records.

'Oh dear,' he eventually says.

Barnum frowns at him.

'A very, very, rich … old lady.'

'So what…?'

'So what, indeed.'

He gets up and stretches.

'I think we need to break the law, Barnum.'

Barnum shrugs. As if.

'Which law would that be, now?' he wonders.

'I think it's time you went to see your aged mother in Berwick,' he is informed.

~

Jane Chappell aka 'Nora' is as well served by electronic surveillance. She hasn't the slightest doubt that her ex-husband would do anything to retrieve his money and get rid of her permanently, if he could, so it's only wise to make sure that she knows where he is at all times.

She is alerted of his movements at a particularly awkward moment, as the young man who is servicing her animal needs is labouring to complete the activities she's required him to do.

He's never going to make a four-star rating, but he's better than the last one.

She waits until he's staggered off to the shower before checking her mobile.

There's a red dot bleeping along a road south out of Edinburgh.

'Tut-tut,' she murmurs. 'Always someone who won't stick to the rules.'

She searches her address book and taps the name *Sandy*, who as usual responds with alacrity.

'Hi, Sis,' he sings.

She ignores this silly and totally inaccurate greeting. Her actual brother would still be in bed at this time of the morning.

'Job for you, Sandy.'

'Yes, ma'am.'

'Idiot ex, heading south from Edinburgh on the A68. Destination unknown, but possibly heading my way. Can you pick it up on your system?'

There's a good few moments before the next response.

'Got him. Just passing through Pathhead.'

'Let me know when he gets where he's going.'

'OK. Have a nice day.'

Nice day? When did that last happen?

Perhaps it might be better if she gets rid of this irritation for good.

She's quite liked living with the codename Eleanora, as it's rather more upmarket than plain Jane … and she's reverted to Chappell, her old surname, as well, although her father was as far away from any church connection as could be imagined. Thinking of him always fuels her anger against all men, but some of them do have their uses.

With that she leaps out of bed and goes to find some breakfast.

She's starving.

⌒

Not long after Tomasz has departed, taking the lovelorn Hengist with him, Magda gets a call from the owner of the removal firm who acquired the painting in a house clearance.

'Old fellow died. No will. Only living relative was a cousin down south who had never met him and didn't want anything to do with the house and contents, so we were asked to do the clearance and put them up for auction.'

Further questioning revealed the old man was in his eighties, which ruled him out of the kidnapping.

No one to ask where he might have got the picture from. Unless…?

She persuaded herself that going to the house and knocking on a few doors was a legitimate course of action even in the lockdown.

In the event it was the woman next door who came up trumps.

'Aye, I ken the picture,' she says, after finding her glasses. 'He had it over the mantelpiece in the living room.'

'Did he ever talk about it? Where he got it from?'

'He did actually,' she frowns. 'Said he'd bought it at an auction.'

'Where?'

'Gala, I think. He often went there. Came back with pots and pictures, generally.'

Magda nods.

'A collector?'

'Aye, I suppose so. Although I don't know where he got his money from. He'd already retired when I moved here.'

'What did he do?'

'I think he was a teacher. Art and design, he said. Some of the paintings were his, I think. He had a few people who came for lessons. The studio was in the attic. I went up there once, when he had a parcel delivered and he asked me to bring it up for him.'

Magda gives her some time to go on.

'A bit scary, actually – the stairs, I mean. Not very good lighting, and a giant bear on the first landing. Bigger than me. Beady eyes staring right at you.'

Magda smiles, thinking of the stuffed creatures that her father had acquired and which still haunted the upper corridors.

'But you don't think he painted that picture?'

'No. He painted people, not landscapes.'

Magda is intrigued, even if he can't have been the kidnapper.

'Do you know any of his students?'

The woman frowns.

'Not really. Just saw them coming and going.'

'Younger people?'

She gives this some thought and shrugs.

'Young and old, I think.'

Magda waits.

The woman frowns again.

'Just a minute,' she says, and goes to the bottom of the stairs.

'Cassie,' she shouts, 'come down a minute and talk to this detective.'

There's no reply, but eventually Magda can hear someone descending the stairs and a grumpy-looking teenager appears dressed in only a long T-shirt and shorts.

She stops halfway down the stairs and stares at Magda.

'What's the matter?' she asks with a sly grin. 'You been robbing banks again, Mum?'

Her mother rolls her eyes.

'Ha ha. Just tell the nice lady about your friend Roz, who went to old Harry's next door for art lessons.'

The girl shrugs her shoulders.

'She only went a couple of times.'

Magda waits.

'She said the other people were weirdos.'

'How weird?'

She shrugs her shoulders.

'Dunno.'

Magda looks at her mother, who just shakes her head.

Five minutes later, Magda is on her way to the friend's address. A very different part of town. The sort of families who pay for their children's education.

She looks out over the valley. Is spring finally coming?

The door opens and Magda turns round and gasps.

There standing in the doorway is a modern-day Ophelia. Long auburn curls and a pale face.

The girl stares at her, a puzzled frown giving way to worried concern.

Magda fumbles for her warrant card.

The girl examines it curiously and then turns to shout for her father.

The stand-off lasts an age, before a surprisingly young-looking man appears. The girl indicates Magda's card, backs away and disappears.

The father glances at the card and nods.

'How can I help?' he asks.

Magda doesn't know where to start.

It turns out that there was a man at the art classes who kept staring at Roz.

Normally she might have been flattered, but he was older than her. Well, probably late thirties.

'You never told me this,' says her father.

Roz just shrugs her shoulders.

'I didn't like the teacher either,' she mumbles.

'Can you remember the man's name?' asks Magda.

Another shrug.

'Can't remember ... Steve?'

'Surname?'

She shakes her head.

'We weren't asked.'

Magda is trying to control her frustration. Why are all young people so difficult?

'You could draw him,' says her father.

They both look at him.

Magda with hope, but the girl with disbelief.

'What? I only saw him twice. Tried not to look at him, because he was always staring at me.'

Magda looks at the father.

He shrugs.

'Go on. Even a sketch might be useful. This is a murder enquiry – a young woman a bit younger than you.'

This really unnerves the girl, and she walks away.

The father shakes his head and manages another smile.

'I'll see if I can persuade her. She's really good at quickly sketching a likeness.'

Magda decides not to frighten him by telling him about his daughter's likeness to the murdered girl. So instead she walks back to her car, convinced she's on to something now.

CHAPTER 8

THE PAST ALWAYS COMES BACK TO HAUNT YOU

Imelda had a bad experience with a dog when she was on her way home from school one day.

The dog came out of a gate that was normally closed.

It wasn't enormous, but it went straight for her. Bit her on her hand and her leg.

She screamed and screamed like Matilda, and the owner came rushing out.

She must have fainted, because the next thing she knew she was in a car on her way to hospital. A passer-by had stopped and decided that was the best thing to do.

Her mother had arrived soon after, full of her usual angry 'Why does this happen to me?' attitude, as if the dog had bitten *her*. She was shouting that she was going to get the owner sent to prison or that she knew some people who would sort both the dog and the owner out.

The nurses took her away, and Imelda knew then that she would leave home as soon as she could.

True to her word, she left the minute she finished her GCSE's and has never seen her mother again.

She hasn't told Tomasz about this. And so, when he reappears with Hengist, she knows he won't understand that his dog is just like any other to her.

Hengist is puzzled.

He senses something's not quite right but is wary of her, which is OK with her.

But she has to agree that he's a fantastic warning system.

She's just fed the horses when he starts growling.

She can't see anyone, even though he's staring up at the hillside.

Tomasz appears bare-chested, just out of the shower, and calls him.

'Come by,' he orders.

Hengist gives a couple more growls and obeys.

Tomasz looks up at the hillside.

'Might be a fox or a stray,' he mutters, but then points up to the summit.

'No. There they are. A couple of walkers, I expect.'

He goes and fetches old Tom's binoculars and confirms his guess.

'On their way to the old lead mine, I think.'

'Maybe,' says Imelda softly, 'but we do have a visitor on their way.'

He turns with the binoculars ready, but the car is nearly up to the gate.

It stops and eventually someone gets out.

'Another one of your lady friends?' Imelda suggests.

Tomasz frowns and shakes his head.

They watch as the woman unhooks the gate and pushes it wide. Gets back in the car and drives up to the courtyard, swerves smartly in and parks up.

They wait.

She gets out.

Tall and slim. Not dressed for this environment, looking more like she's going to a meeting in a city office. Regulation black mask.

Tomasz glances down the lane and then up at the hillside where the walkers can still be seen. In his head, he's calculating the time it would take to get his gun and the routes he might take to escape.

Imelda is doing much the same, but without the gun.

Having surveyed the 'scenery', the woman steps towards them.

'Nice place you've got here,' she says.

Tomasz recognises the quote but can't remember the film, except that it's very violent.

Neither of them speaks.

There's that stand-off silence you get in spaghetti westerns.

She breaks it by coming towards them.

'Charlotte Danby,' she announces.

Tomasz doubts that's true. Sounds like someone out of Jane Austen novel. And he still wishes that he wasn't so exposed.

'What do you want?' he asks, his eyes on the hillside.

'Perhaps if we go inside and I'll explain,' she says, with a smile.

He nods and backs away.

Imelda and the woman follow him.

Inside the kitchen, Tomasz stands by the window and then whispers to Imelda – who then goes through to the main room, where she can look out at a different view.

The woman watches all this with a slight smile on her face.

'Listen, if we just wanted to eliminate you, you'd not know anything about it … would you?'

Tomasz nods his agreement.

'And, anyway, you're much more useful to us alive.'

'Us?' he asks.

She smiles again.

'One job. Lifelong immunity. You and the young lady. A negotiable price.'

He stares at her.

She sits down.

'Any chance of a proper coffee? I'm rather parched, actually. Can't abide motorway service swill.'

Tomasz can't help but smile.

'Why on earth should I trust you?'

She sighs.

'Of course you shouldn't, any more than you felt safe in the hills of Afghanistan.'

He shakes his head.

'Never felt safer in my life there, surrounded by my squad. Even when you were asleep there was always someone on guard.'

She makes a face… As if a woman like her would have the slightest idea.

Silence descends.

Imelda comes back into the room. Reads the stand-off. Shakes her head and goes for the coffee pot.

Apart from her soft movements the silence remains.

She makes the coffee, waits for it to boil. Pours three coffees, gets the milk from the fridge.

The woman takes a sip and smiles at her.

'Is he always such hard work?' she asks.

'Often worse.'

Tomasz shakes his head and sits down.

'Who?'

The woman doesn't smile. She puts her cup down, unhitches her handbag from her shoulder, opens it and takes out a pen and a notepad.

The other two swap sarcastic looks.

The woman writes on the notepad and passes it across the table.

Tomasz looks at her and then at the pad again. He can't suppress a snort and a shake of the head.

'Can't fault the desire. Probably one of the most annoying people in the whole world.'

The woman sighs.

'If you'd only had to spend as much time in his company as I have, you'd have done it years ago.'

Tomasz pushes the paper towards Imelda, who reads it and then frowns.

He shakes his head and smiles.

'She's a Scottish savage who's had a sheltered upbringing … meaning she doesn't read the papers or watch the news.'

'I know who he is,' she says. 'But why him instead of anyone else?'

The woman shrugs.

'We need to move on. Change the rules of engagement before everyone wakes up.'

'Do you mean close down Parliament and set up a police state?'

The woman stares at him.

'What would you care? You'd be elsewhere.'

Tomasz stares back.

'You must think I'm stupid.'

The woman frowns.

'Do you think I'd fall for this as if I'd not get a bullet in the head the day after? Probably sooner than that.'

The woman sighs again and then stands up.

'I told them this wouldn't work, but they're determined to go through with it. You've twenty-four hours to agree or we'll start going down the list.'

She walks to the door.

'Shame, really. Your sister has never looked happier.'

Tomasz explodes, crosses the room, and would have knocked her down except for the gun pointing towards him.

He stops.

She motions him to back off.

'As I said, twenty-four hours.'

She opens the door and backs out.

Tomasz follows her out, to find that the yard has sprouted a cohort of stern-faced men in black. Not black exactly, but no markings or company flashes.

He watches as the woman goes back to her car and drives away. The men fall back in regulation order with not a single change in their faces. As the last three stand watching, there's the sound of revving jeeps. And then they're all gone.

Tomasz, knowing they'll be out of sight by the time he gets to the gate, doesn't bother to go and look after the speeding vehicles.

He turns to look at Imelda, who is looking pale.

Completely out of character, he finds himself taking her in his arms and holding her until she stops shaking.

They go back inside.

That hollow feeling he knows so well, when they were told of an imminent attack or engagement.

He knows it will be filled with that weird, cold composure that gets you through, beats back the fear of instant death – or, worse still, shattering injury.

He takes her to bed.

He never had that in Afghanistan.

⌒

The following morning Ellie is first up, having had hardly any sleep.

She leaves the gently snoring figure curled up in the bed, descends the ridiculously huge staircase and walks along the corridor to the kitchen.

The only other big houses she's spent any time in are the tumbledown relics owned by her uncles. *Tumbledown* is not quite the correct description, in that all three of them are totally different.

Uncle Rollo's is probably the worst, in that he's never kept a wife or lover for longer than five years, so no one's ever managed to put his vast house in any order. He just moves from one floor or section to another, leaving the previous wreckage to moulder. The last time she went, he'd ascended to the servants' quarters on the third floor. It had lots of smaller rooms than down below, so more scope for clutter and forgetting.

Uncle William's is a large farmhouse, so wellies and chickens everywhere are de rigeur.

The only one that is partly organised is the west wing of Uncle Geoffrey's town house, but that's entirely down to the wicked witch, his wife Harriet, who she can never bring herself to call her aunty. Even though she knows the heating is on, it always makes her shiver and want to leave as soon as she gets there.

But she finds Louisa's house is just very still, like it's holding its breath. Not something scary, a sort of anticipation that something is going to happen … soon. And, this early in the morning, it is a bit unnerving. She makes a coffee and finds some cereal, then walks around until she finds the conservatory, with its enormous plants, which seem to love being all cooped up, if their luxuriousness is a symptom of happiness.

She stands looking out at the garden, which she suspects extends all the way to the hedge along by the river. Opening the door a twitch enables her to just hear its murmuring in the distance but it also lets the cold air in, so she quickly shuts it again.

On turning to find a seat, she is startled to see Louisa standing in the doorway.

A blue figure with a pale face.

But she's smiling. Not that fearsome glare, a trick she can still do that turns people into ice inside.

'A woman after my own heart,' she whispers. 'Early mornings alone.'

Ellie grins.

'Not now, though.'

Louisa laughs.

'Sorry. I'll take my tea back upstairs.'

Ellie shakes her head.

'Don't you dare,' she says.

The two of them sit side by side, staring out at the morning mist and the gradual brightening of the line of naked poplars along the riverside.

'So tell me why you're so interested in Hugh de Morville,' Louisa says.

Ellie gives her a stern look.

Louisa smiles.

'I do know who he was. I was married to another history buff, you know. I didn't always do rapt attention and he was good at knowing when he'd lost his audience, so shall I tell you the little I do know and then you can tell me chapter and verse?'

Ellie giggles.

'Am I that bad?'

Louisa gives her a one of her cool looks.

'I'm afraid you are, my dear, just as bad as John was … that beady look in your eyes.'

Ellie frowns.

'Really?'

Louisa nods.

'Oh, yes, but don't worry … I'll give you until my stomach tells me it's breakfast time.'

Ellie stares at her, but then grins again.

'OK. I'll try to do the potted version.'

'Do I need to take notes?'

Ellie shakes her head.

'I'm sure your memory is good enough.'

She does the short version but leaves the most important fact till last.

'However, the most interesting thing is that there is evidence that he did come briefly to Dryburgh in 1200, not long after Richard died at Châlus.'

At this point, Ellie stops and checks Louisa's face.

Louisa smiles.

'Please don't stop, not now,' she whispers.

Ellie frowns and wonders whether she's being patronised.

'Well, that's about it,' she murmurs.

Louisa isn't having that.

'But why? Why did he come here?'

'Exactly,' says Ellie.

'Just to visit his father's grave?'

'Maybe. After all, he was getting quite old himself, probably in his late fifties. He died in 1202. Don't know where or exactly when, just that his niece inherited the lordship of Dryburgh in 1203.'

'So he could be buried there as well?'

'Possibly.'

Louisa remains still, her fingers steepled together like that Dürer drawing she has a copy of in the library.

'But what's that got to do with the message Tata left you?'

Ellie's eyes glitter.

'I don't expect you can read Occitan, can you?'

Louisa frowns.

'No, I don't. Who can?'

'Well, Mali can read it and speak it, like her father, but it's not the same as the language Richard and Hugh would have spoken or written – in the same way that the English of that time was not the same as now, and hardly ever used to write anything down. All the documents I've had to read are in vulgate Latin.'

Louisa gives her another frown.

Then Ellie stands up and goes to stand looking out of the window.

Louisa waits.

The air goes still.

And then Ellie starts to speak.

Quietly at first but then gathering momentum.

A sing-song language, vaguely French. But harsher, more like Spanish.

Louisa catches the odd word because she speaks both French and Spanish quite well.

Ellie finishes.

'What does that mean?'

'It's not easy, even though Tata taught me to read and speak Occitan, because it's poetic and, I suspect, deliberately mysterious. Like a complicated crossword puzzle or a riddle.'

'Is that what Tata left you?' asks Louisa.

Ellie gives her a stern look.

'Some of it.'

Louisa waits.

But the moment passes.

Until it's interrupted.

'I think the English saying is "Like getting water from a stone".'

They both turn to see Mali standing in the doorway still in her nightshirt, a Barcelona number ten, which even Louisa knows is Messi.

All three of them burst out laughing, although Ellie's face is a little sheepish for a few seconds.

Louisa breaks the moment and declares that breakfast needs to be taken and Fletcher needs to be roused.

After they are all watered and fed, Louisa declares that as a legitimate four-person pod they can go for a walk together. Fletcher shakes his head, but the other three know exactly where they're going and that he's going to be the driver.

His last thought, as he turns westwards along the main road, is that being a long-retired police officer with a fair few commendations won't cut any ice with the Borders police officers, but that Louisa's death ray stare might.

⤳

Magda stares at the drawing.

The sulky girl's father has managed to persuade her to do a drawing and has sent it by email.

He's certainly right about her ability. The sketch is superb. She's even caught the staring eyes, which so unnerved her.

Amelia arrives with two teas and glances at it.

'Who's that?' she asks with a frown.

Magda glances at her. Is that a frown of recognition? 'Do you know him?'

Amelia frowns again and Magda offers her the phone. She takes it over to the window and studies it.

Still frowning, she gives it back.

'Not sure,' she murmurs, 'but…'

'Where? When?' Magda prompts.

Amelia shakes her head.

'I think I do, but I can't place him.'

They both sit down. Magda knows not to badger her. People need time for their internal records manager to find the right context, the right place or moment to pin the image on to.

Unfortunately this doesn't work right now, as two of the four children Amelia has brought with her come bundling into the room, fighting over some toy or other.

Magda walks through to the library. She's made it quite clear that she doesn't do children. It's the one thing that comes between them. She knows, or has told herself, that Amelia's weakness with discipline is down to having had an abusive husband, who beat her and all the children on a regular basis.

She waits till the noise has died down before returning.

The boys are at the table, obediently eating their breakfasts.

She gives them a stern look, but they ignore her.

Amelia is at the sink, her hands busy with pots.

She's looking out of the window.

She stops. One hand in the water, the other pushing back a falling lock of hair.

'He was on the help desk at the council offices,' she declares. 'When I went to sort out the council tax – which of course Duncan hadn't paid.'

'I don't suppose you can remember his name, can you?'

'She shakes her head.

'Don't think he said, but he was helpful. Gave me the forms to fill in and who to contact.'

Magda is straight on to her mobile.

'That's brilliant. You're a star,' she murmurs to her as she waits for Gatti to reply.

The two boys look at her with a frown, then grin at each other. They already know that their mother is a star.

⌒

At least it isn't raining.

The four-person pod has arrived at the abbey and parked above the hotel car park, which surprisingly has five or six cars sitting there.

Fletcher frowns at them.

'Aren't hotels supposed to be closed?'

Louisa shakes her head.

'No. They can have people staying, but they have to eat in their own rooms.'

Fletcher shrugs his shoulders.

'It's not as good as it was when it was privately owned. Used to be one of our favourite places.'

The two girls have ignored all this and have vaulted over the low wall and disappeared into the trees.

Louisa helps Fletcher over the wall and then he turns to help her.

'Turning in to a couple of auld gimmers,' mutters Fletcher, attempting a Todmorden accent.

'Speak for yourself, old man,' comes the rasping reply.

They both laugh and set off towards the red stone ruins.

They find the two girls in one of the few buildings still sporting a roof.

Inevitably, Ellie has brought a ground plan, which she's photocopied.

'This is the earliest part still left standing from the twelfth century, the sleeping quarters for the monks,' says Ellie, not reading from any book or a brochure.

Fletcher can't stop a stab of pride and a little recognition of his own stubborn, investigative nature.

They go back out into the weak sunshine.

'It's very unlikely we would be able to find anything here. The abbey was attacked and burnt no end of times. It's a miracle there's anything left at all,' she added.

'Where's Walter Scott buried?' he asks.

'Over there,' she points. 'But he had bits knocked down to make it look more Romantic.'

'I thought it was the Earl of Buchan who did that,' said Louisa.

Ellie smiles like her best student has done some homework.

'You're right. They were both involved: both trying to pervert history to fit in with their Romantic ideas.'

'So where's your man's father buried, then?' asks Fletcher, trying to show he's keeping up.

'Well, the plaque is over there, but we can't be sure that's where he was actually buried, given the Romantic interference,' says Ellie, with a stern look.

They go and stand where they can look up at it.

It's at this moment a voice calls out.

'Hey, what are you doing in there? The abbey is closed.'

A combination of Louisa's haughty connections and Fletcher producing a long-dead police identity card doesn't really convince the local jobsworth, so they retreat back to the car and wait until he stomps away.

'I'm afraid it's little use us trying to find anything here now,' says Ellie sadly. 'There's only one reference to Hugh the Younger ever coming here, maybe to visit his father's grave, but we don't know where it was. There were a couple of attempts in the seventies to dig here and there, but Scott's determination to turn it into a fairy tale is stronger than the truth.'

'Aye, John said much the same,' says Louisa.

They stand silently looking out at the raging torrent the Tweed has become after all the snow has melted and the subsequent continuous rain.

Mali puts her arm around Ellie's hunched shoulders.

'Let's go see the weird sisters,' she says quietly.

Louisa knows what she means, but Fletcher has to wait, while these three 'weird witches' take him there.

It isn't far.

Back up the drive and then down a lane towards the river.

Ellie and Louisa know he won't spot the temple, because most people are too focused on the river and the bridge ahead. Especially today, as its roaring draws you on.

They let him follow them onto the bridge and stand looking down at the fierce currents swirling beneath.

'So where are the weird sisters, then?' he asks above the thunder, thinking it's obviously them.

But Ellie turns and points back at a bunch of trees beyond the bridge end.

He looks where she's pointing but can't see anything but the trees until he realises that some of the straight trunks are pillars and they're holding up a roof. And what's that underneath?

He follows them back and round to a straggly path he hadn't noticed.

Up to the top of a little outcrop and there they are.

Four naked ladies, dancing in the wind.

But they're not all there. Literally.

Only half-shapes of their bodies, cleverly positioned to look whole, but in reality only empty shells.

'Not Scott, I'm glad to say,' says Ellie, 'although I dare say he would have approved. His best buddy Buchan had it done, but not these four winds that are here now. It was a statue of Apollo originally, atop a frieze of the Nine Muses.'

They walk back up the car. But, when they set off, Louisa suggests that they may as well go and check out Mr Wallace while they're there.

Again 'Mr Wallace' means little to Fletcher, but Mali puts him straight by whispering,

'William, as in Scottish hero number one, aka Braveheart,' which isn't much use because he thinks he went to sleep ten minutes in when Laura put the film on.

Unfortunately, he doesn't get to see him today either because the footpath is blocked off with the distinctive blue and white tapes. A young officer officiously gets out of his car to tell them that they can't go in because it's a crime scene.

They don't even get out of their car.

Louisa thinks she heard a body has been found, but hadn't realised it was here.

So instead they're on their way back home, given that a drop into a cafe, or more likely a pub, is still off limits.

However, if you have to go somewhere for a drink and a bit of lunch you could do a lot worse than Louisa's, especially as their noses tell them that something scrumptious is already on its way as soon as she opens the front door.

∼

Ziggy has his teeth into a new mystery provided by the equally mysterious Eleanor de Camville, who is Fletcher's step-granddaughter. I assume this is the correct word, as he was never married to her grandmother, Laura, who unfortunately died a year ago. Try to keep up.

Ellie, as she prefers to be called, is a medieval history student at Edinburgh University, and she's in a relationship with a rather beautiful maiden called Mali. I think she's half-Arab, half-French, and she has the most alluring soft brown eyes I've ever seen. The sort of young woman who regularly leaves men, young and old, bumping into doors and walls after she's passed by.

Anyway, Ellie is a bit obsessive, to say the least.

Her grand-tante and grand-oncle were savagely murdered seven years ago in their cottage in the woods in deepest Limousin.

Since then, she's been researching their past and following up some leads, which she has shared with Ziggy – which, unbelievably, have stumped him. If you knew him you would know that is a rare event.

So now he's totally obsessed with trying to solve the riddles she's given him.

Part of the problem is that the riddles are written in Occitan, a nearly dead language that is getting a bit of a revival in southern France and northern Spain, he tells me. He's played me some people speaking it and it does sound like French or Spanish, but more sing-song.

And – would you believe it? – there seems to be a local Borders connection, hence the photos hanging from the wires in his workroom. It's beginning to look like the previous investigation already, but it has some way to go before the forest thickens and becomes darker the further you go in.

It's strange, really, that he uses notes clipped on to strings, when you'd think that, being a computer whizz, he'd do it all on the screens. Yes, generally at least three, but he says that he needs 'concrete' as well as 'virtual', whatever that means. They're bits of paper and banks of screens, which make the forest.

The local detective Magda Steil doesn't seem to be copied in yet, but she's investigating a recently discovered body in the woods and my money is that they're somehow connected. No evidence at all yet, but there's something about this part of the world where everything seems to be interconnected, no matter how distant they are timewise.

I'm glad Freya has come back to stay with us. At least she's partial to a walk or two, although she's still recovering her strength after the long periods of being cooped up in safe houses and hidden away from prying eyes.

Like Ziggy, she's a bit weird as well. She can't forget anything she's read or seen on a screen. Some kind of hardwiring in her brain, she says.

Don't know how she copes with that. I forget what I've gone for at the supermarket before I get out of the house. Hence all the little bits of paper I leave all over the place.

Anyway, I've done the washing-up, so I'm off out. The sun is shining, and the snow has gone, so I'm going along the riverside, hoping the river has gone down a bit. Some of the paths were under water after the snow melted but that was over a couple weeks ago, so they should be drier by now.

A weak sun lights the way as I'm heading off upstream.

Freya's deep in some book, so shakes her head when I ask if she wants to come with me. So I'm the Lone Walker once again. To be honest, that's how I like it.

CHAPTER 9
PASSING SWEET

Magda is now thinking she's found a possible suspect. She calls the girl's father and asks him to get as many names of other people at the art classes as his daughter can remember.

He comes back to her within the hour.

Eight names. But only first names, of course. But she does remember that one of the older men, someone in his sixties, is a town councillor.

It doesn't take long to track down Jamie Graham.

She gives him a call.

His wife answers, all cheerful, until Magda says who she is.

'Aye, what's the auld villain been up to now?' This sounds a bit wearisome.

'Nothing that I know of, madam,' says Magda, cautious not to get off on the wrong foot.

'I'll get him fer you,' says the woman and silence reigns. For some time.

But eventually a cheery voice comes to the phone.

'Ah didna do it,' he says, and then laughs.

Magda reintroduces herself, and then asks if he remembers going to art classes.

This stumps the man, and there's another pause.

'Aye, of course I do, and I did pay the old man and was happy to do so. He knew his stuff and gave us all a lot of confidence, right enough.'

Magda waits to see if there will be any more.

'You do know he died?' says Graham.

'Yes,' she replies, 'but it's one of his other students we're looking for.'

'I see… Which one? I canna say I can remember all their names. Some people only lasted a couple of sessions.'

Magda can't stop herself from being intrigued.

'Why was that, do you think?' she asks.

There's another pause.

'Well, he was OK for me, but I think some people thought he was … rather slow. I mean, he didn't say much. And, if you asked him a question, he was never quick to reply.'

'What sort of question?'

'Oh, anything. Simple things, like, "How do you make a particular shade of colour?" Or harder stuff, like … composition.'

Magda waits again, but all she can hear is his laboured breathing.

'OK. We're trying to find a particular person,' she says. 'A young man, I guess in his thirties. We think his first name is Gordon.'

There's another pause and then a bout of coughing.

'Sorry about that,' he says. 'Emphysema. Drowning in your own skin, someone called it.'

She can't say anything to that.

'Aye, I ken who you mean, but I canna tell you much about him. He was even quieter than Conrad.'

'Conrad?'

'The teacher. He was a German. POW, didn't go back. I think his real surname was Meissen, but he changed it to Mason.'

'So what can you tell me about Gordon?'

She waits again, as another coughing fit intervenes.

'Sorry,' he says.

'Do you want me to call back?' she asks.

'Nah, I can't tell you much more. He was quiet, didn't make eye contact. If you asked him anything, he wouldn't tell you any more than Conrad. Sometimes he'd just ignore you, like he hadn't heard you.'

Magda wonders what else she can ask.

'Do you know where he lives?'

'No. As I said, he didn't say much, and we weren't encouraged to get to know each other. Conrad would just say hello and then give us a few instructions and then we got going. We were often silent for long periods. Not common in this household, but I came to like it.'

Magda thinks how restful that must have been in comparison with the raucous art classes she remembers with Miss Hainsworth, who could no more control a class of teenage girls than climb Mount Everest. A spindly old stick who often cried.

How cruel we were, she reflects.

'So what did he paint?'

'Oh, that's easy. He was obsessed with Dryburgh Abbey. I think he must have gone there a lot.'

Magda perks up. The burial site overlooks the ruins.

'Really…? Can I ask from what angle?'

Another bout of coughing.

She waits. Poor man.

'Every which way,' eventually comes the reply.

'And … were there any people in these pictures?'

'Oh, aye, just the one. The same woman wandering about.'

Magda catches her breath.

'How do you mean, the same?

'Well, she was just a tiny figure in the distance: thin body, long hair, long dress dragging through the grass. Sort of Romantic, I suppose you'd call the style… Well, that's what Conrad said it was. As I said, the man was a bit weird.'

Magda can hardly believe this.

She wants to ask more, but then realises there are other people she can question.

'Are you in contact with anyone else who went to the classes?'

'Only Jennie Cuthbertson. She'll talk to anyone. She tried to get more out of him than anyone else.'

With that he hands the phone back to his wife, who is able to give her the woman's phone number.

Magda thanks her and says she hopes she hadn't worsened her husband's condition.

'Nah, hen. He's his own worst enemy.'

Magda stares out of the window.

This seems too easy. Leads like this come once in a lifetime, in her limited experience.

She taps in the woman's number.

Although the woman is as helpful as can be, she doesn't add much to the knowledge she'd received from the coughing man.

Except the one time she saw him at Dryburgh, but only at a distance, scurrying away behind one of the buildings and disappearing.

It was only as she is saying her thank-yous that the woman suddenly laughs and says,

'But I didn't tell you that one of his paintings is in the library.'

'What?' says Magda.

'In the town library. They chose it in a competition. As far as I know it's still there, although, of course, it's been ages since it's been open.'

Magda thanks the woman and immediately contacts the library, and then must spend a good five minutes going from one number to another until she gets the chief librarian.

'Why? Yes,' she says. 'Although I haven't been there myself since Christmas.'

Magda sighs.

'But it's not a problem. You can see it online.'

'Where?'

'On our website.'

And, sure enough, there it is.

But of course, as the coughing man said, there is only a slim figure in the distance.

Magda knows there are quite a few paintings like this on the first-floor corridor at home. Hazy romantic scenes with tiny people dwarfed by either the scenery or the weather.

So no chance of seeing a likeness to the body, apart from the long hair.

She's about to give up when she notices some writing at the bottom of the painting. Is that a title?

Passing Sweet?

Meaning?

And then she wonders why she can't see a name.

She rings the librarian back again.

'Do you have a contact number or address for him? Even his name?'

'Well, not at home. I suppose we must have had some contact details for him, but it's quite a long time ago. It was 2015, I think. If it's really important I could search our records. But if it's that far back it will be on our old system, which I can't access from home.'

She hesitates.

'I think his name was Geoffrey. Can't recall a surname.'

Magda convinces her that it is urgent and important, so she agrees to go down to the library that afternoon.

〜

Ellie can't wait to get back and check out the police investigation.

She goes straight to her laptop and to a lot of frustration.

Hardly anything. Just a body found near Wallace's monument confirmed to be a missing woman called Susan Kingston.

Even the reports of the woman's disappearance way back in 2014 are limited.

She stares out of the window.

The big fir trees are being buffeted by the wind.

The year 2014?

Is that just a coincidence?

She can't see how the two events can be connected.

But the remembrance of Tata and Tonton's deaths always makes her weep.

But then she has a thought.

She gets the box out of her bag. Good job Mali is downstairs, or she'd be groaning.

She rechecks the words.

Nothing to indicate Scotland at all.

For someone like Richard or even Henry II, Scotland was just the other side of a ragged line on a map. As far as she knows neither of them ever went there, and William the Lion took plenty of advantage of that.

Is there really a connection here?

Why would a man like him come all this way north? He'd fought all over France and had been to the Holy Land, but what could possibly interest him up here? Why did his father come here, for that matter? It was just a parcel of land handed out as an acknowledgement of his support. Support that was only feudal, nothing to do with his origins or interest in the place itself. He would have only spoken French, not English or whatever the Scots were speaking then. Gaelic, presumably, although William the Lion would have spoken Norman French as well.

The more she thinks about it the more intriguing it becomes. Even the distances involved. On horseback it would have taken over a week to get from the south coast to here. She can't even be sure that he was at Châlus when Richard died, and why would he want to come here other than to visit his father's grave? And why was his father buried here anyway?

She stares out of the window, her head whirling with the questions like the wind outside.

⌒

Imelda is only out feeding the horses for twenty minutes or so, but when she goes back into the house she knows he's gone. No Hengist, either.

When will she ever learn?

Always ends up with the worst sort of men.

She picks up the note lying on the table.

Two crossings-out and a riddle. Typical.

Hasta la vista and something else she can hardly read, so she scrumples it up and throws it away.

She goes to check the van, but it's still there.

She scans the hillsides, but can't see him anywhere.

He has just disappeared into thin air.

But when she goes back indoors she knows the rifle will have gone, and it has.

She stares out of the window.

Does she wait for that woman to return or get herself back to Edinburgh?

No answer comes.

So she's still sitting there ten minutes later.

Her decision made, she goes to pack her things.

She rings up Johnny down the road to get him to look after the horses and an hour later she's on her way, although the thought of where she's going makes her heart sink.

From the ridge, Tomasz waits until she drives away.

Even his cold heart gives a sigh.

But it's for the best.

He can't guarantee that she's any safer without him, but he can't risk taking her with him.

He doesn't really know what he's going to do. Being a dead man walking doesn't do much for your determination.

He's never experienced a quiet life, and doubts he could manage one anyway.

So … going out in a blaze of glory?

He sighs.

No such thing.

Down the other side of the hill he would no doubt be welcome in Victoria's bed, but why put her in danger yet again?

Instead he heads east along the ridge.

There are always other ports in the storm.

∽

Louisa rings Helena.

A quick run through everyone's health and whereabouts takes less time than usual.

'It's no use asking me,' says Helena when Louisa asks about Magda. 'She never tells me what she's doing.'

Louisa understands Magda's good reasons for that but she merely agrees, having nothing to say, especially as she's never ever even contemplated having children.

'I don't seem to have her number any longer.'

It takes Helena some time to find her mobile, and there are a lot of Polish mutterings accompanying this search.

'Damn thing always hides,' she says at one point.

But then there's a sigh.

'It's been on the table all the time,' she says.

But Magda calls Louisa first.

'This is a bit awkward,' says Magda.

'Well, I do have Michael staying with me,' says Louisa, with a small, almost girlish laugh.

Magda sighs.

'Um, I know. That's why I'm calling. Your car and four occupants including yourself were identified at the Wallace memorial car park.'

'Well, we'd been to the abbey and then went up to see the statue and found it all closed off.'

There is another pause.

'Not sure you should be out and about like that.'

'I think we're a pod,' says Louisa, trying not to laugh at such a silly word.

Again there's another pause.

'And the two young things are Fletcher's granddaughter and her partner.'

'Not sure if four unrelated people counts as a pod.'

'Anyway,' says Louisa, ignoring that, 'Ellie wanted to take us, because she wanted to show us where Hugh de Morville is supposed to be buried. It's her ongoing investigation. Part of her course, I think.'

'Who?'

'His son was one of the four knights who killed Thomas Becket.'

Magda had had enough ancient history from her father and so had dropped the subject at school as soon as she could, but she has heard of this story.

'But that was in Canterbury Cathedral, hundreds of years ago, wasn't it?' she said. 'What on earth was she expecting to find here now?'

'Try telling her that,' laughs Louisa. 'She's inherited her bloody-minded doggedness from Fletcher, I think.'

Magda is shaking her head.

'I can't be bothered with thousand-year-old murderers. We've enough trouble catching the more recent ones.'

Louisa sighs.

'Well, good luck. And we'll try to stay at home, ma'am.'

Before Magda can say anything, the line is disconnected.

Was that Louisa making fun of her?

Still, she is now sure the murderer has chosen the burial site because it overlooks the abbey... But where is he?

She can't find any record of him.

Even Geoffrey or Gordon could just be fictional.

She goes back to the librarian.

'Did you have any correspondence with the painter?'

This temporarily stumps the woman.

'Er, well, I suppose we must have done. Let me just think...'

Magda considers where she was eight years ago.

'Meteoric rise through the ranks,' some people might say about her rapid promotion. She knows that many of the male police officers – who she has leapfrogged over – only give her grudging support, while muttering to each other about the 'laird's daughter'. She knows she can point to several arrests and cases she has resolved, but the events during lockdown didn't enhance that reputation. Losing your laptop and phone to an intruder was embarrassing. But, facing a gunman alone in their own home, how would they have reacted?

A voice brings her back to the present.

'His name was Henry Morton. I've got a phone number and an address,' says the librarian.

Magda thanks her and then immediately calls the number.

It's been disconnected.

She checks.

The address doesn't exist either. She realises that even if it was only seven years ago, addresses weren't all digitised and retrievable in seconds like they are now. And why would a librarian check someone's address back then?

Morton? Why is that ringing a bell? And Henry? Nothing like Gordon.

She stares out of the car windscreen.

She's missing some connection.

She starts the car engine, knowing that her brain will turn it around once she's concentrating on something else.

∽

'Louisa Cunninghame,' says the voice.

'Who?'

'Do you know her?'

Not sure how much to reveal, he pauses. Certainly not the disdainful way she treated him. Haughty madam that she was, she was not likely to have changed much since.

'Our paths have crossed,' he decides is the best description.

'So what do you know?'

'Rich. Very rich. Her own family fell on hard times after the war, I think, but she married well.'

'Who?'

'First was some upstart eighties car salesman who was a Tory MP for a while, then he got mixed up in some drug gang warfare. Ended up in prison, I think. She took him to the cleaners … and the driers. The second was a much wiser decision. John Knox, straight as a die. I think he was cannily linked to oil investment and few other offshore ventures. He left her an exceedingly rich widow indeed.'

∽

Fletcher finds Ellie in the library. Books all over the place. Scribbled notes littered like confetti, whereas he always kept everything in his head. He would get nowhere with the current policing of data collection.

He waits till she sighs and turns to look at him.

'Anything?' he asks.

She mutters something that sounds like, 'Cha-cha la fama.'

He frowns.

'*Cherchez la femme*,' she says with big eyes – which is always scary, they're so very green.

'Which one?' he asks.

'*Exactement*,' she replies, and sighs.

He wonders whether this French exam is going to continue, because he's already at his limit.

She leans back and looks out of the window.

How did she get so tall and willowy, more like her father than her dark-haired mother?

He sits down on what he feels might be a hideously expensive yet rickety-looking chair.

There is a long silence.

Motes start to fall, having no breath to carry or swirl them anywhere.

His gaze follows hers as she stares out of the window, although he knows she's looking elsewhere.

'How did you feel about that woman … Fern Robinson?' she asks quietly.

He frowns. Where's that coming from?

'How do mean, feel?' he asks.

She doesn't look at him.

'Did you think she was a monster?'

He wonders where this is going and how much she knows about Fern.

'Not a monster, but clever and elusive.'

The green eyes swivel to pin him to his seat.

'I've read the old news stories,' she says. 'Was it five or six other women?

'Six,' he says, 'but then she turned to men. Another three, at least. That's not counting the copycat killings.'

There is another long silence.

'What were her motives?' she asks.

He shrugs, recalling the arguments and all the press speculation.

'The psychologists eventually called it "Snow White revenge psychosis", or something like that.'

Ellie nods.

'Meaning a sort of misplaced Freudian mother hatred?'

He shrugs his shoulders.

'If you say so.'

She turns to look at him again. This time the eyes are torchlike.

'Did it even get to you?'

He shuffles uncomfortably. What did he feel? Can he even remember? It's not often that someone has interrogated him. But the eyes are still burning into him.

He shrugs.

'I guess ... in the end it's just solving the puzzle. Joining the dots, I think someone called it.'

She turns away.

'But how did you ... or how do you feel about her now?'

Again, he's stumped.

She frowns.

'Did you admire her?'

He stares at her.

'Yeah, in a way, as she was impossible to catch. Always seemed to know how to completely disappear. Like a ghost.'

'But you don't believe in ghosts, do you?'

He shakes his head.

'Not ones that could do what she did to people. Other women...'

'So what about this latest case? The woman found buried near the Wallace statue.'

He shakes his head.

'Don't know yet. Didn't even realise it had happened. Don't watch the news any longer.'

She smiles.

'But you're interested now?'

He grins.

'Maybe … but why are you so intrigued?'

'I'm not, really. It's nothing to do with my research.'

It's his turn to frown.

He stares at her. She doesn't look away. Where does all that stubbornness come from? There's none of his blood in her.

'Do you believe in second sight?'

'Meaning?'

'The ability to perceive things that haven't happened yet.'

'Don't you mean premonition?'

She laughs.

'That as well.'

He grins.

'Not really. I suppose I've always believed that the truth is out there, but often it's hidden behind lies and confusion. "Can't see the wood for the trees," as my sister would say, … although she just thought people weren't looking properly. Bringing six kids up with no support from a drunken bastard, who she eventually kicked out, didn't give her much time for philosophy.'

'So it's all just a puzzle to be resolved?'

He nods, wondering why the revelation about his upbringing didn't even get a flicker.

'The problem with clues is that sometimes you just don't see them. But mainly you misinterpret them or think they're not significant.'

Ellie stares at him and then looks away out of the window.

The silence gathers again, creeping all around them.

He realises they have disturbed the motes. Was he waving his arms about or was it her?

He reaches out and touches her shoulder. Her hand comes up to touch his.

'But she's the exception, isn't she?' she whispers.

He nods.

'Yes . . . because what she did to other women was so . . . unique. If it had been a man, it would have been . . . well not exactly unusual. Like the Yorkshire Ripper. It took a long time to catch him, but that's because the different police forces didn't share their information or have one person leading the investigation.'

'Like you, you mean?

He shrugs.

'Maybe, but my methods weren't liked then.'

'How do you mean?'

He looks away.

'Too many men are like dogs on heat. They're pack animals, each one wanting to know their rank, although some get more ambitious than others. It's the showing off I can't stand. The "Look at me" stuff. The "Being one of the lads" syndrome. Never been that for me. Most men see me as a loner, I expect, which is fine with me. I've never been in a gang. Don't like being told what to do. I get angry . . . but the worst thing is, I've trouble with loyalty. Your grandmother was the only one who ever managed to stop that, and...'

'It's OK,' she says.

He wipes the tears from his cheek and stands up.

'Let's go for a walk, eh?'

So they do.

At what point did Magda feel OK about sharing police information with someone like Sigismund Hook, who she knew from her own research had a significant criminal record? Nothing violent or obscene, but he did have little regard for online privacy, which in his case includes extensive hacking of extremely sensitive government and other secretive sites.

Even in one case from prison, although no one could prove that he had a device or that it was he who closed down the whole computer system, which allowed all sorts of misbehaviour and vandalism until he agreed to reconfigure it. Just for two hours, but no one had any idea how much information and funds other inmates were able to access during that time.

So, as communicating with him online was certainly not a good idea, she wends her way to the White House, where he and his entourage have reinstalled themselves.

Entourage?

Not exactly as weird as him, but still a bit disconcerting.

A woman whose mother was a serial killer who was never apprehended and who could possibly be still alive, and another woman who has a phenomenal photographic memory and who is still suspiciously monitored by secret service agencies frightened about what she might reveal.

The door, as usual, is open.

There are no answering voices, so she carries on through to where the tapping is coming from.

'Hi Magda,' says the man at the screens, without turning round to look.

Eyes in the back of his head as well?

'Anyone else here?' she asks.

'Nah,' he says. 'Over the hills or tramping the river paths, I suspect.'

'Back soon?' she asks.

'Black, three sugars,' comes the predictable reply.

No acknowledgement of a woman's role in this house, she notes, although she knows that he would have said the same to any man and that he has gender issues himself. Not that he's bothered by them, as might be assumed given the bright green dress he's wearing and the shiny black bobbed wig.

When she comes back with the coffee, she's surprised to find him swinging round to take the mug from her.

Trying not to be disconcerted by his make-up and the dark fringe, she frowns at his piercing look.

'So what do you know already?' she asks. No point in being coy.

'Intriguing,' he says.

'The burial, you mean?'

'Uh-huh. The fair Ophelia.'

She shakes her head. That is definitely not common knowledge.

'It's OK. The secret's safe with me,' he says with a sly grin, 'but it's still not a good way to die.'

Magda nods.

They're both silent, respectful even.

'Do you know about the artist?' she asks.

'Well, I know there's a painting involved, but can't make any other connections.'

'Apparently he only painted one subject. A woman wandering among the ruins of Dryburgh Abbey dressed in the sort of long dress she was found in.'

Ziggy stares at her.

'Really?'

She nods.

'Flowers?'

'Which ones?'

'The ones mentioned in *Hamlet*: rosemary, pansies, fennel and daisies…'

'But not violets?' he nods.

She smiles. Can't catch him out.

'No, not violets.'

'What about roses?'

She frowns.

'Yes, there were some.'

Now Ziggy smiles.

'Lilies?'

She stares at him and frowns.

'So it's not Ophelia, then,' he murmurs.

She shakes her head.

'Why not? Maybe he wasn't totally obsessed with that story.'

'Or maybe a different story?'

She glares at him. She's always hated secrets. Her father was the worst. Hiding things in the library was his favourite game.

'Go on, then.'

'The fair Rosamund,' he whispers conspiratorially.

She frowns.

'Who was she?'

'Um … much easier to connect her to Dryburgh than Ophelia, who was Danish and fictional.'

Again she frowns.

'Are you suggesting that overlooking the abbey could be as significant as the nature of the burial?'

He nods.

'There is a possible connection between her lover and the abbey.'

'Who was he?'

'Henry II.'

Now she frowns and shakes her head.

'King of England from 1154 to 1189, but spent most of his life in France, mainly fighting with his sons and bashing the Frogs, although he was as Froggy as them. Born in Le Mans.'

Again she shakes her head.

'So what's the connection?'

'He was married to Eleanor of Aquitaine but also had lots of dalliances, and this Rosamund was supposed to be his great love.'

'So is she buried here?'

He shakes his head, as if she's not following.

'No, she's buried down south somewhere, although she was dug up from the chapel he paid for and put outside with the ordinary folk, because some bishop declared her to be a floozie, who shouldn't be buried in hallowed ground.'

Magda is getting exasperated. Just the sort of long-winded stories her father used to tell.

'But the person who is supposed to be buried there is Hugh de Morville,' says Ziggy, but he's now laughing, while she's put her face in her hands. 'He was the one who founded the abbey.

'Keep up,' he says. 'Only one more connection.'

She looks up. She can't stop grinning.

'You know of course who Hugh de Morville is, don't you?' he says, his dark eyes twinkling with mischief.

She shakes her head but can't stop laughing.

'Of course, I don't,' she cries.

'He was the father of one of the murderers of Thomas Becket in 1170.'

Again she stares at him.

'And?'

'He was called Hugh as well.'

She sighs. How long is this going to take?

'After he'd done his fifteen years' penance he became a trusted companion of Henry's son Richard I, the Lionheart. He was probably with him when Richard died at Châlus after an arrow wound went gangrenous.'

She puts her head in her hands. This was too much.

'So what's the connection to Dryburgh?'

'Not sure, but the whispers among the Holy Grail brigade tell me that some treasure was found at Châlus and that it was spirited away after Richard's death.'

'And brought up here?'

He nods.

'It's possible. Hugh, the younger de Morville, came here a year or so before he died in 1202.'

'But…' Magda wants to scream.

He pauses for the final uncovering.

'I don't know … but Rosamund was buried with "roses, lilies and flowers of the field".'

She stares at him.

He shrugs and sips his coffee. Then makes a face – as by now, of course, it's cold.

Surprisingly, he gets up and goes to make some more.

Magda sits there staring at the paper chains moving slowly in the draught he's made as he goes.

This is ridiculous.

Why would someone murder and bury someone to replicate an eight-hundred-year-old love affair, when the only tenuous connection was that the man's father was supposed to be buried here?

She shakes her head.

Ziggy returns with two fresh coffees.

They sit looking at each other.

'It's too far-fetched,' she murmurs. 'Can you imagine me going to the super with this?'

Ziggy makes a face. He wouldn't bother, she thinks.

'It's precisely these fragile threads that often lead to the truth,' he says in a low voice. 'In any case, why would someone in the Borders be obsessed with Ophelia rather than Rosamund? There's nothing to connect Shakespeare to Scotland, other than *Macbeth*, and there's nothing there connecting to Dryburgh.'

'So we're looking for a history student rather than just an artist?'

He nods.

'What's the guy's name?'

Magda frowns. Why doesn't he even know already?

He shakes his head.

'You're getting secretive in your old age,' he says with a smile. 'Not sharing your information with the squad, not even your trusted Italian stallion.'

Magda can't help but grin.

It's not only that they've been encouraged to work alone if possible, but it's also that she's found it less pressurising to go solo.

'Not sure, that's why,' she answers defensively. 'I'm not even certain of his name, which might be Geoffrey or Gordon, but then the librarian tells me he was called Henry Morton.'

Ziggy laughs.

'There you are.'

She frowns and then realises.

'Henry Mor-ton, aka Hugh de Mor-ville.'

She stares at him. He grins and then the grin fades

'But that doesn't help, does it?' he says for her. 'Not likely to be his real name.'

She shakes her head.

'And it still doesn't tell me why.'

Chapter 10
History

I dropped history in the third year at school.

My 'not-mother', Mrs Henderson (just to remind you, I was abandoned by my real mother, the notorious Snow White Killer, when I was a baby) was pleased about this, as, being a God-fearing Methodist, she was suspicious of non-religious versions of the truth. You know, like there wasn't really a Garden of Eden or a Great Flood. This isn't the case nowadays for Methodists, I understand, but she was nothing but literal in her beliefs.

So I didn't get past the Romans. Or maybe we did do some stuff about the Victorians, but by then I was more interested in what was happening to my body.

Anyway, that's a huge gap. Fifteen hundred years or so. I'm one of those people who doesn't know whether the Spanish Armada was before the Civil War or not, or when either were.

I'm aware there's no love lost between the Scots and the English. Something to do with Culloden and Bonnie Prince Charlie didn't help, I think, but don't know when that was. Also, something about the Clearances? Again, just a blank.

So wandering about in the Scottish Borders is a historical mystery to me.

Someone told me they're all cattle rustlers. But there seem to be more sheep than cows now.

One good thing is they don't have a strong accent and are easier to understand than Geordies, especially when ex-DS Becket is having a rant about something.

'Just a noise,' as someone said.

So eavesdropping on Ziggy and Magda isn't any use. Why do people like them seem to skip whole chunks of thinking from their conversations? It's as if they know the missing chunks but can't waste time saying them.

Again? In another lockdown, which these two are breaking.

Suffice to say, as far as I can tell she's identified a body buried in a wood that has been buried with flowers. This seems to be significant to both her and Ziggy, but they can't agree about which story they're from.

Er...?

Isn't it normal to be buried with flowers?

Don't lots of people throw flowers into a grave?

Not much use, I grant you. Well, no use to the dead person.

Anyway, I'm gagging for a brew, so I'll just have to do that offstage cough trick to announce my presence.

⤳

The arrival of Ursula brings Magda back to the present.

Since she's learnt things about this woman's history, she's at the very least a bit wary of her. Especially the way she seems to creep up on you.

A few quick exchanges and she's out of there.

All that Ziggy has done is muddy the waters, which he seems to have a knack of doing. Just when it seemed she had a handle on the modus operandi he posits a completely different scenario, with an eight-hundred-year-old motive to deal with.

She calls Gatti and asks him to meet her at the burial site.

He's waiting for her at the car park.

For once it's not raining. In fact a weak sun is trying to kid-on that spring is coming. It's not. It's bitterly cold as they walk to the edge and look down upon the abbey. She tells him Ziggy's alternative suggestion, but she can see straight away that Gatti is dismissive.

'Who even knows all that stuff, except people like Hook or other crossword freaks?' he says.

She frowns.

Not his usual response.

She glances at him.

He's looking towards where the huge statue of William Wallace is hidden behind the trees. He shrugs and gestures towards the 'big man'.

'All that hero stuff is just a fairy story about Wallace and Bruce. It was all made up by Walter Scott and his friends.'

She waits to see if this outburst, which is completely out of character, has got any more legs, but he turns and gives her a smile.

'According to DS Johnson, anyway.'

She shakes her head and then laughs.

'And him with a master's degree in history, and all.'

They both return to gazing down at the abbey and its grounds.

It would be quite hidden when the trees are in leaf, but just now it's a good vantage point from which to see the layout.

'Actually, what we're looking at now is different from what Scott would have seen two hundred years ago,' he adds. 'The hotel's much later and the grounds are a lot smaller. The Temple of the Muses is now the Four Winds.'

Magda nods her agreement, having suffered long-winded lectures from her father that she's surprised to find she can remember.

'So what do we think?' she asks.

'My money is on Ophelia,' he murmurs.

She is inclined to agree, but it's all academic unless they can get a lead on the painter.

'Did you check with the librarian to see if she'd got his address?'

He nods his head and then sighs.

'False. No such number. Telephone the same.'

She stares into the distance. Clouds are gathering over the Cheviots.

'Did you check on similar scenarios?'

He shakes his head.

'Nothing recent in Scotland.'

Again, she's stumped.

'So all we've got is a one-off event? No copycat crimes. No repetition.'

Gatti shrugs his shoulders and then gives her a sly smile.

'Actually, the only historical similar murders were those committed by the Snow White Killer, back in the eighties.'

She stares at him.

'You mean the cases Fletcher investigated?'

He shrugs.

'Yes, apparently she always marked her victim's graves with roses, although they were planted rather than actually buried with the corpses.'

'And they were dead before she buried them,' she adds.

He looks away.

'And she was a woman,' he adds, unnecessarily.

'But never caught,' she whispers.

Gatti frowns and shakes his head.

'She'd be in her nineties.'

Magda didn't voice the thought that she'd just been in the company of that woman's daughter. That was too far-fetched to even contemplate. Ursula's a bit strange, but definitely not a murderer.

However, it did make her think that paying Fletcher a visit might be worth a punt.

～

The van pulls up at the gates.

Carter looks down the drive, which disappears into the fir trees twenty or so yards in.

He's not sure whether Louisa Cunninghame is a dog person. But it's not worth the risk, so he continues along the road to a pull in and finds his map. He quickly sees that there's a riverside path going along the back of her property and finds a legitimate way down from the road.

He gets his boots and rucksack out of the back, drives to the car park indicated for walkers and sets off.

It is not a good day for walking, and having a snood ready to pull up is a perfect way to remain anonymous. It's strange how sometimes disasters can be quite helpful in his line of business.

He's brought his camera. Not so much to record anything, but it seems an acceptable indicator of his reason to be out and about.

Eventually he spies the house through the trees.

There's no one in sight, so it's easy to climb the fence and get a bit closer.

He settles down to wait.

The birds return and give him some grief for disturbing them, but soon quieten down when they realise he's not moving about.

It's only then that he remembers he's left his rucksack and the chocolate bars in the van.

Magda realises that she'll be passing the turning to the murdered girl's mother's house on her way, so gives her a call.

The response is the usual dull agreement to see her.

Magda tries to imagine how it must feel. To be alone, knowing your daughter was murdered and buried in a makeshift grave. No explanation or reason. Just a body in a hole in the ground. At least now she'll be able to bury her properly. Have a grave to tend.

The house might have been pretty once, but the garden is untended.

There would be an extensive view if it weren't clouded over.

She knocks on the door and adjusts her mask.

A curtain twitches over to the right.

The door opens and the sad eyes blink. The woman gives a brief nod and Magda steps inside.

In the kitchen the table is clear.

No sign of a breakfast. No newspaper. No TV flickering. No radio. No cat or dog sniffing around. Just a solitary prisoner's cell.

The woman sits at the table.

No offer of a coffee.

Magda is almost overwhelmed by the desolation.

The woman's eyes focus on her.

There's only one question, but she doesn't ask it.

So Magda asks hers.

'Do you know or did your daughter know a man called Henry Morton?'

Magda watches as she consults her memory bank.

She shakes her head.

'No, I don't think so.'

Magda waits.

'Susan didn't have many friends,' she says quietly. This in a monotone. No indication of how she felt about that or why that should have been the case.

Silence ushers itself in again, like an unapologetic nosy neighbour pushing aside the curtain.

'Apart from Roz … but I told you about her.'

'Yes. I went to see her, just recently.'

The woman frowns.

'Does she know something?' she asks.

'No, I don't think so, but she did a drawing of a man who kept staring at her.'

Magda produces the drawing.

The woman stares at it, but she shakes her head.

'Don't recognise him,' she says. 'Have you found him?'

'I'm afraid not.'

'What's his name?'

Magda sighs. Maybe this wasn't a good idea.

'Possibly Henry Morton, or maybe Geoffrey, although we suspect it isn't either of them. Did your daughter ever mention those names?'

The woman stares at her.

'No.'

Magda frowns and puts the pictures away.

'Not much use, is it, then?'

Magda agrees.

The woman looks away.

Magda decides that she may as well go back to the young woman rather than trying to wring any other information out of this mausoleum.

No, not a mausoleum. No photographs of the dead. No paintings or photographs at all. Hardly any ornaments or knick-knacks. Just four plain pale green walls. Only functional items standing about, waiting steadfastly for some limited action.

A living death.
Time stopped.
No future.

As the door is closed behind her, Magda shivers. Like coming out of the morgue.

Poor, poor woman.

She gets back into the car and shivers again.

Stares out of the windscreen.

There's not much more action from the other house either.

No curtains twitching.

No smoke from any chimneys. No one doing a bit of early gardening.

'Cul-de-sac' had never seemed to be so appropriate.

A gust of rain obscures the view. Again.

She starts the car and escapes.

〜

Louisa and her guests are sitting down for a late lunch when the distant bell rings.

The four of them look at each other and do a group frown.

Both Ellie and Mali know it can't be for them.

Fletcher likewise.

So they all focus on Louisa, who frowns and then smiles at him.

'Would you be so kind, Michael?' she says. She was never one to flutter her eyelashes, even as a young girl, and that isn't going to happen right now either, so Fletcher pushes his chair back and sets off.

He returns with Magda, who apologises for interrupting their lunch, but is found a chair and an extra plate and cutlery.

As an uninvited guest it takes some time before she feels it's polite to start asking questions, but they're all curious to know why she's come.

She briefly outlines the case without giving too much away that hasn't already been announced in the local news. Louisa vaguely remembers hearing about it, but hadn't realised where the body was found. And inevitably it's Ellie who is the most curious.

Not having met her before, Magda is struck by the young woman's eyes. A vivid green torchlike glare brimming with urgent intelligence. As she sits between her and Fletcher's equally – if now slightly dimmed – weird eyes (one blue, one green), it begins to feel like a witches' convention.

'But you don't know why this girl was buried looking out over the abbey?' she asks.

Magda glances at the others, but realises that they're all deferring to her.

'Well, no, but what isn't common knowledge is *how* she was buried.'

The others frown at each other, but Ellie's eyes remain focused on her.

Magda clears her throat.

'I'm asking you not to share this information beyond this room,' she says, in what she hopes sounds a seriously stern manner.

They all agree.

She pauses, still uncertain how much she should share.

'At first we thought the murderer had tried to mimic the death of Ophelia … in Shakespeare's *Hamlet*.'

Frowns are passed round the table, but it's Louisa who intones the words.

'There is a willow grows aslant a brook

That shows his hoar leaves in the glassy stream.
There with fantastic garlands did she come
Of crow flowers, nettles, daisies, and long purples,
That liberal shepherds give a grosser name,
But our cold maids do "dead men's fingers" call them…'

They all stare at her, Fletcher shaking his head.

'You're not suggesting she buried herself?'

Magda shakes her head.

'No and it's still subject to other interpretations, but there are other indications that this was deliberate.'

They all wait.

She sighs and then continues.

'Our suspect is known for being obsessed with the abbey. He painted images of it, one of which included a woman with long, flowing hair wearing a long dress.'

'Like Rosetti,' asks Louisa.

Magda nods.

'Is he one of the Pre-Raphaelites?' asks Fletcher, keen to show he's not a barbarian.

'Yes, one of the gang, which included Burne-Jones, Holman Hunt and Millais. I've a copy of his Ophelia on the landing upstairs.'

Ellie is still frowning.

'But what other interpretations can there be?'

Magda looks at her and hesitates. She glances at Fletcher, who is now also frowning at her.

'Ziggy Hook has suggested there's another possibility.'

Ellie gives Fletcher a quizzical look.

'Ziggy Hook?' she asks, pronouncing the names like they're from a comic strip.

He sighs.

'Ah, a bit of an oddball – a computer nerd – but I think he's a good guy.'

She rolls her eyes.

'Actually, he says that you may know more than him,' says Magda with a smile.

'Me?' laughs Ellie, but then sees the smile has gone.

Magda glances briefly at Fletcher, but he's not smiling either.

'Yes. I was told you are studying medieval history.'

Ellie gives her a guarded nod, while still looking perplexed.

'So do you know about the history of Dryburgh?'

'She knows chapter and verse,' says Mali with a sigh. 'How long have you got?'

Now Ellie can't stop a smile, but then she shakes her head.

'Actually, that's not true. I'm only really interested in one particular connection.'

Magda nods.

'Ziggy tells me it's Hugh de Morville.'

Ellie's eyes go wide. But then she glances at Fletcher, who puts up his hands in defence.

'Not guilty,' he says.

Magda nods.

'No, I think Ziggy worked this out himself.'

Ellie is looking from one person to another, but they're all smiling at her.

'Well…' She hesitates. 'To be honest, there's little to tell. Only that he did apparently go there. Probably in 1200. Don't know why, other than to visit his father's grave. He may be buried there, but I've no idea where. And, as you probably know, the abbey has been ransacked and plundered many times, including by Walter Scott and his friends, so…'

Magda nods.

'But there is another possible connection,' she says quietly.

Pins dropping would have made everyone jump.

Ellie stares at her.

'The body we're investigating was buried with flowers.'

Ellie shivers.

'Ziggy tells me that as well as Ophelia, a real woman – called Rosamund Clifford – was buried with particular flowers … which are like the ones we found with this recent body.'

Ellie frowns. The others look at each other.

'But she was Henry II's lover. She died in 1176, I think,' she says.

Magda nods and waits.

Ellie shakes her head.

'That must be just a coincidence … surely?' says Fletcher.

'Which flowers?' asks Ellie.

'Lilies and roses,' says Magda.

'Not what Louisa just said,' whispers Ellie, with a strange look in her eyes.

Magda shakes her head.

No one speaks.

They're all quiet.

'However,' says Ellie, 'there is still a possible connection.'

All eyes focus on her.

She clears her throat and looks at Mali, who raises her eyebrows.

'Hugh de Morville. The Younger.'

Again, she checks her audience.

'It's complicated and there's little proof.'

She takes a breath.

'He was one of the murderers of Thomas Becket. He had to do penance for fifteen years, but then he appears again in 1194 when King Richard was captured and held for ransom. Hugh was also held as a hostage with him. But then, after Richard died, he appears to have visited Dryburgh. It's where his father is supposed to have been buried. We don't know where or when the younger Hugh died, and his lands and titles were passed on to his niece, so it's possible that he was buried at Dryburgh as well.'

'So is there any connection to Rosamund?' asks Magda.

Ellie thinks about this.

'Only that Hugh was one of Henry's close companions while he was having his affair with her.'

Again, everyone goes quiet.

Until they realise Mali is staring at Ellie, who is avoiding her gaze.

Louisa breaks the moment.

'Coffee, everyone,' she says, standing up.

Fletcher stands up as well, indicating he's ready for duty.

The two of them set off to the kitchen, while Ellie goes over to the window.

Magda looks at her phone and thinks she'd better be going.

Mali hesitates, but then goes over to Ellie and puts her arm round her.

Magda decides to go and say goodbye to Louisa.

The two girls stand together.

'What is it?' murmurs Mali, not liking what she thinks Ellie is going to say.

Ellie shivers again.

'*Le spasa, l'anel, le cur...*'

Mali holds her close.

They're still like this when the other three return, Louisa having convinced Magda to stay.

They clock the pose and glance at each other before returning to their seats.

'You two OK?' says Fletcher.

The couple untwine and come back to the table.

Louisa plays mother, except of course it doesn't feel maternal. More like a brisk elderly aunt.

Silence descends after a bout of clinking cups, worried looks and glances.

'What I'm going to say was written in old Occitan,' says Ellie, quietly.

More looks and now slightly worried frowns.

She repeats what she just said to Mali.

Louisa translates in a solemn, teachery voice.

'The sword, the ring, the blood and the chalice?'

Ellie stares at her. She hasn't met anyone else, apart from her professor, who can speak or understand Occitan. She gathers herself and continues in English.

'But the next line says, "If ever the four come together again…"'

The frowns become harder.

She looks at Louisa, who gives her a hard but encouraging stare.

'*Il yo un autre pleuja de sang.*'

~

Carter has managed to gradually creep close enough to be able to see people sitting in what looks like a sitting room. A huge space with lots of big paintings.

He's able to identify the two young women, and can see that the older lady must be Louisa Cunninghame. The older gent must be Fletcher, but then another woman arrives.

They seem to be listening to one of the girls telling a story.

Then suddenly the party breaks up. The two oldies disappear, but then he has to duck down as the two girls come to the window.

Then they all gather together again with their cups.

After figuring out that this woman must have arrived in a car, he works his way through the trees so he can see the car park. He scans all three, reckoning the furthest away was the newcomer.

Bingo.

Galashiels Police car.

What is she doing here?

He decides that following her might be useful, so hurries back to his own car and waits, which gives him some time to find out more about her.

DI Magda Steil.

He drops her into recent news slots and there she is. Investigating a woman's body found in the woods a week ago.

So why has she come here?

The only thing he can think of is that Fletcher might be involved somehow. He knows the old bugger can't keep his nose out of any trouble.

And none of this tells him why the two girls are there.

He calls herself and tells her what's happening.

She sounds as puzzled as he is, but tells him to keep a watch on the girls.

That's fine, but where's he going to stay?

And will it ever stop raining?

⌒

If anyone had asked Magda where her brother might find a bed for a few nights in the Borders, she would have laughed in their face.

'Any woman between sixteen and sixty,' she would have suggested.

Which wasn't much good to the enquirer.

But, in this case, she was wrong.

Jamie Morrison was long retired, living a quiet life in the estate cottage the laird had generously provided for him.

He still had to pay a rent, of course, but he didn't mind that. He just liked to be where he'd been for most of his adult life.

Well hidden up on the hillside, at the end of a dirt track only accessible in a Land Rover.

He still helps with the dogs and the hunts so is doing pretty much what he always did, but without the heavy lifting and sheep-mithering.

He's known wee Tomasz since he was in his short trousers, and he has taught him a lot about surviving out on the moors.

So he isn't that surprised to come back from a walk to find him sitting on the wall.

They shake hands and Jamie offers him a brew.

It is a good half an hour before the conversation stalls and they both sit staring out over the valley.

The one thing Jamie has taught Tomasz is the power of silence.

Or rather giving someone time to think before they speak.

He knew the lad was in trouble as soon as he saw him, but he wasn't about to start digging.

A buzzard floats over, wheeling in the rising updraft.

Its haunting cry breaks the silence.

'I need a place to stay,' says Tomasz.

Jamie watches the bird.

'Aye, I thought that might be it,' he murmurs.

'I can pay,' says Tomasz.

The old man shakes his head.

'Not necessary,' he says. 'Be good to have some company for a while.'

Tomasz smiles.

'Not so sure I'll be much fun,' he mutters.

Jamie shakes his head.

Later, they're sitting outside again watching the sun go down.

Tomasz has produced a bottle of Talisker, but Jamie's only had one sip of his.

'Is it a lassie yer running from?' he asks.

Tomasz shakes his head.

'Not this time.'

Jamie waits.

'Mind you, in a way you're right, but not for the usual reasons. This one isn't after my body … it's more that she wants to use me as a gun.'

Jamie shakes his head but doesn't ask anything further.

'The less I know the better,' has always been his mantra.

He knows Tomasz won't stay long, him being the same restless spirit he'd been as a boy.

And the Talisker is dulling the nagging pain in his abdomen.

He knows what it is, but he has never liked doctors pawing at him.

He's put a fair few animals out of their misery in his life, and he is intent on being the only person to deal with his own demise.

So a day or a week of company will be fine.

Tomasz has also noticed the winces and the careful movement.

Although he is familiar with death in many of its gory or malingering ways, the slow death of cancer frightens him the most, so he resolves to stay only long enough to gather his strength and figure out a way to solve the latest conundrum.

Chapter 11

Encounters

Magda doesn't quite catch what Ellie just said, but she's the only one.

Mali puts her arm around her.

Louisa is for once uncertain what to do or say.

Magda frowns.

'I'm sorry, I didn't get that.'

Ellie tells her in English.

'There will be another "rain of blood".'

'What?' she asks.

Louisa frowns.

'Was that at Château Gaillard?' she murmurs.

Ellie nods.

'The workmen thought it was an omen, but Richard wasn't deterred.'

Magda frowns again. People talking in riddles always infuriates her.

'Richard who?'

Louisa smiles.

'The Lionheart.'

'Oh, yes, all right, but what's this rain of blood?'

Louisa gracefully asks Ellie to explain.

She tells the story again: how it was recorded that there was a 'rain of blood' while they were building the castle in Normandy and the workmen thought it was an evil omen.

Richard rebuffed this and forced them to carry on … but the castle was easily breached and destroyed not long after Richard died.

'So…' murmurs Magda, the frown still pasted onto her forehead.

Louisa says she understands that it is a well-documented phenomenon, with several suggested scientific explanations.

Ellie shrugs, but there's obviously something else.

Mali sighs.

'Go on, tell them,' she urges her.

Ellie looks straight at Fletcher.

'It's one of the things that Tata's message says.'

Fletcher is surprised by a cold shiver. Where did that come from?

But both he and Louisa are hooked now.

Ellie looks away and then back, bringing the fierce emerald gaze to bear on them.

'It's difficult to translate, but basically says that his royal line will end in ignominy and that England will sink beneath the waves into oblivion.'

Magda almost laughs, but Louisa's look silences her.

'Well, I doubt that the Remainers and the forecasters of climate disaster will be surprised by that … but it's been a long time coming.'

'Oh, come on, really,' says Magda, looking at all these serious faces staring at her. 'How long ago was this?'

'It was in 1198,' intones Ellie.

Magda shakes her head.

'That's … over eight hundred years ago.'

Now it's Ellie's turn to shake her head.

'Tata's message is clear. It says that if the four elements are brought together then it will happen sooner rather than later.'

'*Four* elements?' she asks.

'The sword, the blood, the chalice … and the ring.'

'What ring?'

Ellie hesitates again. Even she sometimes thinks she's been press-ganged into some ridiculous Dan Brown movie.

'This one,' she says, and unhooks one of her earrings.

Louisa reaches out to examine it, so Ellie gives her it.

Magda can see it's just a plain gold ring with a few dents.

Louisa looks on the inside.

Mali frowns.

'But I bought you those . . . in the market in Blaye last time we were there.'

Ellie shakes her head.

'I know. I've still got the other one . . . I'm sorry . . . but it was the best way to hide it. In plain view.'

'Where did you get it from?' asks Fletch.

'I found it the first time I went back in after the . . . after Tata and Tonton were . . .' She bites back a sob.

The whole room is utterly silent.

'I knew where it was hidden, because she showed me the summer before, but I didn't know what it was until I read the message at Maître Virondeau's.'

She looks at Mali and holds out her hand, which Mali grasps and holds onto it.

She looks back at Fletch.

'There are some marks, but they're worn away.'

Magda is still far from convinced, which makes the others frown.

'So, what about the sword and the other things?'

Ellie closes her eyes.

Magda looks at Louisa but she shakes her head, puts her finger to her lips.

Ellie starts to mumble some words quietly.

They're not English, vaguely French.

Perhaps four lines of sing-song verse.

Her eyes open.

'I'm not certain, but it says that a certain knight was given the sacred objects and told to take them somewhere safe.'

Again, Magda is sceptical, but she's now beginning to worry about Ellie's sanity.

She's gone very pale and seems to be about to burst into tears.

Mali hugs her closer.

But then her eyes open and the fierce gaze returns.

She glares at Magda.

'I know it sounds ridiculous,' she rasps, 'but if you'd heard Tata talk about it, you'd be very worried.'

Magda frowns.

'Who?'

'My French great-aunt,' says Ellie.

Magda looks at the others, whose looks all indicate she's on her own with that.

So she tries another tack.

'But what's that got to do with this knight? What's his name? Marville?'

Ellie smiles at her.

'It's de Morville.'

Magda stares at her. Is it the man who Ziggy was talking about?

'It's because that he was the one given the task of protecting them, hiding them … by Mercadier, just before he died.'

'Who's he?' asks a now exasperated Magda.

'Richard's right-hand man. He was murdered by King John's men in 1200 in Bordeaux, about the same time that Hugh de Morville made the journey from there to Dryburgh.'

Now Magda is stumped, although she remembers that John was Richard's brother and a bad lot … according to the films she's fallen asleep watching.

This girl has made the links.

It might be possible.

But no. It's all a fairy story. Like in those ridiculous films. Isn't it?

⤳

Carter has reported back.

As he has received no further instructions he's found a hotel that is open for business. Meals only served in the rooms, but that's fine with him.

He gets onto the Wi-Fi, checks out the local 'housewives' and books one in for later.

Other than that he just waits, trying to find something to watch that doesn't send him to sleep.

Meanwhile Jane has contacted Hollis and told him part of the story. Just enough to get his attention.

'You should check out the ongoing murder investigation in the Scottish Borders. I'm sure you can work out the connections.'

She cuts the call before he asks any questions, giving her time to progress while he plays catch-up.

She ignores the follow-up calls and snuggles back down under the bedclothes with her phone, and continues to search for further connections herself.

⤳

Magda has gone back home.

Now that her father is in the old people's home annoying a whole host of rich inmates with his more and more fantastical local history stories, she has gone back to living in the big house. She's immediately rejected the fleeting idea that he might know something about this de Morville character, as whatever he did know is all jumbled up now in incoherent jabbering.

Amelia hadn't taken much persuading to come and live with her after the terrible murder of her husband. The man had been a monster and a wife beater, which Magda was ashamed to admit she hadn't realised. She had just assumed that Amelia's tiredness and sometimes distraught looks were simply the consequences of having such a large brood. This was further confirmed when she realised that they were perfectly well-behaved kids, even though they'd suffered the same aggression from their father.

As she opens the kitchen door she is met with laughter. But the scene that she sees is bemusing.

One of the younger boys – she keeps forgetting who's who – is sitting on the edge of the table while Amelia washes his knee with a bloody cloth and then wrings it out into a bowl of blood.

'Why the laughter?' wonders Magda.

Five faces turn to look at her. Their laughing turns to embarrassed awkwardness and then sheepish grins.

'It's all right,' says Amelia. 'Nothing broken.'

Magda shakes her head.

'We were tray-sledging,' says Miranda, the only girl.

Magda stares at her.

'What?'

'Down the stairs,' says Davy sheepishly.

Now the injured party, James, gives her the injured victim's apologetic face.

'Sorry,' he says.

'Sorry?' she asks, wondering why he should be apologising, while almost simultaneously realising that there may be collateral damage.

'It's all right,' says Amelia. 'I'll pay for the repairs.'

Magda tries to think what might have been in the way of the slalom.

'The giant soldjar,' says Billy, with big eyes, like he can see him now.

Magda looks at Amelia, who tries to grin back at her.

'Sorry,' she says.

Magda's stare evaporates and she bursts out laughing.

'You mean Sir Lopilop?'

It's Amelia's turn to laugh.

'That's what Tomasz used to call him when he was your age,' Magda says to Billy.

She is taken to see the fallen knight and between them they drag him up into one of the bedrooms, where he's laid on the bed to await what looks likely to be some extensive surgery.

Magda dismisses all their apologies and tells them it will be all right, so soon the children all slink away and the kitchen becomes quiet again.

Magda and Amelia are in a close embrace when Helena returns from her afternoon visit to one of her friends.

She's never fazed by this love affair blossoming in her home. She remembers her own amorous adventures back in Poland.

Later, after the children have left the table and Helena has poured them a coffee, Amelia asks if there's any news about the murdered woman. She had been particularly horrified by the idea of being buried alive.

When her father was still at home, Magda never said a word about ongoing cases, because she knew he would have blurted everything out at the next Masonic do or even worse: get straight onto the phone to regale his friends with erroneous versions of the events.

So even now she can't bring herself to say much more than the bare details.

'Not much progress, I'm afraid. The suspect seems to have been very clever at hiding his identity.'

'But this must be nigh on impossible nowadays,' says Amelia.

Magda nods her head.

'You're right. He must have planned this well in advance, using false names and contacts.'

The three women contemplate the difficulty of that.

'Although,' says Magda, 'we're talking about seven years go. It makes you realise how much things have changed. There are far more cameras and tracking facilities now than then. You can't do anything now without being watched and recorded.'

'Even at places like the Wallace memorial?' asks Helena with a frown.

Magda shakes her head.

'Well, no, not actually up there, but there are cameras on all the approach roads.'

'And it's only recently that they cleared the trees from around the statue and tidied up the path and the car park,' says Amelia. 'I was surprised the last time we went, but back then it would have been much more overgrown and less visited.'

'You're right,' says Magda, 'and at night there would have been hardly any traffic. It would only be the Bemersyde folk, and they'd have all been abed.'

They sit quietly for a few moments, and then Amelia fetches the coffee pot and refills their cups.

'But now Fletcher's' granddaughter, Ellie, has offered us another lead.'

Amelia and Helena frown.

Magda realises that Amelia has no idea who she's talking about, so she briefly outlines ex-DI Fletcher's involvement in the previous case and how he was now staying with Louisa, which reminds Helena that she has met him.

'A bit of a card sharp, that man,' she murmurs, recalling a well-hidden king of clubs.

This confuses Magda, so Helena has to confess to the illicit bridge night at Louisa's during the first lockdown last year.

Magda shakes her head, but Helena can't stop a sheepish grin.

'So what's the new lead?' asks Amelia.

Magda wonders where to start.

'Do you know what happened to Ophelia in *Hamlet*?'

Helena pulls a face, while Amelia's face lights up. But then it fades as she realises what that might mean.

'You mean she drowned? How? Up there?'

Magda shakes her head.

'No, but "buried with flowers".'

Amelia frowns and shakes her head.

'But people are often buried with flowers.'

Magda nods.

'Yes, but these were unusual.'

The other two wait.

'But now Ellie has suggested that they could refer to someone historical rather than fictional.'

'Historical?' asks Amelia.

'Someone called Hugh de Morville.'

This only gets a blank look from Helena.

'He's buried there, and maybe his son is as well. Same name.'

'Why does that name ring a bell?' murmurs Amelia.

'He was one of the murderers of Thomas Becket.'

Now Helena is totally lost, but Amelia's face lights up.

'Who will rid me of this troublesome priest?'

～

The White House is eerily quiet when I return from my afternoon walk. Wet through again.

No clicking of laptop keys or pinging or brief chatter.

I go through to see what's up with Ziggy, but amazingly he's not there. So I check his bedroom, where I find him buried beneath his duvet with his eyes shut, quietly breathing.

I leave him alone.

Back in the kitchen I find a note: Ex-DS B on her way minus J. Split up.

I look out of the window.

Well, I never. There's a surprise. If you'd asked me, I'd have said,

'Totally solid.' Two lost souls who'd found each other.

I turn instinctively, to find Freya leaning against the doorjamb.

I wish she wouldn't creep up on me like that.

'You never know, do you?' she says.

I assume she's talking about the news and nod my agreement.

'Well, I'd better start thinking about a meal,' I say.

Freya smiles and disappears.

Typical.

As I fiddle about finding the makings of a meal for four, I recall the first time I met Fletcher and Becket.

Ziggy had figured out where to go, somewhere in the middle of nowhere north of Glasgow. Don't remember how we got there.

We come upon a vision of wartime carnage.

Two strange buildings: one a tower, and the other burrowed into solid rock in a cliff side. The tower is on fire, with smoke billowing out of the roof.

Inside and outside there is an array of bodies.

One man dragging himself away from the tower with bloody knees.

A man on the ground with an arrow sticking out of his chest.

The man who I now know as ex-DI Fletcher comes out of the door of the rock house.

Inside there's a woman standing like a zombie with black hair and piercing eyes staring at us. Two or three bodies on the floor. One with an arrow in his arm and a black hole in his chest.

Ex-DS Janet Becket covered in blood and pointing a very shaky gun at us.

She collapses.

We get her out and try to get as far as we can from the tower, which is now burning furiously from the roof.

The woman in black has disappeared.

The cavalry arrives.

My first experience of government forces who don't wear uniforms and don't speak, only to give rasping orders, which you instinctively obey without question. Something hard in their eyes.

The woman in black was Carole Morgan.

And the figure I briefly glimpsed on the roof of the burning tower was my mother, Fern Robinson.

Neither of them ever seen again.

All this in the matter of less than five minutes.

But burnt irrevocably into my brain, to pleasure my mind for ever.

I realise I've peeled enough potatoes for the Last Supper, and wonder what I can do with them. Cheese and potato pie is the answer. Maybe three pies? Have I enough cheese? Yes, I have.

I suppose people who go through that sort of experience inevitably feel a strong bond of ... what?

'Comradeship' sounds a bit public-school ... not their thing at all. But stronger than friendship. A sort of 'knowing that comes from a shared experience' sounds a bit like one of those phrases you hear from course leaders trying to big up the life-saving importance of financial services seminars.

Don't know. Perhaps I'll ask them.

But I do know I don't have anyone like that.

Although it's that moment one of Ziggy's laptops comes to life and informs us that Ms Violet Cranthorne is calling. That can only mean trouble. With a capital V.

Amelia is still uncertain about her relationship with Magda.

She's grateful for the security and help she's getting after what happened to her husband, but realises that her three boys are missing out when it comes to masculine influence. Is that such a bad thing? Although knowing your father was both a wife-beating sadist and that he was killed as a diversionary tactic by some stranger rather than for being a total bastard will be difficult to explain … eventually. Something to do with … what's that word? Serendipity?

She's faced with this question every time she goes down to feed the horses, who are still living at the house down across the river.

They know she's coming long before she gets there, and she can hear their whinnying as she crosses the bridge.

She forks the hay into the feeding crate and watches as they shuffle and bump each other to get at it.

She strokes a few necks and then goes to the house to check everything is OK.

The front door has never locked properly. One of the many jobs Duncan thought was beneath him.

But, as she enters, she knows someone's there. The heating has been turned on.

What should she do?

She calls out.

'Hello?'

Silence.

She shivers and turns to get out.

'Hi,' says a voice.

She turns.

Tomasz is standing there with that sly grin she's always distrusted.

'What…?' is all she can muster.

'Sorry,' he says. 'Port in a storm.'

She can't think of anything to say.

He comes towards her. She backs away. He stops with a look of surprise on his face.

'Hey, I'm not going to hurt you,' he says.

'What are you doing here?' she asks, trying to be forceful, but knowing her voice is waveringly pathetic.

'As I said, a port in storm. I'm trying to avoid some very unpleasant people who want me to do something terrible on their behalf, which I'm not prepared to do.'

She continues to stare at him.

He shrugs.

'Can't compromise my sister and mother yet again, so … this is the next best thing.'

She feels her shoulders starting to relax.

'But won't they think of looking for you here?'

'Maybe, but the horses are a great alarm system and maybe they don't know about … you and me.'

She can't help but laugh.

'You and me?'

He smirks.

'You didn't seem to have any complaints.'

She shakes her head.

'You're a bastard.'

He nods.

'I don't think my mother would like to hear you calling me that.'

Amelia laughs again.

'I've heard her call you worse than that.'

Tomasz grins again.

'I didn't know you spoke Polish.'

'I don't, but the meaning was clear.'

There's a moment of stand-off. Not exactly the opening of that Charles Bronson movie. No squeaking gate. No fly being trapped in a gun barrel.

But she's the first to speak.

'Well, you can't stay here.'

He shrugs again.

'Why not? I'll keep the place aired. Pay you for the electricity. I won't be using any of your wood, for obvious reasons. Even feed the horses if you like.'

She shakes her head.

'It's not even safe. Don't you think they'll think of looking for you here?'

He smiles.

'They're not that bright. Hiding in plain sight is beyond their expectations.'

She stares at him.

He smiles back.

'Can I take that as an OK, then?' he whispers.

She shakes her head in exasperation.

But what happened next is beyond her explanation.

As she hurries back up the hill, she curses herself. Magda will be wondering where she is and why she's going straight for a shower. Although she got completely wet through coming up the hill, anyway. When will it stop raining all the time?

But fortunately, Magda's gone out.

So it's not until she's letting the hot water pummel her body that she allows herself to think of what she just did.

It wasn't the first time with him.

That was a long time ago.

They'd both just come back from boarding school, and they'd met at a local dance. They already knew each other, as she'd been a friend of Magda's since prep school. She was still living at home further down the valley.

They met at the ruined castle high on the hill. It became their place. She suspects that they were both virgins, despite his arrogance.

But they aren't now.

She'd allowed this to continue as he went from one conquest to another, each time he came home from the fighting, and even when she was married. She'd regretted that mistake the first night of the honeymoon, when she realised that Duncan's charm had been hiding a vicious, sadistic violence.

So meeting up with him became an escape clause that no one, not even Magda, knew about.

And now she's just succumbed to him again.

What if Magda finds out?

No, he wouldn't do that.

'What is wrong with me?' she says to herself.

Why do women fall for such men?

At least now she's taking the pill, which Duncan had forbidden her to do.

Four of the little bastards is enough.

Back in her house, Tomasz reflects on this encounter.

While it satisfied his ongoing desire for her, he knows it's not right.

He's not much better than Duncan.

And now he's sitting in his den. Or what he probably called his darkroom, with a sly smile on his face.

He knows the bastard was good at photography. He won all the local competitions and had a couple of showings in Edinburgh and down south. But that was for his pretty pictures of the Borders, not the obscene stuff covering the walls of this room.

He's ripped a lot of it down.

But in here he can watch the TV and fiddle on his laptop.

So it's in this vile sanctuary that he comes up with the idea.

He's been watching the recent protests and the ongoing rise in the demands for more women's rights.

He surmises he's probably the sort of man they're talking about, although he's never beaten a woman like Duncan did. So perhaps he wasn't that bad.

He recalls the woman by the sea. What was her name? Nina?

No use thinking of her. The spooks will be staking her out.

Imelda was different. No messing with her. She would be all right. But, equally, they'd be shadowing her as well.

So where should he go?

By now it was too late to troll up to the barracks. A court martial was inevitable, although he saw that as a blessing. But not the months or years he might have to endure in prison.

So?

Go out in blaze of glory?

He's momentarily distracted by a news item.

Some ned going on about Union Jacks.

He turns up the sound.

'Every public building to sport one,' is apparently the government's latest wheeze.

He listens as the man drones on about celebrating Brexit la-la land.

And then he's back in the mountains.

Lying on his front, covered in dust and rubble.

They'd been under heavy bombardment for what seems like hours.

He's been sent to take out the gun emplacement at the top of a small rise, but he's not been able to get into a decent position. The little buggers have picked a canny spot.

It's then that he notices the flag.

He doesn't particularly recognise it. There are lots of different tribal rags, apart from the government or opposition stripes.

Like many of them, this one is accompanied by some white-robed rabble-rouser whose voice can be heard occasionally above the noise of the gunfire. They're there to provide encouragement, apparently. They promise a land of milk and honey and virgins for ever, which sounds like a much better reward than if you're a British soldier unfortunate enough to get injured and sent home to bask in the rain outside Marks & Spencer.

They've been told not to take them out, because that just makes them more likely to torture anyone unfortunate enough to be captured.

But nothing's been said about the flags.

He takes aim.

Puff.

Missed.

Again.

No more flag.

Ten minutes later they retreat. He manages to pick off a couple of them as they scuttle away.

It never occurred to him that they'd give up just because he blew away their flag.

Ridiculous.

But it happened more than once.

Whereas he wouldn't go anywhere near one of his own flags, for the simple reason that you would become a target.

What's not to understand?

But now … he's thinking.

He could take out a Union Jack on a town hall or a government building from hundreds of metres away. There would be no enemy fire coming back at him. Plenty of time to walk away. Disappear. Go somewhere else.

The more he thinks about it, the more it makes him grin.

Maximum disruption without any fatalities.

And then he remembers all the fuss about statues.

What fun.

Chapter 12

Connections

Hollis doesn't take long to work out the connections between de Morville and Dryburgh, although even he is dubious about such a tenuous link. A brief trawl through the web's history of Dryburgh reveals a long-running tale of destruction, disastrous backing of the wrong horse and abandonment … and that's before the Romantics took over and prettified it, which also included knocking things down, digging things up and inventing outrageous fairy stories around it. Fat chance that anything buried or hidden in the year 1200 will be still there.

He stares at the screen.

But…

He's also aware that there are plenty of other ancient artefacts found recently that are older than this.

So how is he going to organise a serious search?

He comes back to the dangerous conclusion he's been putting off time and again.

The young woman is key to this.

He knows she's as secretive as can be and that's there are almost certainly some things that she hasn't told anyone.

He also remembers the sarcastic look in that old Frenchwoman's eyes just before he killed her. Almost a look of pity.

He knocks the mug of coffee off the table.

Bloody women.

Two hours later, after another flurry of investigation, he comes back to rereading about the work Erskine did in the late eighteenth century. A lot of digging must have gone on before the new-builds, but he knows that they were careful to keep some structures as they were. It probably involved removing overgrown ivy and weeds, although not shifting whole buildings from one site to another.

He sets about identifying what seems to have survived the longest.

Little from the twelfth century, as far as he can tell. Even the plaque commemorating de Morville the Elder is probably much later.

Completely stumped, he decides that he needs some professional help – something he hates having to get. When he figures out who that will have to be he can't help but smile at what a pleasure it will be to eliminate her afterwards. Having been brought up by his paternal grandmother, he's had a lifelong hatred of stern old academic ladies with their pursed lips and elegant manners.

But first he needs to gather the troops. He'll need some help with this. Funds and logistics first, and then personal involvement. He needs to keep them fully committed as he knows they're all capable of betraying him, even though he has all sorts of personal information that would make them think twice about doing that.

And finally, he must find a way to make the evil witch pay. A slow and miserable death will be such a pleasure to look forward to.

◠

Fletcher comes awake with a start.

Is he in the jungle?

He rubs his eyes.

He's between a huge fern and some other weird plant with enormous green leaves.

But now he can see panes of glass and above him a glass-domed roof, which explains the pattering noise that probably woke him up. Is it raining again?

He recalls one of the few times he met his father. He'd been taken to Kew Gardens. He'd never seen so much greenery. There weren't many trees in the part of Streatham where his eldest sister lived. His mother had died when he was three and his father had already abandoned her. So he'd ended up being added to his sister's brood, which meant that he grew up with her daughters.

He can hear voices.

More women.

He peers through the undergrowth.

Louisa Cunninghame.

He shakes his head.

How did this happen?

Slowly the recent events come out of the woods.

He groans.

Another mystery.

But then he smiles as a burst of laughter echoes around the vaulted roof.

At least it means he can be in the company of his favourite granddaughter. He grabs the arms of the chair and hauls himself to his feet.

Sure enough, Ellie is sitting cross-legged on the carpet, while her lover is carefully plaiting her hair. They both look towards him as he pretends to stagger out of the jungle like some long-lost explorer.

'Damn hot in there,' he murmurs in his best David Niven accent.

Louisa, who is sitting in her favourite armchair, peers at him over *The Guardian*.

'Ah, glad to see that Livingstone's been found alive again.'

The two girls grin at the gruesome sense of humour of these oldies.

Apparently he's missed morning coffee. But Louisa goes to get him some, in the absence of any servant.

Fletcher contents himself with watching the hairdressing activity but declines to voice the sad joke of asking when it's his turn. Although he still has a decent head of now grey hair, it had never been long enough to plait anyway.

With coffee and a couple of slices of toast in front of him, he eventually starts to think of the current investigation.

'So what's next?' he asks.

'Savitri is on her way as we speak,' says Louisa.

Fletcher frowns, but then remembers who she's talking about. A woman who she went to school with, apparently … although he reflects, it's more *inevitably*. Who doesn't she know?

'Remind me who she is again,' he says with a sigh.

'Retired professor of medieval European history at Stirling University,' says Louisa. 'In considerably better mental health that most of the population and not a lady to cross swords with, as I've already warned you.'

Fletcher sighs again. Is it because he was brought up in the company of women that he's doomed to have to put up with them for ever? But then he remembers the men in charge that he had to deal with and shrugs his shoulders.

'Oh, well,' he says. 'I'll try to keep my mouth shut.'

This only meets with a trio of raised eyebrows, so he eats his toast.

In the event, Savitri Kingshurst turns out to be a tiny, birdlike lady who hardly comes up to his shoulder. She is dressed in an Indian manner in a beautiful silken sari and has a dark red spot on her forehead.

She kisses Louisa on both cheeks and offers her hand to the two girls and Fletcher, who has stood up to greet her.

But when she speaks it is with a Yorkshire accent, and he soon finds out she was brought up in Bradford. So he feels a little less overawed by her smiling eyes, which are disconcertingly as green as Ellie's.

She immediately wants to know what Ellie is studying, and then they're quickly swapping book titles and other intellectual Jabberwockery as the other three try to keep up. Well, Louisa does, but soon enough Fletcher and Mali are exchanging glances and raised eyebrows.

So they're a bit caught out when Savitri suddenly pounces on Fletcher.

'I always like to check up on new people before I meet them,' she says quietly, and then pauses with a stern face.

Fletcher frowns at Louisa, who shrugs her shoulders as if to say,

'You're on your own there.'

But when he looks back at his new interrogator, she's giving him a bright smile.

'"My, my," as my mother would say, what a colourful history,' she says.

'Well…' he responds, but then can only look embarrassed.

Ellie laughs and gives him a big grin, which he hopes means she's proud of him.

There is a strangely uncomfortable silence.

Until the green eyes meet again.

'Well, what an intriguing *challenge* you have *ventured* upon, *Aliénor*,' she says quietly, but in a way even Fletcher realises is a specific and accurate usage of both the words and their pronunciation.

Ellie nods, but doesn't turn away from the gaze.

There then follows a prolonged interrogation, which quickly loses the other three in the company. Louisa nods Mali away to the kitchen and the two of them slink off. Fletcher reaches for the abandoned *Guardian* and pretends he's bothered about how QPR are doing while trying to follow some of the exchanges to his left.

As far as he can gather, a lot of it is about the limitations of court rolls as sources of truthful accounts of what really happened. This makes him reflect on the truthfulness of the reports he grudgingly compiled during his time as a detective.

'Not very,' he decides.

On tuning back in he realises they've jumped to the late eighteenth century, which for him is an even emptier vessel. At least listening to Ellie going on about Henry and Richard Coeur de Lion has given him a better handle on the twelfth century, but the late 1700s are a complete blank.

As if his ignorance is written on his face, Savitri turns to him and asks if he wants a résumé.

He nods and then has to concentrate hard as they deluge him with the devastating exploits of Erskine and Walter Scott, who seemed to have invented the idea of romanticising the past while happily obliterating a lot of it.

He's only saved by the bell summoning them all to the dining room.

Although it doesn't stop there, as Louisa demands to be brought up to speed.

It's only as they return to the conservatory with coffees and digestives for the oldies, and Indian sweetmeats brought by Savitri, that he manages to encapsulate what he understands in a brief list.

'Bravo,' says Savitri, clapping her hands

'Inimitable,' says Louisa.

Ellie grins and Mali smiles.

'But that means basically we haven't a chance of finding Tata's hoard … even if it actually was transported here, does it?' he asks.

Savitri shakes her head.

'I'm afraid you're right.'

Ellie frowns.

'Maybe,' she says. 'But that's not what she thought.'

The others are all silent, trying not to look at each other.

Ellie's face is at its most stubborn, which both Fletcher and Mali know is fearsome and often correct.

Louisa also recognises the obstinacy and knows it's not just her grandfather's influence.

The room gathers itself in preparation for what Ellie might say next as her eyes harden, and it's Fletcher who's feeling the heat.

'It's not her hoard … but it is priceless. She told me that the men and women who have protected these secrets for so long would make sure the items would remain safe … whatever sacrifices it took.'

No one is about to contradict this, but nor are they sure what else to say.

Ellie hesitates.

'She told me why they would do this.'

The room stiffens further.

'Because if they didn't and they were found and abused, or destroyed, then the prophesy would happen anyway … but be far worse.'

⌒

The Zoom with Violet is brief.

To be honest, she doesn't look well. Her hair is all over the place and her eyes are both tired and jittery.

She immediately cuts to the chase.

'I've been trying to get in touch with Fletcher and Becket, but the pair of them seem to be offline and AWOL,' she nearly barks.

I'm just thinking,

'Well, they're not on her team. And both are long departed from any legitimate service – if they ever did that, anyway.'

Ziggy is only able to tell her that Becket is on her way here and that Fletcher is probably dozing in Louisa's conservatory without a clue about where he's abandoned his mobile.

This just produces a lot of tutting.

There's a break in transmission, so we only catch the back end of the next tirade, which consists of,

'Need to get in touch with her sharpish,' and then she's gone.

I look at Freya, who shrugs her shoulders. She's not an action girl, after all. More a memory bank. You could ask her what she had seen on a screen or saw written down and she could tell you word for word, but the spoken word is not her forte.

For once, Ziggy's not immediately on five screens at once.

He's just sitting there motionless.

My instinct at moments like this is to go and make a brew, but for once I think I'll just wait and see. Although, being with these two, you can never tell what's going to happen next.

Inevitably, it's Ziggy who reacts first.

He swings round on his stool.

I've long become used to his transformations, but the lipstick and eye make-up are always a bit of a shock. I guess I should have figured this out from the bizarre hairstyle he's concocted. I do my best not to do the goldfish routine but miss the first few words.

'… believe what's going on.' He pauses and shrugs. 'We're heading at full steam towards a Nazi regime, and we seem to be the only people who are able to even recognise it.'

I'm not that sure this includes me, as I wasn't aware of a recent proliferation of swastikas everywhere.

I hesitantly ask about this.

Ziggy shakes his head, and the ridiculous cheap wig bounces like a pom-pom.

'Don't need them, do we? We've already got the Jacks, the three lions, and all that World Cup and Olympics bollocks.'

Not having seen him get as wound up as this for some time, I've nothing to say.

Freya has shuffled nearer to the door.

'So?' I venture.

'So bugger all,' he replies, and swings back round to his screens.

Freya has now disappeared.

I dither.

But then I hear the front door open and a voice calling.

It's Janet.

I go to greet her and take her through into the kitchen.

I sense a certain tension and her eyes are a little too bright and flittering, but she manages to smile and talk about the journey.

'So what's he up to?' she eventually says.

I shake my head.

'Not sure, other than going on about us all becoming Nazis, apparently.'

She grins.

'Oh, yeah. Can't wait,' she grunts.

I stare at her.

She laughs.

'If I get to wear the uniform,' she adds.

I can see that she would look dead sexy in a black Gestapo outfit, but don't fancy it myself.

We go through into the front room, where Freya is installed in the big wing-back chair reading a book.

She gets up to give Becket a hug and there's a bit of small talk as they catch up with trivial stuff, all the while avoiding mentioning what's happened with John.

So that gets us to an awkward silence.

Becket looks out of the window.

The rain has finally stopped, and the weak sun is trying for a guest appearance.

'It's not him, it's me,' she says.

She's not looking at either of us, so we exchange glances. Another long pause.

'He's happy just taking the dog for long walks and looking after the sheep.'

Not a lot I can say about that. I'm afraid of dogs, although his dog was OK, and I don't understand sheep.

Freya avoids my glance.

Becket stands up.

'So I'm going for a long walk now. Either of you want to come?'

I'm always up for a walk, so I find my boots and we set off.

Without saying where we might go, we trudge along the road towards Amelia's house. I tell Becket about the rearrangements. And about Amelia taking her brood up to the big house.

Becket manages a smirk.

'Very cosy,' she says, but then points at the horses, who have just noticed us and are giving us a wary once-over.

'Still keeping them, then?'

'Yeah. I've seen her down here a few times, sometimes with the kids.'

We carry on until we're nearly level with the gateway.

I point beyond it to where the bridge is hidden behind a line of trees.

'We could go across the bridge and walk back along the other side. It's probably less than a couple of miles.'

She follows me down the drive and past the house. The horses follow us, thinking we might be heading for the barn, but we disappoint them.

Becket nods at the curtained windows.

'Not a happy place,' she murmurs.

I can only guess, but the stories are that the husband was a bastard and deserved what he got.

We carry on.

It's not until we get to the bridge that Becket stops and looks down at the rushing water.

'It's been even higher,' I say. 'Nearly burst its banks last week, apparently.'

Becket nods back at the cottage.

'I think there's someone there,' she whispers.

I frown.

'You mean in the cottage?'

She nods.

'Just a feeling,' she says. 'Let's keep going. I'll call Magda when we get back.'

We wander along the track.

I can't think who might be there.

But we don't talk about it. Walk on in silence.

Becket is good at this.

And I like her for it.

∽

Magda is sitting in her car in the lay-by near the house of the dead girl's mother.

She's trying to think of the right questions, which might get the woman to remember things that might be relevant. There must have been some clues that would have indicated her daughter was in a new relationship.

A different hairstyle? Spending more time getting ready to go out? New clothes? Make-up?

She starts the car and drives to the house.

Again she has to wait until the wary face appears in the narrow gap.

Again there is the reluctance to let her across the doorstep. She's starting to think that maybe the woman has got something to hide.

But the room hasn't changed. It's as lifeless as it was the previous times.

Magda asks the questions she's thought of, but the woman merely shakes her head until the questions peter out.

So she determines to give the woman some more time.

It must have been a good few minutes before she coughs and then gets up and goes to the girl's bedroom.

'I found this the other day,' she says when she returns. 'It was down the back of the drawers.'

Magda takes the proffered magazine.

Not the usual girls' stuff. More upmarket country lady material. The sort of thing that Amelia might have perused before she had children.

She flicks through it until some pictures catch her eye.

Notices that the corner is turned down.

Images of a redhaired gal standing in various 'natural' poses outside a country mansion. Dogs and horses in the background. Tweeds. A Porsche on the drive. Not her style at all.

She shows the mother, who shakes her head and sighs.

'She never wore stuff like that. I bet it costs the earth,' she says with a frown.

Magda checks the date. It's the month before the girl disappeared.

'Do you know where she would have got this from?' she asks.

The woman shakes her head.

'You could try the shop on the high street. I think she went in there. But then you could buy that anywhere, couldn't you?'

Magda nods her agreement and asks if she can take the magazine.

The woman shrugs her shoulders one more time, and Magda's out of the house and into the car.

She's just about to start the engine when she has another thought. Goes back to the house and asks the now irritated mother which hairdresser the girl used to go to. She drives straight back into town and heads for the shop – forgetting, of course, that they're all shut.

'Bugger,' she says, but then taps the telephone number into her phone and waits.

'Hi,' says a slurry voice.

It takes some time, but eventually she sets off to go to see the woman at home.

She's expecting a hairdresser's home to be neat and tidy, but this woman isn't coping with lockdown at all well.

Her own hair is straggly and unwashed.

She's reluctant to let her indoors, and so Magda interviews her on the doorstep. She shows her the magazine and the photo of the girl.

The woman frowns.

'Yeah, I remember her. She wanted to look like one of them toffs. I told her it would take months before she could have her hair like that. Silly tart. I imagine she was seeing some rich guy who was trying to get into her knickers.'

Magda thanks her and escapes.

Drives round three corners and pulls in.

Does this mean she's been looking in the wrong places? That the man is more likely to be in the circles that she herself might frequent? More like used to frequent. When was the last time she attended any of those sorts of events? Hunts, balls, dinners in brightly lit rooms. She'd never liked them, even when she was younger. Always seemed false to her. Just hiding the reality of what that woman just said. Awkward public schoolboys trying to impress you, while you knew they hadn't a clue.

How or why did this girl get involved with any of them?

Maybe he saw her at the art class and then somehow persuaded her to go out with him.

And then persuaded her to change her hairstyle.

She shakes her head.

It's all too unlikely.

But?

So what now?

Where else could they have met?

Seven years ago?

She needs to go home and talk to Amelia.

⤳

Once he's thought of it, Tomasz begins to make plans.

The solution to his lack of mobility is resolved when he discovers Duncan's bike in the shed. It's more modern than the bikes he's used to, but he quickly gets a hang of the controls. At least it will get him further south fast enough, and then he can find something else. Even public transport is anonymous.

He's still got one of Victoria's guns, which is serviceable for what he needs, and it fits perfectly into Duncan's fishing bag. He adds the fisherman's jacket and cap to complete the disguise, which he can't help but giggle at. He's never understood the attraction of sitting for hours on your own on a riverbank for little reward.

He's still got some cash left and a couple of cards belonging to his 'escape' accounts, which at the most recent attempts seem to be still alive.

He stands in the kitchen and checks his kit.

But then he finds himself staring out of the window up the hill at the big house. He realises that it must be one of the few places that anyone can see from a distance.

He ponders the possibility of never going there again.

After all he's been through, he's not frightened of dying. He believes he's absolutely used up his nine lives and then some.

Without feeling it's at all maudlin, he finds some paper and begins to write a message to his mother and sister.

He foregoes any trite professions of love. He's let them both down too often for that. But he is intent on his funeral not including any military pomposity.

So no list of tours, accounts of dubious bravery or any other lies.

What he's done was mainly out of a ridiculous belief in his own invincibility, which he's known for some time to be just down to luck and the laws of probability.

He gives all his inheritance to Magda. Apart from a few thousand here and there to Imelda, Victoria and other female friends, who he's dragged through all sorts of trouble.

Three dollops of five thousand pounds to the three muckers he abandoned in the Aegean.

Apart from them, no other military at the funeral.

No uniforms allowed.

His ashes to be put on the bonfire in the garden.

No hymns, no music, no trumpeting last post.

Nothing in the local rag.

As he sits there at this other man's table he finds himself moved to tears.

Not for himself.

More for the flimsiness of life in general.

He wipes his face and stands up.

The two things he'll regret most of all, he's just realised, are leaving the dog and the horse.

He puts the letter in an envelope and then in his jacket pocket.

Not yet, he thinks.

But soon.

Chapter 13

Getting Nowhere Fast

Magda is up early the next morning.

Finds herself standing at the open door, looking out over the valley.

Will it ever stop raining?

What was all that about last night?

She can't remember having a row with Amelia ever, never mind since they've become an item, as one of her mother's acquaintances has called them.

And it wasn't really a row.

She'd asked her if she was all right, because she seemed a bit quiet at dinner time.

The response was abrupt.

'Why wouldn't I be?' and a sharp look before looking away.

Later, when they were getting ready for bed and she'd been to the bathroom, she came back to find her at the window naked, looking out over the valley.

She went to put her arms around her but felt her flinch.

It was only a momentary reaction and then she turned around and embraced her.

They climbed into bed.

Amelia said she was upset because she'd been down to the house, and it had brought it all back. The murder, but also how awful her relationship with Duncan had been.

Magda tried her best to reassure her, but eventually they just lay there until they fell asleep.

When she wakes up Amelia is still sleeping, so she creeps downstairs without waking her.

None of the children have appeared, so she makes herself some breakfast and is now wondering whether she should wake her.

This proves unnecessary because she appears five minutes later carrying the youngest, who's had a bit of nightmare and has woken her up.

She seems fine now and gives Magda a watery smile.

'Don't worry. I'm all right,' she says.

The other children arrive one by one, so further conversation is impossible.

So Magda gets onto her laptop and researches possible venues that the man might have attended. She finds hunts, balls, shoots and weddings and assembles a catalogue to show to the young woman … what was she called?

She stares at the bookshelves.

Roz. Of course.

Is that just a coincidence?

Is that Rose or Rosalind? Or Rosamund?

She doesn't know.

She finds the number and calls.

A woman's voice.

Magda explains who she is.

There's no response.

'Hello?' she says.

'Yes, what do you want?' says the voice, which has now gone cold and defensive.

Magda is puzzled.

'Excuse me, who are you?' she asks.

'I'm her mother and I don't like you upsetting my daughter, frightening her.'

Magda is both intrigued and a bit angry with this, but tells herself to be calm.

'I'm sorry if that's the case, but we are investigating a murder, Mrs Lambert.'

'She's been having nightmares,' says the woman.

Magda wants to ask what they're about, but stops herself and pauses.

'Have you caught the man yet?'

'No, we haven't,' replies Magda, biting her tongue on the next response.

'So why are you hassling us?'

Magda hesitates.

'I don't think that's true, madam.' She makes herself say. 'We're dealing with a cold case here, a murder that happened seven years ago. The girl was a friend of your daughter's. It's only sensible that we try to find out as much as we can about what happened back then.'

The woman is silent, but Magda can sense the gritted teeth.

'I've only two questions, actually,' she continues.

A sigh.

Magda takes her chance.

'Is Roz a short name?'

'Rosamund,' replies the mother sullenly. 'It was my grandmother's name. So what?'

Magda holds her breath and composes herself.

'Was Roz wearing her hair long and curly seven years ago?'

There's an intake of breath.

'What are you saying?'

Magda hesitates. There's a fine line between using moments like this to elicit potentially important information or losing the trust of a witness. She figures that she isn't going to get a better chance than this with this woman, so she goes for it.

'Have you a photograph of her from that time?'

For a moment she thinks the woman is going to slam the phone down or shout at her, but there's only silence.

'Hello?' she asks quietly.

A long pause.

'Yes, she did … and she said the man did ask her if they could meet up some time.'

Magda held her breath.

'But she says she didn't.'

They're both silent, thinking what the other must be thinking.

Magda knows what she must do.

'I'm sorry, Mrs Lambert. Given what you've just told me, we will have to interview Roz. You can, of course, accompany her, but we need to do this soon. Today, if possible.'

There is another long pause, but eventually a sigh of defeat.

'All right, but can we do it at home?'

'Of course,' says Maga, glancing at the kitchen clock. 'Is eleven OK?'

'Yes,' says the woman, 'but please don't come in a police car.'

'I wouldn't do that, Mrs Lambert,' she says.

'Good,' comes the reply and the line goes dead.

Magda stands staring at the clock.

It's one of the few things her mother managed to salvage from her home before it was destroyed by the Russian advance in 1944. She's always refused to have the crack mended, even though it disfigures the number nine.

Magda wonders whether taking Gatti will be helpful or not. Only … meeting the woman on the phone hasn't really given her a good idea of what she's like, other than defensive. She's seen him use his natural charm and dark looks to good effect in the past. Especially with difficult women suspects. She decides it's worth a chance and gives him a call.

He agrees to meet her at the house.

⁓

As Magda sets off down the lane to the main road a woman is getting out of a car in the forest car park. She bends briefly to say something to the driver then shuts the door.

The car drives away.

She walks slowly along the road until she spots the footbridge and figures out where the path must be.

Anyone local watching would have been intrigued, as she's not dressed for the countryside.

The long black coat is serviceable and the boots are all right, but the long dress is a bit flimsy … and her hair? Well, half of it is a brassy blonde and the other side of her head is shaved to the skin. But it's the make-up that would have caught their attention: dark eyebrows, heavy mascara and black lips.

She stops at the middle of the bridge and stares down at the river. It's very full after all the rain and snow over the last month or so.

After continuing on she eventually gets to Amelia's house and goes in uninvited.

Inside, she looks round. Little sign of occupation apart from the heater. She doesn't remember him being so tidy. Maybe he's gone, having dragged her down here in the wilderness once again.

She calls out.

Tomasz appears at the door she's just come in through. They both smile. Eyes shining.

They embrace.

He takes her clothes off.

And reveals the whirl of dragons and snakes, eyes and claws grappling with each other in a whirl of fierce vengeance.

She undresses him. Like a formal dance without the music.

His body is devoid of colourful images, but there are scars. Battle wounds. One that was badly tended, leaving a faded purple mark.

The coupling begins gently enough, but quickly morphs into a raging battle.

Violent.

Unforgiving.

Afterwards they share a joint.

And sit staring at each other, her leaning against the sofa, him against the wall.

'I can't stay here,' he says softly.

She nods.

'Where will you go?'

He shrugs.

'England, I'm afraid.'

She pulls a face.

'Who's the target?'

He grins.

'You could say … the Queen.'

She raises her eyebrows, but then shrugs.

'Why not?'

He laughs.

'Does that mean London?'

He shakes his head.

'Not necessarily. "She's everywhere and nowhere, baby."'

She stares at him. How old is he again?

'Why the Queen?' she asks. 'A lot of trouble to kill an old biddy.'

'Not her in person,' he whispers in a hoarse voice.

She frowns again and then he explains.

She stares at him.

'What will that do?'

'Nothing much to start with. But then, when the copycats follow, it could become a riot. Especially when I start taking out a few heads as well.'

'Heads?'

'Old white stone ones. Metal ones.'

'Ah,' she says. 'I see.'

Later, they lie asleep.

Her curled up, him on his side.

The moon creeps out from behind the towering clouds and surveys them.

Silvery corpses on a much-abused bed … about to be abandoned one last time.

Ziggy has been trying to contact Violet, but with no success.

I suggest he alerts the Bristol police.

Not his usual style, I have to admit, but he reluctantly agrees.

An hour later they get back to him. And ask a lot of questions before telling him that she's been found dead.

We are all stunned.

'But didn't she have the highest level of protection?' Freya asks, as though she knows what she means by that.

Ziggy nods his head in agreement. But he thinks it's pointless telling the local Bristol police about that, as they'll soon be taken off the case.

Which is what happens. And then he gets interrogated. How did he know something was wrong? How does he know her? Who else has he told? Et cetera.

Later he manages to find out that it was a blow to the head. When he asks about the alarm he's told it was deactivated, and who does he know knew about that?

It's only later that he realises he has received a message from her, via a separate connection she's set up – which seems to be in code, because it doesn't make sense.

He prints it out.

He and Freya puzzle at it. He on his computers. And she covers sheets of paper with words and diagrams and scribbling out.

Janet spends a lot of time on her mobile. God knows who she's speaking to.

I know she knows a lot of people you wouldn't want to cross or meet in a dark alley. Not that she'd tell me their names, anyway.

I make the coffee. Dole out the biscuits and sweets.

This is how it gets done.

I know my place.

~

Magda and Gatti are sitting in her car. The rain is belting off the car roof.

They're not outside the girl's house yet but are a couple of streets away, discussing the way they should start.

Often it's assumed that women officers are more likely to elicit difficult information or confessions from female suspects, but Magda has seen what her sergeant can do. Something to do with the softness of his voice and, she suspects, his soft brown eyes. She's not at all comfortable with this and has never said anything about it to him.

They agree that she will start then seamlessly pass over to him, so that she can focus on the young woman's reactions.

She'd prefer to do this without the mother present, although she thinks it's unlikely that she'll agree to that.

Gatti seems to have sensed the awkwardness of this and glances out of the window.

'But,' he says, 'this "girl" is actually twenty-four years old.'

'Yeah, well, it's not her immaturity I'm worried about … more that the mother knows or is hiding something.'

Gatti frowns.

'Like what?'

Magda stares out of the window.

'Not sure. Just a feeling. Something's not quite right.'

Gatti waits.

'The father looks really young… Maybe he isn't her father. Maybe that's the problem.'

Gatti checks his mobile. Magda thinks she's pretty sharp with the Internet, but she knows he's done some extra training.

It only takes a few minutes before he's showing her a list of divorce records, including the mention of Lambert vs Lambert.

But the more interesting thing is that this was in 2012, two years before the disappearance of the daughter's friend.

'So is that a connection?' he asks.

Magda shakes her head.

'Not according to the files.'

'OK. So we've two teenagers, both without their real fathers. I wonder when the stepdad came on the scene,' she says.

Gatti shrugs. Not easy to check that out.

'Was he a suspect at the time?'

Again, it doesn't take him long.

'No mention of him.'

They both look out of the window.

Magda hates these cases. People with screwed-up families. It's rare to get any truth about anything from either side.

She sighs.

'So we're back to asking the girl if the man at the art classes pursued her after she stopped going, or if he showed any interest in her friend.'

Gatti frowns.

'She's not likely to confess to that in front of her mother, from what you've told me.'

Magda nods.

'But she is twenty-four. We could insist on talking to her on her own.'

He shrugs.

She sighs.

They drive round to the house.

The door opens and the mother gives them a stern look.

The daughter is in the kitchen. The 'stepfather' is nowhere to be seen.

Magda asks the mother if they can interview the daughter on her own.

The woman bristles but surprisingly gives in, although she does tell her daughter not to be intimidated by the police.

Magda sits at the kitchen table.

Eventually the girl joins her, after giving Gatti a brief stare.

Magda begins by asking her to try to remember what happened seven years ago.

The girl sighs and then gives a well-rehearsed summary, which implies that she knows nothing more than she's already told them.

She slumps back in the chair and glances at Gatti.

He smiles.

'So you never saw him again?' he asks.

She frowns.

'No.'

He pauses.

'What about Susan?'

'What do you mean?'

'Did he transfer his attention to her?'

'What?' she laughs. 'Why would he do that? She didn't go to the art class. How would he even know about her?'

'He could have followed you, could have seen you together.'

She stares at him and shudders, but then shakes her head.

'I don't think so ... although...'

Gatti waits.

The girl looks at Magda, who just gives her a straight face, but then looks back at Gatti.

'OK. Maybe something might have happened.'

The two police officers are silent.

The girl stands up, goes to the window.

'We had an argument, and we didn't see each other for a week or so. It was the holidays, so we weren't at school.

'What was the argument about?'

She shakes her head.

'She asked me about the man.'

'The man in the art class?'

'Yeah. I told her he was a creep.'

They wait.

'That's all?' asks Gatti.

She puts her hand behind her neck and pushes her hair to one side.

'I told her she wasn't his type.'

'Why not?' he asks, almost smiling.

She stares at him.

'Because she had short hair.'

Gatti is still, but his smile doesn't go away.

'Not like yours,' he murmurs.

The girl's face hardens.

'No, not like mine.'

Magda can hardly breathe. The two people in front of her are locked in a staring battle.

Gatti breaks it with a look away.

'So what happened next?'

'What do you mean?' the girl asks.

He looks back at her.

'Did she let her hair grow long?'

The girl nods.

'She tried, but it wasn't like mine. It took ages … and then she disappeared.'

Magda becomes aware of the mother standing by the door.

The girl gives her a hard look.

'They didn't ask me that before, Mum. And, anyway, why would that be important?'

She looks back at the detectives.

The penny finally drops.

She bursts into tears.

Back in the car they're both staring out of the window.

'Does this mean that Hook's prognosis might be correct?' she asks.

He nods.

'Not that it helps us or helps find the murderer,' he murmurs. 'How do you track down someone who has a fetish for a long-dead woman?'

Magda turns to look at him.

'Does Google keep a record of who has looked at a particular website?'

Gatti nods.

'Unless you regularly delete it.'

'So can we ask it to check who's been on a particular site?'

'I think so. But, if he's deleted it, no.'

She sighs.

'Why does it have to get so damn complicated?'

Gatti shrugs.

'From what we've found out so far, I suspect that this man is clever enough to hide his tracks, especially digital ones.'

'So how else are we going to find him?'

Gatti is silent, fingering his phone.

She starts the car.

'How many times do you think people have asked Google about Henry II and Rosamund?' he asks.

She shrugs.

'They've had 1.3 million hits,' he says.

Magda feels like banging her head on the steering wheel.

⌒

Hollis is furious.

Neither Marchant nor Sudeley would agree to going to Scotland. His threats only made Marchant laugh, and Sudeley just ended the call. He has a stronger hold on Barnum, but he started whining on about the Covid restrictions as if he'd not already broken them. So he reminded him about the long list of his other more serious crimes.

He doesn't contact Jane, although he suspects she keeps track of his movements. Maybe if she turns up it might be an opportunity to get rid of her as well.

Barnum agrees to meet him in Kelso in a hotel that is open for key workers.

The journey to the Borders passes without interest, although the further he goes north the more he remembers how much he hates the place. It's always cold and the people are miserable. England would be better off without them hanging on to their coat-tails, whining on about their rights and independence.

He puts his foot down and roars up the A1.

~

Eventually Ursula calls Louisa and tells her the news.

Fletcher can't believe it.

'But…' he says. 'She must have had the highest level of protection. Unmarked police cars, phone taps … as well as the maximum level of risk alert.'

Louisa can only shake her head.

'Apparently the alarm system had been turned off.'

Fletcher pulls a face.

'She wouldn't do that.'

The two girls and Savitri are nonplussed, not knowing the woman or how influential she had been.

'Apparently Sigismund says she called the other day and sounded unusually angry, almost hysterical.'

Again, this is met with frowns.

Fletcher attempts to explain who Ziggy is, until he gives up and looks to Louisa.

'He's a computer man,' she says, as if that's enough, but then adds, 'He's rather unusual. A bit crazy.'

Fletcher laughs.

'He's also confused about his gender,' he adds. But then, on seeing the looks he's getting, he shrugs his shoulders.

'OK. He likes wearing dresses and make-up.'

Louisa's stare tells him to stop digging, so he shuts up.

'But why now?' murmurs Louisa.

Four blank faces stare back at her.

She orders them all to get ready for a walk, and they're soon straggling along the riverbank. Louisa is leading the way chatting to Mali, mainly in French. Ellie and Savitri are deep in historical discussion, while Fletcher dawdles along at the rear, stopping now and again to watch the swans or the dabbling ducks.

He's standing watching a heron when he realises that they've turned back and are coming towards him.

As they get level with him, he murmurs more to himself than them.

'People called her the Stork,' he says.

They all stop.

'Not to her face, of course. She was too scary to do that.'

Not one of them can think of anything to say.

Ellie puts her arm through his.

'I'm quite sure she saved me from harm more than once,' he continues, and is surprised to feel a tear running slowly down his cheek.

He rubs it away and shakes his head.

The five of them watch as the heron decides that it's had enough. It launches itself into the air and, after a couple of desultory flaps, glides off downstream.

It starts to rain.

They take Fletcher back to the house without much more conversation.

He is parked in the conservatory, and Louisa and Mali go to fix some lunch.

Eventually Ellie goes and sits with him, but there's no conversation. It's only then that she realises how old he looks, slumped in a wicker chair, like someone in an old people's home.

'How can that be?' she wonders. 'How could he get so old and feeble-looking? What is he thinking? Someday he'll be gone.'

He must have realised that she's staring at him, and he looks up as though from a sleep.

He sees her worried face and frowns.

He sits up in his chair.

'Wassup?' he asks.

She wipes her eye.

'Hey,' he says. 'I'm not dead yet.'

She gets up and goes to sit on his lap like she used to do as a girl.

He holds her tight, and they're sitting like this when Mali comes in to tell them that lunch is ready.

She's taken aback for a moment but then it's all laughter, and Fletcher is pretending to be an old gimmer chasing them back inside.

They arrive with screams and giggling, to find Louisa and Savitri looking at them like two bespectacled head teachers.

No explanations are given or asked for, but the conversation is more downbeat than usual.

Afterwards Louisa gives Magda a call.

She hasn't heard about Violet and is shocked to hear the terrible news.

'But wasn't she heavily protected? she asks.

'So everyone thought, but apparently the security system was disabled.'

Magda shakes her head. She can't think of what to say.

'Anyway, we're having to look after Michael. I think it's hit him hard, although of course he won't admit it.'

Again, her knowledge of Fletcher is only recent, if disconcerting, and so she can only offer her commiserations.

∾

Gatti suggests that one way to find the suspect is to assemble a collection of old photos from newspaper and magazines from events like hunt balls, meetings and other similar gatherings, which they can then show to the girl.

Magda is happy to leave him to do this thankless task, especially as it may include embarrassing pictures of herself, which she tells him she doesn't want to see.

He tries not to smirk, but she just laughs.

She decides she'll go home early and make a lovely tea for Amelia and the kids.

Although when she's standing in the supermarket, she can't think what that might be, until she embarrasses both herself and the young woman with a couple of kids in tow by asking for her advice.

With bags full of spaghetti, ice cream, cakes and biscuits, she arrives at the house to find them all charging around chasing Hengist, who, completely out of character, has stolen one of the steaks Amelia was preparing for dinner.

Suitably chastised, Hengist is sent to the barn and Amelia has stopped laughing at Magda's provisions.

They are totally unsuitable, apparently. Hasn't Magda paid any attention to Amelia's rigorous regime, which is dedicated to trying to bring up her children to be healthy? Not obese and spotty, like most other children seem to be?

To be honest, she hadn't.

Anyway, afterwards they're sitting watching the sun go down, with a glass of her father's best Armagnac in their hands.

'Did you find the man at the council?' asks Amelia.

Magda frowns.

'Which man?'

'The one in the drawing.'

Magda shakes her head.

'He only lasted a week, apparently. Didn't turn up the next Monday. His details turned out to be false. No such person.'

They stare at the sun as it dips below the skyline.

'But why would someone do that?'

Magda frowns.

'Good question. Although that's how he operated. Always covering his tracks.'

Amelia considers this.

'Yes, but why did he get a job at the council?'

'No idea. We've asked what information he would have been able to access, but their first response was, "Hardly anything."'

'How about people's addresses?'

'We asked about that. They said, "Not really."'

'But he was able to access their system, wasn't he?'

'How do you mean?'

'Well, I asked him about our council tax.'

'And?'

'It was under Duncan's name, not mine.'

'But he still found it?'

'In a few seconds.'

Magda frowns.

'I'll go back to them,' she says.

They sit there silently.

Magda's hand creeps across to Amelia's arm.

She looks across at her.

She's silhouetted in the dying light.

But then she frowns.

'What's that light?' she asks.

Magda looks where's she's pointing.

'It's your house.'

Suddenly there's a blossom of flames followed by the blast of an explosion.

They both stare in disbelief.

CHAPTER 14
OF MICE AND MEN

Magda is astonished at the destruction of Amelia's house.

As the saying goes, it left barely one brick on another.

The problems for the fire brigade were made worse by the panicking of the horses – who, thankfully, hadn't been in their barn, but the flames and explosions had terrified them.

The first fire engine arriving at high speed along the lane had made things worse, as two of the terrified creatures had got over the fence and had met them hurtling along with lights flashing and siren blaring.

But eventually they got the fire under control, and the next morning all that could be seen were the blackened remains. The only surviving building was the garage.

The cause was quickly but mystifyingly identified as being an old electric fire, which must have somehow set off a piece of curtain or the sofa. Amelia told Magda afterwards that she thought they'd got rid of it ages ago.

The lead officer comes to talk to Amelia and asks if she knows how that could have occurred.

She shakes her head and says she can only think someone must have realised the house was empty and was dossing down there.

'When were you last there?' he asks.

'I go every day,' she says, but then adds, 'although I never go in the house.'

He waits.

'So yesterday evening was the last time,' she says.

The officer gives her a questioning look, but she doesn't waver.

'Bad memories, I'm afraid,' she says. 'To be honest, I'm sort of relieved … but I didn't do it.'

Magda puts her arm round her and gives the officer a look.

He looks from one to other. It's obvious he's suspicious.

'I can vouch for that,' she says.

He nods and says that he will have to put this in his report, but then gives them another look.

'Was the place insured against accidental fire?' he asks.

Amelia stares at him until a frown comes onto her face.

'Actually, I've no idea,' she says. 'My husband did all that sort of thing.'

He gives her another enquiring look.

'He died last year,' she says. 'I've got the papers somewhere.'

He nods.

'Well, it's your problem, but I'm going to call it 'Cause unclear' for now. We'll be carrying out further investigations, but you must let me know about the insurance as soon as possible.'

Amelia's face has gone blank, but she manages a nod of understanding.

With that the man turns on his heel and walks away to his car.

'Pompous arse,' says Magda under her breath.

Amelia bursts into tears.

Back at the house they sit at the table. Amelia has found the house papers but can't find any insurance policy.

'Who did Duncan use?' asks Magda.

Amelia shakes her head.

'I've no idea. You know what he was like. "Man stuff,"' she says with a sneer, but then bursts into tears again.

Magda puts her arm round her again, but she shrugs it off.

'Bloody bastard,' she snarls. 'It would be typical if he hadn't insured it. He was always cutting corners and doing dodgy deals. He thought he was so clever. Bastard.'

Magda stares at her.

She's never seen such rage from her.

'All that effort I put into that place. I did all the painting, the wallpapering, finding the nice second-hand furniture, getting the cheapest workmen to come. He never lifted a finger and scoffed at everything.'

She paces up and down.

'And now he's left me with nothing.'

She screams.

It's only then that they both realise there's a line of terrified faces at the kitchen door. The little one is starting to cry.

Amelia stops in mid screech and rushes over to them.

There's a lot of Amelia saying 'Sorry,' and, 'Mummy's just upset,' before everyone calms down and a picnic is created.

Throughout this Magda has never felt so useless. First she stares in disbelief, and then she doesn't know what to do with upset children or how to make a picnic.

Later, when the kids are playing outside, Amelia looks up from clearing away the debris.

'Sorry about that,' she says with a wan smile, which then turns into a grin. 'Never seen you so scared,' she says. And then, with a lascivious laugh, 'You obviously didn't know that I can be a bit of wildcat.'

Magda doesn't know whether to laugh or shake her head.

Amelia gives her another big-eyed leer and comes slowly towards her.

What happened next Magda was never to forget, but it changed their relationship irrevocably.

It was only when they come back downstairs that she checks her phone for messages.

Two from Gatti.

One that the chief wants to talk to her and the second that a stranger was seen crossing the bridge to Amelia's earlier yesterday, and that the description fits someone they know about.

She calls him straight away.

'Who's the suspect?' she asks without any preamble.

'"A tall woman in a long black coat, with a weird hairstyle,"' he quotes.

'One side shaved,' guesses Magda.

'Yup,' says Gatti, which sounds odd in his accent.

'OK,' she says. 'Meet me there in half an hour.'

He agrees and she turns to look at Amelia.

'It's Tomasz and his slut girlfriend,' she says, defensively.

'Well,' says Amelia, 'they've done me a big favour,' and she waves a paper at her.

Magda frowns.

'Johnny at the solicitors has just emailed me a copy of the house insurance paid for last year, and it's still valid. He assures me that I'll cop the proceeds, especially if it's someone else's fault.'

Magda doesn't know what to say, although she's thinking how that brother of hers might have done something right for once. Even if he has had to commit a crime to do it.

And, of course, he's long gone and an expert at disappearing.

⤙

Imelda doesn't know England very well, apart from a few visits to London and various gigs and festivals in places she can no longer name.

So arriving at the Yorkshire seaside is a bit a culture shock. A bit like Portobello, but far tweer. Everyone seems to be over sixty and there are a lot of ice cream sellers open and little shops selling tat. Is that OK?

When Tomasz was researching on the Internet he landed on the council pages with a photo of the councillors, who looked like the residents of an old people's home.

They stopped and bought an ice cream and walk along a promenade.

'I haven't done this since I was a six-year-old,' she says, staring out at the sea, which is surprisingly calm. Little waves flopping onto a clean stretch of pebbly sand.

'Where's this statue?' she asks, as she looks for somewhere to put her ice cream paper and then shakes her head. 'This place is turning me into a granny,' she explodes, and throws the paper onto the ground, where it's whisked away by a gust of wind.

Tomasz grins, but then nods at an actual granny, who has put her foot on the paper and is now bending painfully down to pick it up.

Imelda glares at him but finds herself going over, apologising, and taking the errant paper from the old lady, who smiles and carries on, pulling her little trolley as she goes.

She finds a bin and comes back, to sit sulking as best she can, but then bursts out laughing at the ridiculousness of it all.

Throughout all this Tomasz has just sat and watched like some doting grandad, but now his face hardens.

'Let's go and find the statue,' he says, and pulls out his mobile.

It doesn't take long, and now they're standing next to a rather grander old lady. She's looking a bit overweight and is holding onto a stick and a ball as though she's waiting for the class to calm down before she starts some game or other.

Tomasz glances round.

Couldn't be better.

It's surrounded by various four- or five-storey buildings, one of which is sporting a Union Jack on a tall pole.

'That's the council offices,' he murmurs.

'Looks like it's derelict,' she says.

He shakes his head.

'Nope, it's still operational … although it's not been open to the public during the lockdown.'

He turns full circle, looking for a suitable vantage point.

'Let's go and have a look at a hotel bedroom or two,' he says, as he sets off.

Imelda follows him, thinking a comfy bed would be welcome after the last few nights on various lumpy ones.

But he's more interested in the top floors and the views.

⌒

Fetcher isn't sleeping with Louisa.

He's OK with that.

He is over seventy and can't remember the last time he had sex.

Oh, yes, he can.

But he'd rather not.

He shudders.

He reflects that his love life – no, let's be honest, his sex life – hasn't been the most fulfilling part of his existence.

Before he met Laura he'd stopped counting the number of one-night stands he'd had. This wasn't out of arrogance, but rather more from embarrassment. If he'd been a woman he would have been called a tart, but he knew the proper words were *philanderer* or *womaniser*.

So Louisa maintaining her dignity is fine with him.

But that doesn't exclude frequent visitations in the early morning. Louisa doesn't need much sleep nowadays.

She always wears her rather grand dressing gown, bought in an eye-wateringly expensive shop on the Champs-Élysées many years ago, and slips quietly in beside him before placing her cold feet on his legs.

No apologies for that, and no grumbling from him.

This arrangement has continued even though they have visitors, including his granddaughter, who he'd rather did not know about this arrangement. But he suspects she does, and that it would only make her giggle.

This morning Louisa is early.

A quick glance at his watch tells him it's just before six.

He sighs and rolls over, as though he's not up for a conversation.

Louisa ignores this and begins her peroration.

'So we can't get back to Dryburgh until after 30 April,' she murmurs.

There's a pause.

He's expecting a '*but*'.

'But I'm going to have word with the chief constable about that and tell him we have some important investigations to conduct.'

Again, Fletcher waits. There will be a coda to that as well.

Sure enough, but it's a girlish snigger.

'If you only knew…' she says.

He waits.

'Well? Are going to tell me?' he grumbles.

'Certainly not,' she snaps.

Fletcher sighs and snuggles further under the covers.

There's quite a long pause.

'Shall we say an indiscretion with a lady whose reputation is more than a little tarnished?'

Fletcher can't help but laugh.

'Do I know her?'

She sighs.

He doesn't know anyone else who can do such sarcastic sighs.

'Way out of your league, Michael dear.'

He grunts.

'Why do you always say that?' he grumbles.

She sighs.

'She's the daughter of an earl and worth a fortune.'

He turns over.

'So what's not to like?'

She sighs again.

'Actually, I don't think you would like. She's had more facelifts than the Sphinx.'

'Who?'

She shakes her head.

They lie there silently for a while.

'Are you worried about Eleanor?' she asks quietly, repeating her rather pedantic way of pronouncing both the second 'e' and the 'a' separately.

Fletcher glances her way. She's staring right at him over her glasses.

He grins.

'She's fine. A lioness.'

Louisa's gaze softens, and she shakes her head.

They lie in a comfortable silence for some time.

As if she's aware they're awake, talking about her, Ellie appears at the door with a tray of freshly made coffee still in the pot, two cups and a bowl of unnecessary sugar.

She grins and puts the tray on the side table and does a daft curtsey.

'Dismissed,' says Fletcher, in his best Edward Fox impression.

'Yes m'lud,' comes the reply, and then she's gone.

Louisa shakes her head again but can't hide the smile.
'You're blessed. You know that, don't you?' she says.
He nods, and gets up to pour the coffee.

Downstairs, an hour later, they find Ellie deep in conversation with Savitri, with books, papers and laptops on the dining room table.

A brief earwig tells Louisa that they're talking in Occitan, so she leaves them to it and goes to see about breakfast.

Fletcher has already got started, and soon they're shooing the investigators off the table and sending Ellie to wake up Mali.

After what seems quite a long time they're beginning to wonder where they are, but then an angry Ellie comes in and attacks her breakfast.

The three oldies glance at each other, not daring to ask why she's fuming, but then Mali arrives.

None of them have seen these two have a row, although Grace has said to stand back when it happens.

But the room grows colder by the minute, until Mali can't stand it any longer.

'My mother is coming back from Beirut and wants me to go home … so I'm trying to see if I can get a flight.'

Louisa looks at Fletcher and then back at the angry young woman.

'I'm not sure you'll be able to do that,' she says.

'That's what I've told her,' rasps Ellie.

Mali ignores that and looks at Louisa.

'I know it's going to be difficult, and I'll have to stay in quarantine. But I haven't even asked yet, so give me a chance.'

They all look at her sympathetically, except for Ellie, who finishes her plate and gets up to take it to the kitchen and doesn't come back.

Mali leaves her unfinished breakfast and leaves the room without meeting their eyes.

The three of them look at each other with raised eyebrows.

'My best advice is to keep our noses out,' says Fletcher.

The other two nod their heads, and the conversation moves on to what they might do for the rest of the day.

As it happens, the solution is unexpected.

Mali's mother has had to change her flight and come to London, so at least Mali can go and see her, even if it's through a Perspex glass wall in some quarantine facility.

The two girls seem to have reached a truce, and Ellie is helping Mali pack.

It's all done quickly, and by ten o'clock they're waving her off down the drive.

They retreat indoors from the rain and Ellie and Savitri return to their investigations, while Louisa reads the morning paper and Fletcher eventually goes for his riverside walk.

As he stands watching his adopted personal heron, he asks her what she thinks.

He doesn't know for certain that she is a 'she', but it feels like she has that elegant nonchalance that many women have, which inevitably brings him to the worrying question about what has happened to Violet Cranthorne.

It's not a question of who would do that to her. He's sure she made plenty of enemies in her long career in the cut-throat world she inhabited, and no doubt some of those people were now engaged in pretending to find her killers. But their tracks will be well covered, alongside a high level of immunity even if it becomes known who they were.

He sighs.

The heron launches herself into flight.

'Just like the Stork,' he whispers, recalling her elegant presence and shaking his head at the extinction of yet another one of the powerful figures in his own life. Last year it was Adversane. Now it was her.

He's still staring into the past when a figure comes into view along the path.

～

Hollis wonders how he ever agreed to include Barnum into this venture. The man is a complete idiot.

He's just knocked on his door and come in, complaining that there's no dining room and that they must order the food to eat in their bedrooms.

Hollis just stares at him until he backs away and goes to look out of the window.

This silence continues until Barnum comes to sit down opposite him like a sulky teenager.

'So what are we going to do?' he asks.

Hollis is as usual on his laptop, and for a few moments continues to ignore him.

The silence gathers.

Barnum fidgets.

Hollis fingers the screen.

'Did you bring your gun?'

Barnum stares at this little bastard, who's ruined his life.

'Of course I have,' he snaps.

'Is it loaded?'

Barnum stands up and walks to the window.

'OK. This is the plan.'

'At least it means they're doing something,' thinks Barnum, as they drive off half an hour later. Although kidnapping sounds risky. What if the girl fights back? What about the other people? And what then? Where are they going to take her?

He's not voiced any of these concerns or asked about Jane. He's sure she's keeping tabs on them somehow.

⌐

Apparently it's about something called 'Operation Ramillies.'

Ziggy explains that this was one of battles in the War of the Spanish Succession.

'When was that?' I ask.

It's easy,' he says. 'BROM5679.'

'What?'

'Marlborough's victories. Ramillies was number two, so 1706.'

'Who?'

He turns to look at me with a grin on his face.

'Ah, that's why it was easy to crack the code.'

I look over at Freya, who merely gives me a weak smile.

'Winston Churchill is Boris Johnson's favourite hero ... and he was the Duke of Marlborough's eight times grandson.'

I shake my head.

But now Ziggy is frowning.

'But that's too easy,' he murmurs, and turns back to his bank of screens.

There's the usual fluttering of fingers as he goes from one keyboard to another.

I always take this as a sign that I may as well have disappeared, so I go anyway.

While I am standing in the kitchen looking out at the sunshine and thinking I'll go for another walk, I realise that Freya has followed me.

She puts the kettle on and stands by the cooker.

'It's as we feared,' she says softly.

'We?' I ask, without turning round.

She comes to stand next to me and puts her hand on my shoulder.

'I mean what a lot of people fear.'

I turn to look at her.

She's smaller than me and as thin as can be. Sometimes I worry that she's ill. After all, she only eats like a sparrow, and hardly anything you could call substantial. No meat, no chocolate and no chips. I'd be dead in a week.

'You mean the dumb blonde revolution, as Ziggy calls it.'

She nods.

I sigh again. What can I – we – do about people's gullibility?

The kettle boils. I pour the hot water into the teapot, realise I've forgotten the teabags, add a couple and give them a stir.

I take the tray into the front room and place it on the table. Freya follows me like a shadow, and then we're sitting down facing each other.

Neither of us speak for quite some time.

'I'm worried,' she says.

I frown, knowing that she has a far greater understanding of what's going on than most people. When I first met her last spring she was even thinner, and on the run from shadowy agents who thought she'd expose their plans. She remains under the protection of the fearsome Becket and John combo, for reasons still undisclosed.

'Can you explain it to me?' I ask.

She looks out of the window with a frown.

'I'm out of the loop now, but basically . . .'

She hesitates and looks back at me, as though she's considering whether I'll understand a word she's on about.

I smile.

'Keep it simple.'

What she then tells me in a long and detailed account, but somehow elegantly explained, is how a so-called free country like ours can be very easily turned into a police state. How the older generation, the others who voted for the current government, will go along with that until it's too late. How the young and non-white communities will attempt to fight back and be violently put down. How the news channels will be constrained far beyond how they are now. Channels 4 and 5 will be taken off the air, many BBC newsreaders will be replaced and lots of journalists and commentators will be arrested. The offices of The Guardian will be attacked and closed down. All this has been planned, rehearsed and updated for many years now.

By now I'm shaking my head.

'They won't get away with it,' I say.

Freya gives me a thin smile.

'I've seen the papers outlining the scenarios. The figures and deployment of the armed forces. The manoeuvres that they have practised. It may be just a wet dream for some people, but it's clear that for others it's very real.'

I can only just stare at her.

But there's more.

She now explains how the current smokescreen of Covid operations has so far hidden the real effects of Brexit. And that come autumn, when there's a surge of returning expats – those who voted for Brexit and who now find themselves literally being deported back to the UK, some of them abandoning property and belongings along the way – will join the ever-growing army of unemployed people. When the support funds are stopped the government will claim that they have to resort to emergency measures to save the country from revolution. Parliament will be dissolved, and many opposition MPs will be arrested. Schools will be closed, and hospitals will become unable to cope.

Eventually she comes to a halt.

All of this is said in a calm and matter-of-fact manner, as though she were reading me a bedtime story.

She stands up and goes to the window.

I don't know what to do or say.

But then I'm aware that Ziggy is standing in the doorway.

He's leaning against the doorjamb, a pen stuck in his mouth.

He's obviously been listening to this for some time.

He looks at me.

Nods his head and turns away.

I look back at Freya silhouetted at the window.

How quiet it has become.

I realise I'm crying.

⁓

Hollis and Barnum have left the van in a lay-by a few hundred yards from the entrance to Louisa's driveway.

Even though many of the deciduous trees are still sensibly holding their fire in the prolonged winter conditions, there are plenty of fir trees to hide their advance to a position where they can see through some of the windows.

At the south side there's a huge old-fashioned glasshouse, which is full of luxuriant foliage protected by the glass and, no doubt, some heating.

They make their way round until they're on the riverside aspect and can see a couple of heads bowed over a large dining table.

Hollis looks at them through his binoculars and confirms that one of them is the young woman. He knows there are at least two other people in residence. But then Louisa Cunninghame could easily afford any number of live-in servants, so he's thinking of using the police identity cards to gain entrance and then playing it by ear.

He knows this will be risky, and that ex-DI Fletcher is a notoriously loose cannon, but doubts he's carrying a weapon in this situation. Cunninghame herself no doubt has a shooting armoury, but it's likely to be properly under lock and key. And both of them are in their seventies, and neither of them are to be seen. The unknown woman looks the same age as them, and the two girls shouldn't be a problem.

Still no sign of Fletcher. Could he be out for a walk? Is he the sort of person to do that? Not likely.

So alternatively, they could gate-crash the two at the table. Disable the older woman. Get out with the girl. Shots into the ceiling if anyone else gets in the way.

It's at this point that a car pulls up in the driveway and beeps its horn.

The two at the table disappear and then reappear at the front door with Lady Cunninghame and Fletcher. There's brief kissing and hugging, then the girl's friend gets into the car and is driven away.

The girl and the older woman reappear at the big table. Fletcher comes out of a back door and sets off towards the river on his own. The lady is nowhere to be seen again.

So back to plan B. Burst into the dining room and get the girl.

Chapter 15
Gang ⊙ft Aglay

Watching Barnum trying to emulate a soldier zigzagging to the doorway makes Hollis nearly burst out laughing, until he remembers that he's relying on this imbecile to carry out their plan.

So, with anger surging up into his chest, he grits his teeth and follows him.

He catches up with him, and the two of them eye each other on either side of the doorway.

Hollis glares at him, while Barnum gives him a puzzled look.

They both become aware that no birds sing, but then a quick glance from Hollis confirms that the two women at the table are still wrapped up in their conversation.

Hollis nods Barnum to try the door handle.

He pulls a face but then gingerly reaches out to test it.

It turns easily enough.

Barnum looks back at him. Hollis nods.

The attempt to burst in like he's seen in Bond movies gets Barnum through the door, but then he bumps into the side of a low, heavy table and goes sprawling onto the floor.

As he scrambles to get upright and rescue his gun, Hollis steps in behind him and levels his gun at the two astonished faces staring at him.

Barnum gets to his feet and retrieves his errant weapon.

There is a brief silence as the two women try to comprehend what's happening and Barnum looks for reassurance to Hollis, who waves him to go towards the women.

'We're not going to harm you,' says Hollis.

Fear has now replaced astonishment in the two women's eyes.

Ellie glances at Savitri, whose lips are tightly closed and who now gives them a stern look of determination.

She stands up.

Barnum looks at Hollis, who points his gun at the older woman.

The noise of the gunshot is ear-splitting.

The two women flinch but Savitri remains standing, while a picture behind her collapses onto the floor with crash of splintering glass

Hollis fires again.

Savitri slumps back into her chair with a small cry.

It's only a flesh wound, but there's blood streaming down her arm. She looks back at him in fear.

Hollis gestures to Barnum and points at Ellie.

He goes over and grabs her by the arm.

She's terrified. But she is still staring at Savitri.

He drags her to her feet.

Hollis comes over and picks up her laptop and her phone and puts them in their bag.

Savitri is breathing heavily. Blood trickles through her fingers as, trying not to faint, she presses the wound.

There's a brief moment when their eyes meet, but then he backs away and puts the bag over his shoulder.

He gestures to Barnum to bring Ellie, but she struggles free and pushes him away.

Hollis grabs her. He puts his arm round her neck and starts to back away towards the window.

'Let her go,' says a voice.

Louisa is standing at the doorway, holding a pistol with both hands and pointing it directly at Hollis. He glances at Barnum, who is staring at Louisa, his gun shaking in his hand.

There is another loud explosion.

Even Hollis's face is briefly shocked, but that's nothing like the horror the three women go through.

Whether it was intentional or not he's blasted Barnum's head open. Bits of flesh, skull, brain, and a wash of bright red blood hit the wall and all around where he was standing, before his legs collapse him onto an armchair, so that he ends up with his legs crossed one over the other as though he was about to have an afternoon conversation … which is no longer possible.

Ellie stares in horror but is roughly pulled back by Hollis, who uses her as a shield to get her through the outside door, while firing a flurry of shots towards Louisa, who has dodged back behind the door.

Once through the door he grabs Ellie by the arm and drags her through the bushes.

There's no sound of Louisa following them, but he urges her on.

'Does that mean she's dead or wounded?' is all Ellie can think.

They reach the car.

He opens the boot, pushes her in and forces the door shut.

She's too terrified to resist. Images of blood and burst flesh fill her head.

She can hardly breathe.

The car rocks as the man gets in, and then the engine roars and the wheels skid as it surges forward.

She holds her breath, thinking it's going to crash, but then it's crunching on the gravel, turning this way and that, before they're out onto a smoother road and onwards.

Where is he taking her?

Her head fills with the nightmare scenario she's just witnessed, and she screams.

But there's no one to hear her as the car disappears along the road.

The trees sway in the breeze, and eventually the birds start to chirp again.

Back in the dining room Louisa is on her phone, unable to stop it shaking as she tries to talk sense to an operator. Savitri has slumped forward onto the table but is still breathing. The body of the man in the chair has stopped twitching.

Having made the operator believe the situation, Louisa puts the phone down and goes to see how Savitri is doing. She's still conscious and the blood has stopped streaming. She shakes her head at Louisa and they hold on to each other.

The police cars and the ambulances arrive one after the other. Armed officers burst into the room. They all glance briefly at the hideous mess in the armchair, and then some are dispatched to search the rest of the house and the grounds.

All this is in a whirl of barked orders and rushing bodies until everything calms down.

The body is covered with a plastic sheet. Savitri is taken into the library to have her arm dressed and to be checked all over. Louisa eventually stops shaking and they are brought cups of tea.

It's at this moment that Fletcher is ushered in, having been roughly accosted as he came back from the river.

He clocks the covered body but is then taken to the library, after scanning the room for the one person he's really terrified about.

'Where's Ellie?' he says angrily.

Louisa can only shake her head.

'The man took her,' she manages to mumble.

Fletcher stares at her.

'Who?' he asks.

Louisa shakes her head.

He turns to look at the police officers.

An older man in plain clothes comes forward.

'I'm DI MacPherson,' he says. 'We've put out a call to find them,' he adds, before Fletcher can say a word.

Fletcher nods his understanding and looks back at Louisa.

'Have you any idea why they've done this, sir?' asks the detective.

Fletcher grits his teeth.

'Yes, but you'll not believe me.'

The detective frowns.

'Something that happened over eight hundred years ago.'

⁓

Gatti is waiting for Magda at the burnt-out remains of Amelia's house.

He's had another look round and is now standing at the garage door.

He's not sure that the car has been used since Amelia went to live with Magda. It's obviously not the one that Duncan was killed in. He thinks that it has already gone to the crusher, having been examined after the shooting.

He knows that it wasn't Magda's brother who killed him and doubts they'll ever know who did. They were told to forget about it by the Special Branch guys who took it away.

He turns to look at the horses, who are ninnying at him.

He's not going anywhere near them.

They're probably hungry, but what can he do about that?

Magda's car swishes down from the lane and comes to a gravelly stop.

She gets out and immediately makes her way towards the hay, which he realises he didn't even see.

He waits while she forks some hay over the fence and the horses jostle each other to get at it.

Satisfied, she comes over to him with a smile on her face, but then it fades.

'Anything to indicate the weird couple have been here?' she asks.

He shakes his head.

She sighs.

'Typical of my brother, I'm afraid … always burning his bridges.'

'We've no evidence he was here,' he says.

She nods.

'And they've not taken Amelia's car.'

He shakes his head.

'So how are they getting about?'

Gatti pulls a face. He knows her brother is more than capable of stealing cars.

'Nobody's reported a missing car?' she asks.

He shrugs.

'Not yet.'

'Well, I doubt that either of them would use public transport.'

Gatti gestures at the horses.

'No,' she says. 'All present and correct.'

They stand watching the creatures as they continue to tussle over the hay.

Suddenly Magda strides back into the garage.

He follows her.

She's gone to the back and is moving stacks of junk and other detritus.

'Duncan's bike isn't here,' she says, and pulls out her phone.

She presses one button and stalks back out of the garage.

When he catches up with her he hears the end of the call.

'So you're sure it was there,' she says, and then curses.

She turns to him and nods.

'Amelia thinks it was there the last time she looked. But she's no idea what make it was, or the registration, just that it was green.'

Gatti frowns.

'Maybe one of his friends?'

Magda gives a sour laugh.

'I'll ask her to think about that, but it won't be a long list.'

It takes very little time for someone to tell them what make it was, but he has no idea of the registration, so Gatti gets on to licensing.

Nothing.

As Amelia keeps saying, he didn't pay for anything he thought he could get away with and he only used it to ride along the drove roads or on that racetrack near Peebles.

⌁

As it happens, Tomasz is now driving the third vehicle he's 'borrowed' in the last twenty-four hours. A rather nice VW Beetle, which has been lovingly cared for. He found it in a back street, and soon they're crossing over the North York Moors in bright spring sunshine.

There are lambs tripping about in the fields and Imelda's found a CD in the glovebox, which she's now singing along to.

Tomasz shakes his head, having no idea who the singer is – never mind the song.

He's decided that Leeds might be a better place to cause a bit of trouble. He's read that there are quite a few statues and buildings associated with slave traders.

It's only as they're sitting in a lay-by having a sandwich and some juice that Imelda turns the news on. More trouble in Belfast as the Brexit foolishness reopens old wounds.

She quickly changes the station to something else.

He stares out of the window.

Perhaps the stupid fool will cause the revolution himself, he says to himself.

Later they're lying satiated on a rather uncomfortable bed in a Premier Inn on the outskirts of Leeds.

Tomasz is staring at the ceiling.

Imelda goes for a shower.

He turns the TV on and searches for Scottish Borders news.

He sits up, immediately alert.

He hears,

'Murder in the sitting room,' with a brief flash of an old photograph of the Cunninghame residence.

He presses the sound button just in time to hear that the police are looking for a young woman who has been abducted by one of the suspected killers.

He turns the sound down.

What's that about?

He lies there thinking about Louisa Cunninghame.

He's only been to her house a few times.

His mother and father went there regularly while Louisa's husband was alive. Can't think of his name.

Once he'd even gone instead of his father to partner his mother at whist. They weren't the only people there. Four tables, as he recalls.

Thanks to Helena's sneaky tricks they didn't do too badly.

But what he does remember clearly is the feelings he had for the lady herself, although he was aware that he wasn't the only man who couldn't keep his eyes off her.

She sashayed around in a shiny blue dress that barely concealed her figure. Blonde hair falling to her bare shoulders and those striking blue eyes, although they always looked like she was laughing at everything and everybody.

As far as he remembers her husband died and left her everything.

But maybe the break-in wasn't about the rich pickings.

He considers calling his sister, but then remembers he would be compromising her yet again.

But he could call Amelia.

It makes him smile that they were together, although that might mean she was off limits now.

He dabs his phone. The number isn't saved because he knows it off by heart.

Nearly gives up after a long wait, but then it's answered.

'Yes,' says a breathless Amelia, which rouses his loins immediately.

'Hi,' he says.

There's a pause.

'What do you want, you bastard?' she says, sounding like she's gritting her teeth.

'Don't let my mother hear you calling me that,' he says with a chuckle.

She doesn't respond to that.

'I've just heard about the fracas at Louisa's.'

This stops Amelia in her tracks.

'So...?' she asks.

'Well, is my beloved sister on the case?'

Another pause.

'I've no idea. Was it you?'

'Not this time,' he murmurs.

Silence.

'Do you know who the young woman is who's been abducted?'

'No, I don't. Why are you so interested?'

He hesitates.

'Anyway, they're after you for stealing Duncan's bike. Serve you right if they catch you.'

'I was only borrowing it,' he says.

'So why did you burn the house down as well?'

'What?'

'You left the little electric fire on.'

'Oh dear.'

'Actually, you did me a favour. I'm going to collect the insurance.'

He laughs.

'Happy to oblige.'

Neither of them speaks for a moment or two.

'I've got to go,' she says.

'Say hi to my sister,' he murmurs.

She cuts the call.

She stands there looking out of the kitchen window.

The kids are running around chasing Hengist, who's caught a rabbit. Normally she'd be out there shouting at the dog. But she stands watching instead. Or, rather, reminiscing, which stirs her loins.

She knows that Magda has been summoned to join the investigation, but she had made a face when she heard that DI MacPherson was already at the scene. He's only just come back from suspension after an incident involving some woman complaining about his behaviour, which was no surprise to anyone.

'How much longer is he going to survive?' she'd asked.

With a sigh she goes out to try to save the rabbit.

Magda is sitting in the car, trying to stop gritting her teeth.

The thought of having to liaise with Donny MacPherson is hardly bearable. She said as much to DCI Irvine, but he just frowned and told her to do her job.

She gets out of the car and walks into the house, where she's taken to see the bloody chamber. MacPherson is smirking as he checks to see how she copes with the atrocity, while she's reminding herself that she's a farmer's daughter and has seen far worse.

In any case the pathologist has finished his preliminary investigation and has set off back to the lab to await the retrieval of the body, which is happening as she arrives. Just the mess of blood all over the armchair is enough to confirm the horror of it.

She goes back to talk to MacPherson.

'The superintendent has told me to take over,' she says.

MacPherson glares at her.

'It's on my patch,' he snarls.

She stares at him.

'I suggest you take that up with him.'

He gives her one more stare and then turns on his heel and storms out.

'Oh dear,' says a voice.

She turns to see Louisa Cunninghame standing at the doorway. Paler than usual, and making certain that she doesn't look toward the bloody mess all over her furniture.

Magda indicates that they should step out into the hall, and then Louisa invites her into the library.

She repeats her version of what happened.

Magda glances once at Fletcher, who is fidgeting with the curtains, while another older woman is sitting with a bandage on her arm.

'If anything happens to my granddaughter—' he says, when she turns to him after Louisa comes to a halt.

Magda nods her understanding and hesitates.

'Why would he take her?' she asks quietly.

She watches as he and Louisa exchange glances, but it's the older woman who speaks.

'Because of what she knows,' she says.

Magda turns to look at her.

'My name is Savitri Kingshurst,' says the woman. 'I'm the professor of medieval European history at Stirling University, and I was helping Eleanor with her investigations into her family history.'

Magda frowns and looks back at Louisa and Fletcher. They both nod.

'It's true,' says Fletcher, 'which means that this man must know about it. Why else kidnap her?'

'And take her laptop,' Louisa adds.

Magda stares at them.

'So what about the dead man?'

They both look at each other and then Fletcher shrugs his shoulders.

'One less to divide up the treasure with.'

Magda's eyes go big.

'Treasure?'

Savitri groans.

'It's not treasure, Michael,' she says, almost crossly.

'That's what that man probably thinks it is,' he says quietly.

Magda looks from to the other.

'You mean what you were talking about the last time I was here?'

∽

It was only when I came over the little rise that I saw there were two cars parked at what was left of Amelia's house.

As I watched I realised that one of them was Magda's.

The way she was moving about while he stayed still and watched her made me suspect he was her sergeant. I've heard he's a rather dishy Italian.

The fire has absolutely destroyed the house.

But now I see her going into the garage, which seems relatively unscathed. He follows her to the door. But then she reappears, and they stand talking for a few minutes before both getting back into their cars and driving away.

I continue along and walk past the horses down to the bridge, thinking I'll go back along upstream and come back across the next bridge, but then I can't resist going up to see how Amelia is getting on.

I arrive to find her chasing one of their dogs round the garden, but she gives up as I appear.

She stands there red-faced, then bursts out laughing.

'Bloody dog,' she says. 'The only person who can control him is even worse than he is.'

I'm assuming she means Tomasz, although I've no idea whether he's even in the country. Ziggy hasn't mentioned him for ages.

She invites me in for a cuppa.

The floor is covered with toys, but Helena smiles at me from the kitchen sink without any sign of an apology.

Five minutes later the three of us are sitting out on the top terrace admiring the afternoon sun lighting up the valley. We can just about hear the kids screaming and yelling somewhere behind the house in the trees. But neither of the women seem concerned, so I try to ignore them as well.

'There's been a murder, I think,' says Amelia.

'Where?' asks Helena.

'Don't know,' she says. 'All Magda said was that she's having to take over from some other DI, who is "a sexist bastard".'

I look at her.

She shrugs.

'There's a lot of them about.'

We sit there drinking our coffee.

The friendly silence is broken by a phone singing. It's a rather odd choice of ringtone.

Amelia jumps up and goes back to the kitchen.

Helena just raises her eyebrows for a moment and gives me a tired smile.

'I'm still trying to get used to all this hustle and bustle,' she says, but it's obvious she's enjoying it, even if her accent does make it sound rather more menacing.

Amelia reappears with a frown on her face.

She goes back to her seat while we both wait apprehensively.

'Apparently there's been a murder at Louisa's, and Fletcher's granddaughter has been kidnapped.'

We both stare at her.

She can't tell us any more, and without more information the conversation dries up.

Eventually Helena stands up and gathers up the abandoned coffees. Feeling a bit intrusive, I say I need to get going and set off down the hill.

Back at White Cottage, I tell Ziggy what I've heard.

Of course, he already knows and has far more information, which isn't good.

'They've no idea what car the kidnapper's using and there's nowhere near enough cameras around here to catch him. But I'm on to it.'

The flashing screens should have told me this, but they're changing so fast I can't even see what he's watching until he stops one and stares at it.

He's only managed to get access to the local speed camera network. How?

He's focusing in on a still frame of a particular car. But then an ID pops up, and he dismisses it before going back to a mesmerising stream of alternative cars on roads.

Freya has now appeared at my shoulder and we look at each other.

Without any other information we decide to leave him to it.

We go to sit out in the unusual sunshine, which is just about warm enough not to need a coat.

'Apparently...' Freya begins and then looks at me with a frown. 'Ziggy tells me...' Again, she stops and sighs.

'This girl – Fletcher's granddaughter, although he's not really her grandfather, who's called Eleanor – is researching some family history, which is linked to Dryburgh Abbey.'

I frown at this. Why is he investigating this? I thought he was more interested in finding out what has happened to Violet.

Freya seems to comprehend my confusion.

'He's had to give up tracking the Violet investigation as it's been comprehensively blacked out, even to him,' she says.

I consider this for minute.

'Can't think that's ever happened.'

'Exactly,' she murmurs. 'He says he doesn't want the men in black arriving, so he's decided to keep out of it for a while.'

'But surely that makes it even more suspicious?'

She nods, but then shrugs her shoulders.

∽

Ellie is trying hard to control her breathing.

The car is being driven fast along winding roads. Lots of bends and gear changes. Climbs and descents ... which must mean he's keeping away from the main roads, where he'd be picked up on traffic cameras.

So does that mean he knows the Borders well?

Or maybe he's using a satnav that's giving him routes to follow.

She shifts her position to stop her legs cramping. Maybe agreeing to go reluctantly with Mali to the yoga classes might have come in useful after all.

Which only makes her cry.

But then the thought of what might have happened to her if she'd been there fills her mind with dread.

She tells herself to think about what's going to happen when this man decides to stop.

What has he done with her phone and laptop?

Presumably he thinks there's something on them that he wants or suspects she has.

Does that mean he knows about the story?

How can he?

What can she do?

Then it comes to her.

Uncle Rollo.

She remembers the occasion clearly.

She'd taken Mali to stay with him at his wonderful but ramshackle mansion in Shropshire.

Her cousins weren't at home and, unusually, he was without a partner, so he took them fishing and then for a night at the theatre. Lots of late-night drinking and tall stories.

But then one morning, while Mali had gone for a run, he suddenly asked her how she was getting on with her investigations.

She'd looked at him. What did he know?

He tapped his finger on the side of his nose and beckoned her to follow him.

They went upstairs and along one of the long corridors into a room that had a fancy lock device.

Inside it was like nothing else she'd seen in any of his other rooms.

State-of-the-art electronics and computers.

It turns out that back in the day, when he was in his Bowie pyrotechnical phase, he'd got heavily into computerised light shows and then carried on with other things.

'Don't do the light shows any longer,' he says. 'But I've kept up with the latest developments, and I think I've got something that might interest you.'

She watched as he fiddled about with a couple of laptops, then indicated one of them.

'Imagine you lost your laptop,' he says. 'And you don't want people to find out you've been storing huge amounts of pornography.'

She'd stared at him as if he were mad.

He laughed and then became serious.

'Or in your case, secrets from the past…' he said softly, his blue eyes boring into hers.

That was even more disturbing. What did he know? Had Tata told him what she'd told her?

He smiled.

'Don't worry. I know Tata told you stuff she never told anyone else. I think she decided that you were the most reliable person to pass on the family secrets to.'

Again she must have frowned.

'So here's the thing. Suppose there are people out there who've got a sniff of what Tata knew and want to find out for themselves?'

She'd shivered at this, although Tata had warned her there that were people who would kill to have what she knew. So she listened.

He showed her how to set up your laptop with two versions. So that if you lost your laptop or if someone stole it you could protect your secret stuff and, even better, a message would be sent to him to start tracking the machine wherever it had been taken.

Is that already happening|?

No, she thinks. Only if the man turns it on.

As if he knew what she was thinking, the car stops.

She feels the car sag as he gets out. Hears him walking about. On gravel?

He walks away.

Where's he going?

Has he taken the laptop with him?

She waits.

'What's the time?' she wonders. She's never worn a watch. Just like they didn't work on Tata, they don't work on her either. She figures out that it must be mid-afternoon by now.

She tries to think where he might have driven to. Less than half an hour's fast driving. Would she be able to smell the sea?

She listens.

Is that the wind?

No other sounds.

Somewhere remote?

She shivers.

Has he just abandoned her?

Will someone find her?

Has he already opened the laptop?

Will Uncle Rollo pick up the message?

He could be drunk, or out of it.

She shivers again.

What if the man doesn't come back?

She's only wearing a T-shirt and jeans, and it's been going down to minus ten at night recently.

She gives the back seat a shove.

There's some give there.

She shuffles round so that her feet are up against it and tries to give it a firm kick, but it doesn't have much effect.

She has another few goes but then stops. It isn't working.

She begins to sob

CHAPTER 16
KIDNAPPED

Magda is standing next to her car, which is parked alongside all the other police vehicles on Louisa's drive.

At least there's plenty of space, and there's no need to be concerned about rubberneckers. One car at the end of the drive will suffice for now. Although when the press get wind of it, if they haven't already, then there will be a problem, because they'll be coming through the trees and from the riverbank in droves.

The super's already on to that, and has told her to hurry up with the onsite investigation. And, if necessary, to bring suspects or witnesses to the station.

She's already certain that neither Louisa nor any of her guests will be up for that, and she doesn't think it's worth asking them.

Her main concern is to get the search for the young woman and her abductor up and running.

It's still not clear why this has happened or why it's been so violent.

She knows the girl, Ellie, is investigating the historical events that might have a connection to the girl's burial.

Bizarre. Not your usual student obsession.

An eight-hundred-year-old copycat killing?

She shakes her head again. Ludicrous.

Rico gets out of his car and makes a face.

There's nothing on the road scan.

He doesn't need to say how unusual this is, given the scant number of traffic and surveillance cameras there are in the Scottish Borders – most of which is open moorland or forestry.

But none of that is much use anyway, when they've not even got a registration, name or make of car … although the scanners are now assessing the cars seen in the vicinity in the last hour that are not locally registered. Fortunately, as lockdown is still in place, there won't be that many, except on the main through roads. In a few weeks' time the place will no doubt be overrun with visitors. But nothing so far.

She goes inside to find the retired detective. She's seen him before on-screen during the investigations last year and knows he can be difficult … and now this concerns his own granddaughter she expects his response to be excessively prickly.

She finds him with Louisa in the conservatory.

The initial glare isn't welcoming, but then he sighs and sits down.

She decides that sitting down herself is the best course and waits, to let him open proceedings.

At least he doesn't start asking whether she's done this and that, which is a relief.

'She's a resilient young woman,' he says, and then he has to look away.

She waits.

Without looking at her, he continues.

'She's often … feisty. But she can also do cunning, so don't underrate her.'

Magda waits to see if there's anything else, but he just turns to stare at her.

Despite the intensity of his eyes – one green, one blue (she's seen them before, but it's still weird) – she meets his gaze.

'Do you think it's true this man might want to abduct Ellie ... because of what she's investigating?'

He looks away.

'I'm probably the most stubborn, cynical person you're likely to meet ... but yes, I think it's possible.'

She waits.

He turns and looks at her.

'It's also possible that he's one of the people who murdered her aunt and uncle seven years ago...'

Magda's eyes grow big.

'What?'

He looks at his hands, which are clasped in front of him. But then he stands up and walks away, to stand looking out of the window.

She glances at Louisa, who is sitting rigidly in her chair like she's at deportment class, which is something she probably did have to go to when she was the missing girl's age.

Is that shock? No?

There's only the slightest indication from her that she should wait until Fletcher composes himself.

So she waits.

It's only a minute or so, but it seems a lot longer, before he speaks again.

'A rain of blood.'

Magda frowns and looks over at Louisa again.

No response.

Her eyes give nothing away. They never have.

'I'm sorry,' she says, thinking this might refer to what has just happened. The scene was particularly gory.

Fletcher turns and looks at her.

'I'm not sure that's why he did it, but it fits in with the story.'

Magda stares back at him, really confused.

'In what way?'

Louisa interrupts.

'It's another version, right enough.'

And then she goes on to explain how the recent atrocity that she witnessed resembles both what happened to Tata and Tonton and what happened at Château Gaillard eight hundred years ago.

Magda stares at her in disbelief.

The room becomes very still.

Fletcher is at the window, Louisa is sitting like a still-life portrait and Magda is feeling like she's in the headmistress's room waiting for a pronouncement.

She gathers herself.

'Are you seriously telling me that this … this murder was staged?'

She glances at Fletcher, who hasn't moved.

'That he brought his … his … associate, so that he could kill him in such a … an appalling manner?'

Louisa's stare doesn't falter.

Fletcher turns round and looks at her.

'Why did he shoot him in the head?' he asks.

Magda stares.

'Why didn't he shoot at me?' asks Louisa.

Magda looks at her.

'But he did.'

'Not then. I can't be sure he meant to do it, but it's extraordinary either way.'

Magda waits to hear if there's anything more, but they're both staring at her with stern faces.

She shakes her heads in disbelief.

'But that's absurd,' she mutters.

'If Ellie were here, she'd be certain,' says Fletcher. 'It's just the sort of thing she calls 'only connect'.'

Magda looks from one to the other, but neither of them is looking at the other.

She shakes her head.

'So what can you tell me about the murderer?'

'You mean apart from a description?' asks Louisa.

Magda frowns again.

'Thin lips,' says Louisa. 'Always a sign of a suppressed childhood. Probably regularly beaten or abused. Pale hazel, almost yellow eyes. Thin, naturally blonde hair. Going bald. Shorter than he'd like to be – shorter than me. Underweight. Bad teeth. Sallow skin. Probably doesn't get out much. Not the sort to sit in the sun. Sits more often than anything else. Probably doesn't sleep very well. Suffers from stomach cramps. Has a poor diet. Obsessive, obviously.'

Magda stares at her and then can't help but smile.

'Can you manage to place yourself at every future crime I have to investigate?' she says, without thinking it through.

Louisa doesn't grace that with anything other than one elegantly raised eyebrow.

'It would be useful if you could come to headquarters to help with that.'

She's aware that the Indian lady is clearing her throat behind her

'I have already drawn a likeness,' she says quietly.

Magda goes to look and then shows it to Louisa, who takes one glance and then smiles.

'My goodness, Savitri, is there no end to your talents?'

The woman smiles self-consciously and makes a face.

Louisa gives it back to Magda.

'I don't need to go. This is perfect.'

Magda shrugs. She knows not to argue with her.

She's aware of Fletcher's simmering tension throughout all this and turns to look at him.

'I know you want to be doing something, get out there, but...'

He nearly sneers but manages to contain himself to a stern shrug.

'Just find her,' he growls.

Magda doubts that will stop him from doing something but decides not to say any more.

She walks down the hall and goes back outside to find Gatti, who is on his mobile. She raises her eyebrows, but he just shakes his head and continues talking.

She goes to the front door and looks out at the assembling SOCO crew getting their equipment out of their vans, while the mortuary guys are coming towards her with their bag and stretcher.

They nod to her as they go past, and one of then throws his half-smoked cigarette onto the gravel.

She shakes her head at him but he just grins.

She then smiles to herself, thinking about the bollockings he's going to get if he does anything like that inside Louisa's house.

What to do next?

Why is it that she immediately thinks about Ziggy Hook?

She reaches for her phone and dabs in his name, knowing full well she shouldn't be doing it.

~

Ziggy puts the call on to speaker, so that we hear it from the kitchen.

We listen in increasing horror at what has happened.

After Magda has quickly described the events, she then asks if he has any ideas about finding the killer and the young woman.

Ziggy just mutters that he's on to it already and the call ends.

We both know not to bother asking him anything and sit, wondering what either of us can do.

Freya is, as usual, standing looking out of one of the windows. She's said that staring into the distance is the quickest way to clear her mind.

I'm more the 'doing the washing-up in moments of crisis' sort of thinker.

So apart from the clinking of pots and the chattering of Ziggy's numerous machines the house is quiet.

'From the little we've been told I'd say this man is an excessively careful forward planner, meaning that he has at least three or four options if the plan goes wrong.'

I'm thinking that that's not like me. After finding out I wasn't who I thought I was a couple of years ago, I've found certainty a rather nebulous thing.

'You mean different escape routes?' I ask.

She nods.

'Yes, but also thinking about alternative communication and connectivity.'

Not sure what that involves, I stare at her. She probably means more than just another laptop or phone.

But Freya's on the move.

I follow her into the hall, where she goes to the little bookcase that holds all the local maps.

Having selected four or five, she goes back into the kitchen and starts clearing the pots I'd been drying. I help her.

She starts with the OS Explorer that includes Louisa's house, but then adds the Berwick map alongside it.

I've no idea what she's looking for.

Where would someone have planned to hide out with a hostage and a car?

I'm just thinking that my 'mother' must have been brilliant at this, as she was never caught. 'Like a wraith,' was how DS Becket described her ... which makes me wonder where she is.

Janet, that is, not my mother.

Who is possibly still alive.

Which makes me shiver.

I'm brought back to the real world when there's a rustle of maps.

Freya has folded up the local map and is now studying the Berwick one.

I was thinking that he'd be somewhere remote, in the wilderness, but of course, hiding in a crowd is much better.

I go to stand next to her.

I've no idea of the population of Berwick-upon-Tweed, but it looks well spread-out, merging here and there with smaller villages.

It's also no doubt a popular holiday destination. Sea, castle and countryside are all available.

So lots of B & Bs, holiday lets, hotels.

Many of them unused. Left empty for over a year or so.

He might not have booked it, just found one left empty.

No, that's too risky. He couldn't spend time searching for one.

Definitely already booked or found.

But where?

Freya's now staring out of the window.

Without thinking, I'm heading for the kettle.

⌒

Imelda's staring out of the window at the flashing scenery.

It's not often that she's been on a train recently.

She was surprised when they abandoned the VW a good way from the station and walked.

Tomasz has adopted a rather fetching woolly hat and glasses, while suggesting she covers up her hippy clothes with a dreadful second-hand raincoat.

She declines to tell him that she is undisputedly not a hippy.

They're going back to Berwick to see what they can do about finding a missing girl, as this seems to have taken precedence over the flag and statue assassinations.

Why he's so bothered about some girl he's never met she's not sure, but it's more probable that he feels he needs to help his sister out after all the trouble he's caused her.

She's beginning to feel as if she's just a passenger in all this and asks herself why she is still on board.

As if he's inside her head hearing this debate, he turns and looks at her.

'You know you can bail out any time?' he says.

She looks at him and then looks back out the window.

⌒

Fletcher doesn't know what to do with himself.

Louisa is redressing Savitri's arm.

'Go for a walk,' she says.

He shrugs and goes to find his coat.

The house is still crowded with SOCO people going hither and thither in their white costumes.

Magda has disappeared, leaving her soulful-eyed sergeant looking lost.

Fletcher sidles up to him.

'Any developments?' he asks.

Rico looks at him.

Magda has told him to beware of what he says to this man because he is the most dangerous of loose cannons even when he was in service.

He smiles at him.

'Nothing that I've been told,' he offers.

Fletcher stands next to him as the body of the headless man is being carried out.

'Not much of a photofit for that one, then,' he says.

Rico shakes his head. Gallows humour has never been his attitude.

'Mind you, planning to blast the face of your sidekick has to be a first, wouldn't you say?' Fletcher continues.

Again, Rico can only wince. It's so bizarre that he still can't accept it was deliberate.

'But at least you must have some ID or a name, even if it's false.'

Rico resolutely stares ahead, mouth closed.

Fletcher waits. Then laughs, shakes his head.

'But you don't, do you? He wasn't carrying any.'

Rico still doesn't respond.

Fletcher laughs again.

'So it was intentional. He brought him along to kill him *in situ*. Told him not to carry anything. Made him empty his pockets.'

Rico turns to look at him.

'I can't divulge anything to you, sir,' he says politely.

Fletcher nods.

'But this means that my granddaughter has been kidnapped by one sick and very devious bastard.'

Rico stares at him. What can he say?

It's at this moment that Fletcher realises who he needs to talk to, and so without another word he walks away.

Rico is left feeling unsure of himself. He didn't tell the man anything, but he seems to be intent on doing something. Perhaps he ought to warn Magda.

Fletcher has tracked down his mobile.

He calls Ziggy.

At least this guy is as direct as they come. He almost has as little respect for correct procedure as he has.

'Hi, Fletch,' he says.

Fletcher doesn't remember giving him this honour, but grunts him a greeting.

'What do you know?' he asks.

'Specifically?'

'Where has this monster taken my granddaughter?'

There's a significant pause.

'Well, the plods haven't a clue, but I'm figuring Berwick.'

'Why so?'

'There are only two towns of any size nearby. Galashiels is closer but not easy to escape from, while Berwick gives him a variety of escape options and a lot of empty guest houses and holiday lets.'

'Agreed. So how can we find him?'

There's a brief hesitation.

'I'm monitoring a shedload of cams and focusing on the out-of-town ones just now. But without any ID or car reg, it's a bit haystack needle.'

'Uh-huh. So what can I do?'

'Might be good to have someone on site.'

'You've got it. I'm on my way.'

'Are you armed?'

'Not yet, but I know a lady who can sort that.'

'She's no lady,' comes the response, with a gravelly chuckle. 'She's one scary witch.'

'I didn't hear that, but I'd rather she was on our side.'

'Keep your mobile on. I've set up a link that will track you wherever you go.'

Fletcher grunts and ends the call.

He's not sure about what Ziggy's just said, or how he could have done that. But, if that's the backup, he's somewhat reassured. Going out on a limb is his stock-in-trade, even though he knows he's getting too old for it.

He goes to find Louisa.

Ten minutes later he's driving away, having convinced some young officer that he's just going to the local chemist for some vital women's articles.

In his pocket he can feel the weight of the revolver Louisa has given him. It's ages since he's felt a gun in his hand and he can't stop the ripple of fear it causes.

So he's not there when Louisa gets a phone call.

It's Rollo.

They've never met, but Ellie has talked a lot about him.

Louisa has to admit that he doesn't sound like her cup of tea, but Ellie obviously likes him.

'Hi,' he says. 'Can I speak to Ellie?'

She's a bit put out by his directness, but then realises he must somehow have heard.

'I'm afraid you can't,' she says.

There's an intake of breath.

'Is she OK?'

Louisa hesitates, not knowing what to say.

'Actually, no,' she says. 'She's been abducted.'

'I thought that might be the case,' comes the worried response.

Louisa is puzzled.

'How did you know?'

'I put a tracker on her phone and her laptop last Christmas. It just pinged me about five minutes ago.'

'Oh, does that mean you know where she is?'

'The phone doesn't seem to be working, but the laptop is in Berwick. To be exact, in a house on the seafront nearby in a place called Spittal.'

Louisa is thinking what to do next.

'Are you there?'

'Yes. I'll have to let the police know … and Michael's on his way as we speak.'

'You mean Fletch?'

'Yes, I'm afraid I do.'

'Bloody hell. Is the old bugger armed?'

'I'm afraid he is.'

There's a pause.

'Has he got a mobile with him?'

'Yes, but I can't see the number while I'm speaking to you.'

There's a sigh that she interprets as 'Exasperated man, not that young any longer, who thinks everyone ought to keep up'.

'I can send you it as soon as we end this call,' she says.

'OK, do that,' he says, and cuts the call.

'Charmed, I'm sure,' Louisa thinks, and does as she has promised, but probably not as fast as he would.

Then she considers telling Magda what's happening and decides it's best she knows, so tries to contact her.

No reply.

So she must laboriously leave a text, which she hates doing. Fiddly little letters always trying to tell you what you're writing before you've even started.

～

Ellie hears the man returning, crunching back along a gravelled path.

She tenses as the footsteps stop right next to her.

She hears the bleep of the key and then the boot opens up.

He backs away, but waggles a gun at her.

She clambers out.

He indicates to walk to the right.

When she scans the immediate surroundings she's surprised to see a high wall, and then the other way is a carefully manicured garden that has two other walls all round it. No sign of any other houses. Is that sound the sea?

They're walking towards a large house with a few steps leading up to a terrace. There are two windows, one either side of a large door, which is slightly ajar.

They go in.

If this house is abandoned it can't have been very long ago. But then she shudders, thinking perhaps the poor occupants are lying dead somewhere, their blood still congealing.

He indicates a low armchair in this sitting room, and so she goes and sits down.

He drags a chair from beside a table and sits down facing her.

He puts his gun on the table and gets out a packet of cigarettes, then offers her one. She declines with a slow shake of her head.

He produces a lighter and lights his cigarette, puts the lighter away and then takes a long pull, before leaning back and exhaling the smoke above himself.

All the while he's staring at her.

Nothing special about his eyes. Just an indeterminate colour, maybe a smudgy brown. His nose is small but otherwise his features are indistinct, as if he's designed them to be unremarkable.

'Well, I doubt that we have much time, so the sooner you tell me what you know the better,' he says.

She realises she's sitting on the edge of the seat and now shuffles back, but at the same time she smells his breath as he releases more smoke into the air.

She wrinkles her nose and looks away towards the window.

The noise is shattering.

The shot echoes round the empty room. She is so startled that she can only duck back into the seat, which is rather pointless.

When she opens her eyes, he's pointing the gun at her.

'Have you ever been shot before?' he asks.

She manages to shake her head, which seems unnecessary.

He laughs. An odd screechy sort of noise, like he doesn't laugh very often, but not normal.

While standing up, but still levelling the gun at her, he fetches her laptop from the table.

He offers it to her and she takes it from him.

'Go on,' he says.

She opens it up and props it on her knees. It's awkward, but she assumes that's why he's asking her to do it like this. She can hardly jump up and run away.

She hesitates, knowing what she does next is crucial.

He laughs.

'Don't even think of saying you've forgotten your password,' he growls.

She taps it in. The screen comes on.

He watches her.

'OK. Open up your files on the treasure.'

She frowns at him.

He sneers at her.

'Or whatever you call the research you're doing.'

She carefully taps in the code she knows will alert Uncle Rollo, although she hopes that his device has already told him something's not right.

The man indicates her to pass it to him. She shuffles forward but he stands up and grabs it from her, and then wags the gun at her to make her sit back in the chair.

He takes the laptop to the table and puts the gun down next to it.

But then he picks it up again and points it at her.

'Just understand that I've no reason now to keep you alive, so don't think of trying anything.'

She glares at him, but he just makes a face and then starts tapping on the laptop.

She tries to estimate how long it will take him to scan all the files, but she can't even remember how many there are.

Her essay is already twenty-odd pages and there are all the website copies, articles, and other evidence she's gathered.

But of course the secret stuff is on a completely different programme, which isn't available without closing the machine down and starting it up again with a different security code.

She's no idea where Uncle Rollo might be right now, although she's pretty certain that he's not out of the country. Last time she spoke to him he was having a party. Totally illegal, no doubt, but then he's never paid much attention to the law.

He also knows some very unpleasant geezers, who he's employed to sort out people who've upset him. She has never approved of this at all … until right now.

She waits.

The man's fingers flitter about the keyboard.

It's obvious he's very expert.

She glances round the room.

Whose house is this?

Are they lying dead in some other room?

Just then she notices the paintings and then the cross on the mantelpiece.

Back to the paintings.

Is this a vicarage?

Her eyes go big.

Before she can think it through, she blurts the question out.

'Have you killed the vicar?'

He stops and glances up at her.

'Course I haven't. He died last year. Silly bugger kept going to old people's homes. Got the Covid. Died in the first wave.'

She frowns.

'So how…?'

He looks up again.

'Not difficult. Even you could have found it.'

She glares at him, but then must hide her grin that he's alerted Uncle Rollo and doesn't know it.

But what's he going to do? He's down in Leicestershire. A good four-hour drive, even with him at the wheel. Who might he call? Does he know Fletch is up here? Does he even know where Louisa lives?

She looks back at the man.

Who is now staring at her.

'It's not all here, is it?' he snarls. 'Is it encrypted somewhere else?'

He picks up the gun and points it at her.

She closes her eyes.

CHAPTER 17
TO THE HILLS

Magda is fuming.

DCI Irvine has just expressed his frustration at the investigation going nowhere fast.

They have a body, but so far no identity. Fingerprints are negative. A homicidal monster wandering about on their patch with similar total anonymity. He was apparently wearing gloves, although it was only Louisa who recalls this.

The drawing that Savitri had done is now all over the news and the Internet, but there are no responses so far.

She walks back to the car and sits there, trying to calm down.

'Bugger that,' she says, and contacts Ziggy.

'*Nada*,' he says. 'He's good.'

Magda grits her teeth.

'My boss is going crazy.'

Ziggy only snorts.

She gets out of the car and walks to the roadside.

There's a pause. She can hear his fingers tapping.

'I'm searching disused buildings, empty houses to let or unsold. You wouldn't believe how many there are.'

She thinks.

'Isn't there some way you can trace the girl?'

There's a brief silence.

'How?'

'Mobile? We've asked her mother for a photo, which didn't go well.'

She winces at the memory of the phone call after Fletcher had told the girl's mother what had happened. She hadn't screamed or yelled at her, but the icy way she said she was already on her way was enough to make her fear the worst kind of distraught mother situation.

'Yeah, I've seen it. I don't think it's very recent. Hasn't her friend got a better one?'

Magda could have kicked herself.

'I'll get in touch.'

'Her mobile is dead. Meaning that it's not only turned off but also that the SIM card is destroyed. As I said, he's good.'

Magda didn't want to hear that again.

'Let me know the instant you get something,' she pleads, knowing full well how risky this is.

This is made worse as she sees Rico staring at her from the car.

She goes over and gets in.

He stares ahead, waiting for instructions.

'I've no bloody idea,' she whispers. 'What do you think?'

It's only then that she sees she has a message.

⤳

Ellie stops sobbing.

Her face stings where he hit her. She can feel the blood drying on her chin.

She's now lying on the floor, tied to a big old wooden chair. The ropes are cutting into her ankles and she can only wriggle her hands, which are hurting like hell.

He's gone outside without saying what he's doing.

She's tried to shuffle along the carpet, but it's hopeless.

She tells herself to stop and think.

Where's he gone?

Has Uncle Rollo got the message?

This isn't how she wants to die.
What can she do?
What would Fletch do?
Then she thinks about her mother.
Which only makes her cry again.

Is that him coming back?
Try to stop trembling.

He comes in with a smile on his face.
Bends down and strokes her cheek.
'It's OK, my pretty,' he says in a creepy voice.
But now he's standing up and dragging her up too.
'It's OK. I've arranged to borrow the neighbour's car.
He won't be needing it any longer.'
She looks at him in horror.
What does that mean?
He unties her from the chair and makes her stagger
out of the door and through the garden.
Out in the back alley there's a different car, with its
boot open.
Despite her struggles she's unceremoniously pushed
in once again.
The door is slammed shut and she screams.
He bangs the boot door and tells her to shut up.
She hears him walk away.
Is he going to leave her there?
It seems like forever.
She can hear seagulls calling. Are they near the sea?
Eventually he comes back, gets in the car and sets off.
Where's he taking her now?
She starts to cry again.
What can she do?

The car is now picking up speed, but not enough to
indicate a motorway. So they are still on minor roads. There

are lots of bends and changing of gears. The car is old, not automatic. Where did he find it?

What can she do?

It's then she remembers what Uncle Rollo said.

Even if her battery runs out, he's put a bug in the laptop that he'll always be able to trace.

She closes her eyes.

Mali's sad face comes into her head.

She weeps.

＞

Magda is furious, yet grudgingly excited that she's got a lead.

Fletcher is doing his Lone Ranger trick again and is probably going to get himself and the girl killed.

She's not told Rico more than to just drive to Spittal with the siren on when he needs it. He's given her one worried look but then does as she asks.

She doesn't know exactly where they're going but Spittal isn't that big, after all.

She contacts Ziggy, who's now trying to spot Louisa's car, which Fletcher has borrowed.

Has she told DCI Irvine? No, she bloody well hasn't. Does she think she's going to get sacked after this? She doesn't bloody well care.

Rico puts the siren on as he approaches the A1 bypass.

Lorries scrunch to a halt.

He's over and tearing down to the zigzag under the bridge. Down the tiny lane out onto the sea road. Along the main street. Is that the church?

Is that Louisa's car?

It's not parked how she would want it to be. The driver's door has been left open.

They're both out of the car and running. Rico is way ahead in a few strides. They burst into the church. No one in sight. Deathly quiet.

They go out through the vestry door. A back alley. A long, high wall.

Maroc indicates a doorway.

It opens onto a walled garden. The vicarage?

The door is open.

They rush towards it but are stopped in their tracks as Fletcher appears and leans against the wall.

'Too late,' he gasps, and sits down on a low wall.

Magda nods at Gatti, who goes into the house.

She sits down next to Fletcher, who is breathing heavily. She hopes he's not going to have a heart attack.

'Too old for this lark,' he gasps.

She smiles and holds his hand.

Rico reappears and shakes his head.

The three of them take time to get their breath.

'Where has he taken her now?' she asks.

The two men look at each other, but they've no idea.

'There's a chair on its side on the floor and there might be spots of blood, but I'm not sure,' says Rico.

'But why here?' asks Fletcher, 'and where's the vicar?'

'Good question,' says Magda and nods at Rico, who makes a face and then realises what she means.

'I'll go check,' he says.

He's only gone five minutes, during which time Magda's on the phone trying to find the name of the vicar.

Rico reappears, but Magda already knows.

'He died last summer. No replacement yet,' she mutters.

He shrugs his agreement.

The two of them look at Fletcher.

'Car?' he manages.

Rico's on the phone again.

Magda goes outside and contacts Ziggy.

'A car leaving here within the last half hour or so. No idea what make. Could be going north or south or inland.'

She knows Rico's asking the same of their control, but now she's taking it personally. She'll show that bastard Irvine, with or without HQ support.

⤳

We're both aware that things must be hotting up as Ziggy's starting to bash his equipment and swearing in Czech, which always sounds like a bird fight.

Freya shrugs and goes to stare out of the window. But then she turns to look at me, which is always disconcerting.

I give her a frown.

She sighs.

'You know what?' she says.

I wait, getting trepidatious. What's she going to say?

'I used to think it was just me, but since I met Ziggy I've realised that we're all screwed-up oddballs.'

I pull a face, but then realise that at least that's true of him and me.

She frowns and puts her right hand round her other thumb to show she's counting us off.

'I'm blessed with having a memory that won't let me forget stuff. Not a blessing, but a curse.'

She dares me to disagree with that.

I can't.

First finger.

'You only found out who you are when your 'not-mother' died and you discovered you're the daughter of a serial killer … who's never been caught and might still be out there.'

I look away.

She continues. I look back. Second finger.

'Ziggy is the weirdest guy I've ever met, who's well on the way to becoming a cyborg.'

This is immediately confirmed by the part-human, part-machine noises blaring out from next door.

I wait.

Third finger.

'Ex-DS Becket: a violent and unpredictable cold-hearted man-killer.'

I'm minded to put up a sturdy defence of her, but then realise she's more than capable of doing that for herself.

Little finger.

'Ex-DI Fletcher?' she sighs.

I almost laugh.

'Mr Unpredictable: a selfish, short-fused maniac who always thinks he's right.'

I nod. Spot on.

Second hand. Thumb.

'On to the local suspects: "Lady" Louisa Cunninghame. Well named as the cunning vixen, but actually a cold-hearted sexual predator.'

This makes my eyes go big. I wouldn't dare to say that in case it got back to her.

First finger.

'DI Magda Steil. Also sexually screwed-up, who both hates and adores her soldier brother…'

Second finger.

'Tomasz, a professional assassin, haunted by distant images of people's heads exploding.'

Third finger.

'His weird lover, Imelda, who can't decide what animal or snake she might be.'

Little finger.

'Their mother, Helena. Not a nice little old Polish lady, but a violent dispatcher of Russian thugs.'

She hesitates, thinking.

'The next generation coming through: Eleanor de Camville. Have you seen her eyes? Witchy or not?'

I shake my head. I'm not going to argue with any of her fingers.

She sighs.

'What's not to like?'

What can I say? Although I could argue that I'm only on the list because of my mother. I was very ordinary before that, and I don't think I've changed that much. I only get dragged along by other people who are on the list.

But, before I can ask her to rectify, Ziggy gives a whoop. There's a crash of machinery and the front door opens on cue to deliver the said cold-hearted killer, DS Becket, who has a disarmingly happy smile on her face. Which fades as she clocks the looks on our faces.

∽

Louisa is wondering if she could impose on Mrs Kenworthy to come and do some cleaning up after the predations of the murderous intruders and the subsequent visitation from the scenes of crime people.

She's about to pick up her phone when it starts to ring.

She frowns, wondering who this might be as most people normally use their mobiles now.

Might it be the local press, who might have got wind of what has happened by now? She doesn't want to speak to them.

But she can't resist the noise.

'Hello?' she says.

'Hiya, Lou,' says a voice she recognises, but can't immediately place, whilst outraged at someone who dares to call her by that diminutive.

'It's Tomasz,' he says.

'Oh, hello,' she manages, wondering where he is and what he knows.

'Have they found the girl yet?'

This answers that question.

'No, I don't think so . . . where are you?'

'Approaching Berwick. Am I on the right track?'

Her head is spinning with this. What does he think he's doing?

'Er, well, I'm not sure. They're not telling us anything.'

'Right. Keep schtum. I'm onto it.'

'Um, are you sure you should be doing this?'

'Well, it's better than shooting at flags and old heads.'

'What?'

'I suppose it's my sense of duty. I'm thinking I might take up the Robin Hood approach. Righting wrongs, etcetera.'

With a laugh the line goes dead.

She realises that Savitri is staring at her.

'Who was that?' she asks.

Louisa shakes her head.

'An outlaw,' she murmurs, then shakes her head again.

'The world's going crazy,' she adds and then realises Savitri is crying. 'Post-traumatic stress', she thinks and goes to comfort her.

⌒

Ellie can tell that they've now left the outskirts of a town and travelling continuously uphill. She's managed to finger a hole through where the back seat joins onto the top of the boot.

She can see trees rushing past, and now they seem to be up on to open moorland. This goes on and on for what seems ages.

Not knowing the area at all, she's no clue to where they might be going. It's grey and looking like rain, so there's no sun to even tell which direction they're going in. And, in any case, she's lost any sense of the time.

Where can he be taking her?

Even if she had her phone, she doubts that it would work up in this wilderness.

Where's he going to find a signal up here?

Maybe he doesn't need one.

After what seems to be an endless, meandering journey, the car takes a sudden shift off the road onto a gravel track. Then through some more trees, looming over both sides of the track. Out into the light again, and then it comes to a stop.

She feels the weight shift and then hears him scrunching across gravel. Then there's a knocking sound.

A door is roughly pulled open and a deep voice is saying something she can't understand. Was that a foreign accent?

The voices are cut off as the door is shut.

She waits.

Just the wind.

She gives the boot a kick.

Was that it loosening?

She kicks it again.

There's a definite give.

She wriggles round and tries to fiddle with the lock. It's pretty rusted.

She struggles back again so she can give it a good kick. Her neck hurts, but she keeps kicking. The gap is widening. Her neck hurts even more. She gives it a good rub. Has another kick. Something snaps. She turns round and gets her shoulder under it and pushes as hard as she can. The lock breaks and the lid lifts up.

She scrambles out. Falls on to the ground. Staggers to her feet and looks around.

It's the middle of nowhere. Apart from the immediate building there's not another house in sight. Only dark green forests and yellowy brown hills in every direction.

She stumbles away from the car.

The building next to her isn't really a house, just a large shed with a big old army truck sort of joined onto it. But the most striking thing is the huge aerial sticking up into the air. Must be ten metres at least. She looks away from it, back down through the wood the track cuts through. She looks the other way, where the track continues further up into the hills.

She shivers. The wind is bitingly cold. The sky is a mass of huge grey clouds, so rain is imminent. Dressed as she is, she knows she won't last long if she makes a run for it. So what to do? Why has he come here?

Who is the man who lives up here? And why does he live here?

She goes round the other side of the car and peers in through the window.

Her laptop isn't visible. He must have taken it in with him. The ignition key as well.

What should she do?

She scuttles across to the side of the hut. There's a window, but she doesn't think that's a good idea. She crawls along the other way until she can get underneath the truck. It's obviously been there a long time. In fact, now she examines it, she realises it's really ancient, like those army trucks you see in Second World War films. So what's it doing up here?

Just then, she hears a door open and voices.

She watches one set of legs, her abductor's, walk back to the car.

'Bloody hell,' she hears him say.

She hides behind one of the big lorry wheels.

She hears him stalking around the lorry and then off around the shed.

What should she do?

He's stopped now.

'Come on out, you silly bitch,' he shouts. 'You'll freeze to death out here.'

She has to acknowledge that's true as she's already unable to stop shivering, so reluctantly she crawls out and stands up.

He stares at her and then laughs.

'Come on in and meet Gerd. He likes a bit of female company now and again.'

She walks slowly towards him and he gestures towards the door.

She ducks down and goes inside.

⁀

Jane tells Sandy to meet her in a car park in Melrose.

It's a long time since she's been there, but it's still got that slightly 'Nose in the air, we're rather special' ambience she remembers.

The car park is surrounded by trees, and she spots his car in the far corner.

She pulls into a space on the other side and gets out her phone. She can see he's resting his head. Probably having a nap.

She calls him.

He responds with a pleasing alacrity.

No need to tell him which car she's in yet, although he's scanning the other cars as she talks.

'Any updates?' she asks.

There's a pause.

'The cafe in town is open,' he says.

She hesitates. Why not? It's not as if anyone here will recognise either of them.

'OK,' she says. 'I'm in the red Volvo over to your right.'

He glances towards her and gives her a wave.

Five minutes later they're sitting outside the cafe, where they don't need masks.

It's some time since they've been in each other's physical company, like many other people ... and it's a bit strange.

She's looking at him and notices his sandy hair receding ever more from his forehead. She doesn't mind that, unless its someone trying to hide the fact with a silly comb-over. Otherwise he looks like any other forty-year-old sporty type. Trainers and a fleece jacket.

He's trying to not stare at her too intently. She's turned a few heads already with her dark Italian-style looks. Her long black hair is pulled back in a tight bun, exposing her sharp-featured face and steady gaze.

They wait in silence for the coffees to arrive.

The town isn't as bustling as he imagines it would normally be, even this early in the season. So it feels quite relaxed, although plenty of people are doing their shopping.

The coffees arrive.

She smiles at him.

He sighs and takes a sip. It could be worse.

She waits.

He's told her what he knows about the shooting at Louisa's. Although names haven't been mentioned by the police yet, they're both pretty certain that the dead person must be her husband Barnum and that Hollis has kidnapped the de Camville girl and disappeared.

Given what he knows about their relationship he's not expecting her to be mourning his demise, but as he glances at her he wonders whether this changes anything.

He clears his throat. She turns to look at him.

'Have the police contacted you?' he asks.

She shakes her head.

'A tad disappointing, actually. Or maybe they've not been able to identify him yet.'

He frowns.

'I can't imagine why not.'

She sighs.

He's wondering whether she'll benefit from his death, although he knows she's been bleeding him dry for years.

'Still, let's not worry about that. Where has the evil weasel taken her?'

He looks away. She's not going to like what's happened.

'He's cleverer than I thought,' he admits. 'Off the radar since leaving the house. I was keeping up with the police tracking, but they've lost him too.'

She smiles at him.

He shrugs his shoulders.

'Then maybe we need to go to the scene of the crime.'

He looks back at her.

'Fortunately for you, I happen to know the lady. She went to the same school as my mother.'

'Of course she did,' he thinks.

She glances away.

'It's some time since we last met, but I'm sure she might welcome some support. It must have been awful having to witness a murder in your own home.'

He stares at her.

How can she have found out what has happened? The reports merely say that the police are investigating a sudden death at the house.

She gives him another of her crocodile smiles.

'I've already called her, saying we just happened to be in the area and asked her if there was anything I could do.'

He waits, trying not to do goldfish impressions.

'She's invited us over for afternoon tea. You're my latest beau.'

He can't help but laugh.

'Beau?'

'Well, I hope you've got some more suitable clothes to wear.'

He pulls a face.

'My suit probably needs pressing.'

'No,' she says. 'You know I prefer the rumpled look, darling. Let's just assume you're my bit of rough instead.'

He stares at her again.

She gathers her bag and scarf and stands up.

'Come on, or we'll be late.'

He follows her back to the car park and is surprised when she links her arm through his.

'Just practising,' she says.

⌒

Gerd turns out to short for Gerhard.

His father was in a prisoner-of-war camp up here in the hills. He didn't go back after the war finished. Married a local woman, and Gerd has ended up back here after losing his job after the crash in 2008.

He was a trader on the stock market. One of the smaller fish who were fed to the sharks by the Tories.

She doesn't ask, but on seeing her look he explains the mast was for what he does now.

'What I used to do before, really. Shifting funds from one pot to another,' says the man. No trace of a German accent.

Ellie's wondering why he's even bothering to tell her this or why her kidnapper is sitting watching her with an enigmatic smile.

She makes a face.

'It also tells him when anyone comes within a million miles of this place, so we'll get plenty of time to disappear.'

She gives him a glare.

He leans forward on his chair.

'All you have to do is tell us what you know.'

She shrugs.

'I don't know anything.'

'Ah, but you do,' he snarls. 'Your Tata told you things, didn't she?'

She stares at him in disbelief and then looks at the other man, who just stares back.

'I don't know what you mean,' she stutters.

He bends down and picks up her laptop, places it on the table and swivels it towards Gerd.

'The other thing you need to know about my friend here is that he can find stuff on computers that even the Microsoft guys don't know about.'

She stares back at him. Even if they torture her, they can't get at what Tata gave her.

But then he stands up and comes towards her.

She backs away, but he's too quick. Too strong.

Lying on the floor, blood still filling her mouth from where he punched her, she watches as he fingers the ring he's ripped from her ear.

He shows it to Gerd, who has worryingly bright eyes.

'This is one of the four items we need.'

Ellie crawls to the wall, and sits up with her back to it, pinching her nose to try to stop the bleeding.

Hollis glares at her, but says nothing when Gerd offers her a box of tissues.

He passes the ring to him. Gerd takes it and finds an eyeglass to peer at it.

'How do you know this is the real thing?' he asks.

Hollis shrugs.

'She's wearing it on her right ear … and look at the way she's glaring at me. Pure hatred.'

Ellie can't disagree with that, but tries to maintain it, rather than allow the smirk that's hidden behind it to get through.

'What she doesn't know is that I have one of the other three items already.'

She frowns.

He slips his hand into his inside pocket and brings out a small box. He opens it carefully and produces a small silver tube.

She can't imagine what it might be.

'Eight hundred and twenty two years ago, Richard the Lionheart died at Châlus.'

She stares at him.

'According to the custom of those violent times and the concerns of dying princes, he ordered that his body be buried with his father's at Fontevraud, his innards at Châlus, and his heart at Rouen, thus ensuring that his birthright and his inheritance would pass to his estranged brother, John.'

Ellie couldn't help but gasp at the words and the way he said them. He obviously knew a scary amount of stuff that she thought very few other people had even heard about.

He stares back at her.

She frowns and then realises what the tube must contain, but daren't believe it.

He nods.

'Yes, my dear, nine years ago some scientists opened up his coffin. They took samples.'

He waves the tube at her.

'Including his blood. Dust by now, but identifiable.'

She stares at him. She can't believe it. How did he acquire that?

'Money always finds a way,' he whispers, and then laughs and places the tube back in its box and then into his pocket.

Gerd stares at him.

'I don't believe that,' he says. 'Surely it wouldn't be of any use. It must have decayed beyond any kind of biological existence.'

Hollis shakes his head, his eyes still shining.

'There's enough other evidence that there are spores of the flowers used in the embalming process. So yes, it's still possible that it has kept its power.'

Again Gerd frowns.

'But what use will that be?' he asks again.

Hollis looks back at Ellie. A look that makes her shiver. Is he mad?

'Go on, you tell him.'

She looks away.

He grabs her by the arm, which hurts.

'Go on, Professor. Tell him.'

He lets her go. She rubs her arm and glares back at him, trying to hold back the tears.

'You're mad,' she rasps.

He laughs. A laugh that confirms it. His eyes are glistening. His lips a rictus of excitement. And now he repeats the command.

'*Vasi, mestra, ditz-lui.*'

She looks away. His Occitan is better than good.

Gerd frowns at this man with the staring eyes, thinking the girl is right, but then he hears her whispered words.

'A rain of blood.'

Chapter 18
The Chase

Sandy was expecting something grand but is still impressed by the wall of pines hiding the venerable beeches, which are still deep in winter slumber.

Jane is surprised to find no cars parked on the drive, although this might indicate that they're not going to find any other visitors.

So she doesn't expect to find a little Indian lady smiling at them as Louisa takes them into the sun-filled conservatory that she remembers.

With the introductions all done, Louisa leaves them to go and fetch tea and scones, which Mrs Kenworthy has brought with her. She is valiantly still trying to get some order into the blood-spattered sitting room, although Louisa has told her she's not going back in there until the carpet and the furniture are replaced.

The Indian lady seems a bit distracted and flinches at every movement. So, when Louisa returns, Jane asks again if she's sure this is a convenient time and says that they're only passing through.

Louisa looks at Savitri, who gives her a weak smile.

She sits down a takes a deep breath.

'Well, actually…'

Jane and Sandy share quick glances.

Louisa gives them a quick summary of the terrible events they've just been through, but without telling them about Fletcher, as she assumes he'd like them to leave him out.

'Oh dear,' says Jane. 'How awful.'

'The worst thing is not being able to do anything,' says Louisa, while now wondering what he is getting up to.

Jane shakes her head and then glances at her watch.

'We must go, Sandy. I've said we'll be at Alex's for half four.'

She gives Louisa a sad smile.

'But if there is anything we can do, you must say. We're staying in Berwick tonight with some friends.'

Louisa shakes her head.

'The police seemed baffled, but I'm sure they're doing their best.'

Five minutes later they're in the car driving away, but she tells him to pull in at the first lay-by.

She sits still for a few moments staring out of the window.

'Where the hell has he taken her?' she rasps.

Sandy stares out of the window. It's raining again.

'You've got his mobile number. Call him.'

She glares at him.

'Then he'll know we're after him.'

'How about if I call him?'

She stares back at him.

'He'll just ignore it. He won't recognise the number.'

He nods, but then turns to look at her.

'Are you sure? I've got a gizmo on this that can check where someone's calling from within seconds. If I can keep him talking long enough I'll be able to get it to work. And, best of all, he won't be able to see where I'm calling from.'

She frowns.

'Why not? Give it a go.'

She tells him the number. He taps it in, presses send and taps the sound enhancer.

It rings.

'Yeah?' says a voice, which she instantly recognises. And shudders.

'Hi, Dave,' says Sandy.

There's a pause. Sandy holds his breath.

'Who is this?'

'Dave. It's Mike, where are you?'

The line goes dead.

Jane frowns at him.

'Was that long enough?'

Sandy taps and scrolls away.

'Gotcha!'

He shows her the screen.

A blue dot flashing on map. He pulls the focus out so that she can see some names, including Hawick.

'Where is that?' she asks.

He pulls it out further and points at another dot flashing.

'That's us,' he says pointing at it.

He taps a few more times and the two dots are joined by a wriggly blue line, which says 43 miles and 68 minutes.

She stares out of the window.

'He'll be armed . . . and I mean machine guns. Long range rifle and the rest.'

Sandy grins.

'Aren't we all?'

She gives him a serious glare.

'This will be it. Terminal.'

Sandy shrugs.

'What's not to like about that.'

She continues to stare at him and then looks away.

'Okay, let's do it.'

Janet Becket is used to unprepared and awkward ups and downs in her life. You know the sort of thing where you open a door expecting smiling faces glad to see you, to find some thug waving a gun at you with his hand round the neck of your friend.

Well, it wasn't that bad, because we do smile and then Freya gives her a hug, which surprises her even more.

'What's going on?' she asks, with what you could only call a dubious frown.

Before we can even begin to explain, Ziggy's shouting at his screens.

'Bastards!' Is the only intelligible word.

Janet shakes her head.

'Same old same old,' she breathes and puts her bag down.

Freya and I look at each other asking who's going to try and explain.

I shrug at her and she sighs.

'Well . . .'

I have to say she's very succinct.

'So, some guy's kidnapped Fletcher's granddaughter, the one with the scary green eyes, and now he and the rest of the world are screaming around the Borders trying to find them.'

Freya nods.

'And . . .' continues Becket, wondering if she should be finding her gun straight away.

Ziggy calls out.

'Do you know the road from Hawick to Newcastleton?'

'Where?' asks Becket.

'Did you bring your car?' he asks.

'No,' she mutters, knowing full well he won't even hear that.

'Armed and dangerous?'

She looks at us and shakes her head again.

'I reckon fifty-five minutes, you'll probably do it in forty-five,' comes the disembodied voice.

She shakes her head again.

'Are you serious?'

'Never more so. The girl will become superfluous at some point. I'm not sure what he thinks she knows that he doesn't know.'

Again, she stares at us.

'Is this just me? The Lone Ranger again?'

'Nah. I think Magda and her bag carrier are on their way. But they're starting from Berwick so they'll take over an hour and drive more slowly than you, and they don't know where they're going.'

Janet stares at us in disbelief. But she finds her bag and searches though it until she pulls out her gun wrapped in its holster.

She looks at us two and we both shake our heads.

'Fine,' she says, taking a wire out her pocket. She sticks it in her phone and then the other end in her ear, while walking through to where Ziggy's encased in wires and machinery.

She tests the connection with Ziggy and then hesitates.

'Hang on a minute. How do you know where she is?'

'Uncle Rollo.'

She frowns.

'Who he?'

'An old rocker I know, who happens to be the young lady's uncle.'

Becket stares at his hunched back.

'And?'

'He's the one who put a tracker and protection on her laptop.'

'Why?'

Ziggy shrugs.

'I guess he thought this might happen one day.'

Becket persists. She is after all a retired, or what she prefers to call an 'asked to go quietly' DS.

'Why?'

Ziggy now swivels round to face her.

313

'Because the young lady has ancient secrets, which some people would torture and kill her to acquire.'

We're now all staring at him. And trying to ignore the dishevelled state he's in, the black rings round his eyes and the disconcerting mixture of costumes he's wearing.

Janet looks back at us and shrugs her shoulders.

'Ancient secrets?'

'Think Holy Grail.'

She looks at us again with a look of disbelief.

'Is this for real?'

We do a collective shrug.

'Why does this happen to me?'

I give her what I assume looks like a wan smile.

'Yeah, right,' she sighs. And then without another word she's gone.

I close the door.

We can hear Ziggy talking to someone else. Probably Fletcher.

Mayhem would seem to be the most likely outcome.

Only glad we're here, not out there, up in the hills.

～

Tomasz was coming down to the Spittal turning when an unmarked car sporting a blue flashing light cuts right across the A1 junction and speeds off west.

He turns right to follow them. This causes Imelda to bang her head as she wasn't expecting to turn that way, nor at such last-minute acceleration.

She screams and holds her forehead.

'What the—?' she yells, then realises she's bleeding.

She shows him the blood on her hand, but he ignores her.

She curses and finds a cloth.

Following a police car isn't the easiest thing in the world, but he now settles down to just keeping up.

Imelda's forehead has stopped bleeding, so he indicates the map that they found in the car.

She scrabbles through it and glances outside a few times until she sees a road sign with a number.

After finding the road she puzzles at where they might be going. At the moment it's towards the A697, which would take them south to Newcastle, so probably not that way. Or north to Kelso?

Straight ahead are lots of tiny roads through the Cheviot foothills. Not sure they're going to get anywhere fast through there.

But that's the way Magda's going.

So what's the hurry?

Where's the action?

Who are the bad guys?

⁓

Hollis stares at the phone.

Who was that?

He tries to source it.

Blocked.

Meaning someone's on the way already.

He curses.

'We've got to go.'

Gerd looks at him.

'Who was that?'

Hollis looks at him.

'Have you got an alternative hideaway?'

Gerd nods.

'Of course.'

'We gotta go.'

He glares at him, hesitates.

Gerd produces what looks like a WW2 Sten gun out of nowhere.

'Well, you'd better get started, then,' he says quietly.

Hollis stares back at him.

'I don't know who you are or why you stopped here, OK?' says Gerd.

Hollis nods and then grabs Ellie by her arm.

'And you didn't even see the girl, right?'

Gerd shakes his head.

'Come on. We're off to find the wizard,' he says with a snarl.

She tries to pull away, but he hits her across the face again. She screams. He punches her in the guts. She would have fallen, but he drags her to the door.

Outside he half-carries and half-pushes her to the car, opens the damaged boot and forces her in. She lies there groaning and holding her stomach. He finds some rope and ties the boot shut as best he can.

Gerd watches from the doorway. His eyes are slits in his face. He's holding the gun, which he's pointing at Hollis all the time.

He watches as he gets into the car.

It jumps forward and then sets off, but then comes to a juddering halt. Hollis climbs out of the car. He waves and with his other hand he throws something towards Gerd, who fires a couple of shots before ducking back inside just before there's huge explosion. Hollis gets back in the car, laughing and accelerating away at the same time.

'Bloody Germans,' he screams as he changes gear and swerves left onto the road.

Ellie's groaning in the boot of the car. She's hardly conscious. Can't tell whether her cheek hurts more than her chest.

At the top of the hill Hollis calms down and concentrates on driving as fast as he can on the long, winding descent.

It's only as he sees the derelict railway coaches that he remembers they're still there. On just a few hundred yards of the old railway line, being kept alive by a bunch of spotter nerds. How sad is that in the middle of nowhere?

⟿

Becket is the first to arrive at Gerd's.

It's not as if she hasn't arrived before at places that have already been blown up or occupied by an enemy known or unknown.

She pulls up at the edge of the clearing.

She notes the recent crater and the damaged pieces of what might have been a Land Rover. There's no other vehicle in sight, so maybe the bird has flown.

She checks with Ziggy.

It's a poor connection.

'I'm here but there's no sign of them, although there's a mangled Land Rover still smoking.'

'Reg?' asks Ziggy.

She looks through her binoculars and reads it out.

There's a pause.

'Gerhard Ritter,' he mutters.

She waits, knowing that he'll be doing a lot of multitracking.

'OK,' he says. 'That's interesting.'

She sighs.

'Don't tell me. He's a spy.'

Ziggy laughs.

'No, just a hacker. Been arrested a few times, but they've not been able to pin anything on him. He's code red, meaning he's a potential high-security risk.'

She grunts.

'So what do we do?'

'Leave him alone. He's probably armed, and he's the sort to lay mantraps and other devices.'

'You mean the bird has flown?'

'Not far. Heading south.'

Becket reverses carefully, avoiding a big ditch.

Inside the shed Gerd relaxes.

But if this person has found him there will be others following, so it'll be best to disappear for a while.

He gathers what he can't do without and goes out of the back door. His nearest hideaway is only an hour's walk away.

⁓

'I've lost him,' says Sandy, as they come to a halt in what Jane is thinking the middle of nowhere.

'Where's he going?'

He shrugs, looks at the map.

'It looks like he's going back down south. This road will take him eventually to Carlisle.'

She shakes her head.

'No, I don't think so. This is all about whatever's at Dryburgh. This is just a diversion.'

He frowns, thinking,

'Why up here?' Apart from there being a terrible connection.

'Give me the map,' she says in a commanding tone.

He hands it over, fearing the worst. Her temper isn't something he likes, although he isn't averse to the sex that often follows. Even thinking of that possibility is enough to arouse him enough to require a bit of adjustment.

She frowns at this and then laughs.

'You're safe up here. It's too bloody cold.'

He grins sheepishly, but then points back down the valley.

'Is that the cavalry?'

She squints into the distance.

'Drive on,' she urges him. 'Find us somewhere else. See who else is following. If they've tracked him this far, they've probably got a better tap on his movements.'

⁓

Five minutes later Rico pulls off the road and points at the mast.

'Is that where they are?'

But Magda is talking to Ziggy.

'Yeah. We can see it.'

She listens again.

'OK, we're on our way.'

She nods up the hill.

'They've gone on and are just cutting back over to the A7.'

Rico frowns.

'So why come up here?'

She shrugs.

'No idea. Diversionary?'

He looks back down the road before pulling out, thinking,

'This is a waste of time. Why don't they catch up with them and take them in for questioning?'

He glances at Magda but she's staring out the window. What's she thinking about?'

Mrs K has given in and contacted a cleaning firm before going home.

Louisa merely nodded her head.

She's not even sure she can ever go back into that room and is actively thinking of other arrangements. It's not as if there aren't other possibilities. The usage hasn't changed since John died.

She pours herself a stiff G & T, knowing Savitri won't have one, and goes into the conservatory. Generally this enough to calm her, no matter what is happening elsewhere. But it doesn't seem to work this time.

Everyone else is rushing about trying to find, save and protect Eleanor, but it's her obsession that has brought this down on herself. Sometimes the look in those green eyes is frightening. She's only just twenty years old, for heaven's sake. Most of her contemporaries are worrying about their hair and not going out for the last year or so.

She senses movement behind her, a rustle of silk.

She turns to find Savitri standing in the doorway.

'Are you all right?' she whispers.

Louisa summons a weak smile.

'Yes, of course, only wishing for a quiet life.'

Savitri stares at her for a moment and then a smile appears.

'Not the Lady Cunninghame I know,' she says.

Louisa has to laugh.

'Maybe I'm getting old.'

Savitri shakes her head.

'Not the woman I'm looking at.'

Louisa laughs again.

The two of them embrace.

Back in the room, Savitri goes back and picks up one of her books.

'I'm not sure, but I think I've found something rather exciting. Although it's been in front of us all the time.'

Louisa frowns.

'What do you mean, "exciting"?'

Savitri beckons her over.

She points at a picture in the book and then picks up another book and opens it at a page she's turned down.

The first picture is a copy of a painting, which Louisa recognises. She knows it's quite famous, because it shows Walter Scott sitting with a gaggle of other famous writers and painters he's gathered at Abbotsford.

It's very posed.

The other painting is of the same vintage, but she doesn't know it or who the people are.

She looks at Savitri.

'This one you know, yes?' she says, pointing at the Abbotsford gathering.

Louisa nods.

Savitri points to the other one.

'This was painted at about the same time, but it's set in a house in Massachusetts.'

Louisa frowns. Her knowledge of US history is non-existent, she realises. Is that after the War of Independence?

She looks back at Savitri.

'What's the significance?'

Savitri pointed at one of the men in the second painting.

'This is David Erskine, Earl of Buchan.'

Louisa gives her a stern look.

'You mean Scott's friend?'

Savitri nods, and then turns a page in the first book to show the ruins of Dryburgh.

'Yes, they're buried a few yards from each other,' she says quietly.

Louisa smiles.

'Everyone knows that.'

Savitri makes a face.

'They were friends, but Erskine went a bit mad before he died. Scott even made a joke about the way he was laid in his coffin.'

Louisa nods. She's heard that story, but she's puzzled by why Savitri is showing her these pictures.

Savitri, her eyes shining, now gives her a strange look.

'But what else can you see in these paintings apart from the people?'

Louisa does as she's asked.

She can see a painting on the wall above a fireplace, and on a table to one side there's something like a large vase or an urn. But that's all.

She points at them.

Savitri gives her a strange look, but then without another word produces a different book and opens it at the same image, but without any colour.

'This was an earlier sketch.'

Louisa stares at it.

'Look at the vase,' whispers Savitri.

Louisa looks again and then shakes her head. There's only a much smaller vessel. A dish? She can't tell what it's made from. Is it decorated?

She looks at Savitri, who offers her a magnifying glass.

Up close she can see a swirling pattern. Waves?

She looks back at Savitri and frowns again.

'What are you saying?' she asks.

'What if I tell you that I recognise that pattern?'

Louisa's getting a bit frustrated now.

'Which is?'

'It's Jewish script. Or, to be more exact, Aramaic.'

Louisa shivers, but doesn't know why. She's not been to church for years.

'*Mia chi*. It means "living waters". It's a reference to at least two stories in the Bible but is generally quoted from the Gospel of John, where Jesus was talking to a woman who is fetching water.'

Louisa is completely lost now.

'What are you telling me?'

'What would you call such a vessel?'

Louisa can't think what she means.

'A bowl? A dish?'

'Think religious,' prompts Savitri.

'Goblet?'

'Older.'

Louisa rubs her forehead. She doesn't want frown lines, but then it dawns on her.

She stares at Savitri and shakes her head.

'You're not serious?'

Savitri just stares at her.

'You mean a chalice?'

Savitri nods again, but then points back at the Erskine painting.

'What do you see here?'

Louisa looks again.

There are more items in this painting. More vases, flowers, framed portraits. A coat of arms. A sword. Even some flags.

She looks back at Savitri, who reaches over and points at the sword.

'What era do you think that sword comes from?'

Louisa hated history at school, because the teacher was a very creepy old lady who smelt of lavender.

'No idea, but it's not a pirate cutlass or a fencing blade,' she offers.

'Twelfth century,' whispers Savitri.

This time Louisa doesn't frown. She just stares.

She stands up and turns away.

'You mean like Richard the Lionheart would have used?' she tries to say, without it sounding ridiculously melodramatic.

'Exactly,' comes the cold reply.

Louisa goes over to the drinks cabinet and pours herself a large Scotch.

Her head is whirling.

She turns to look back at Savitri, who is sitting looking at the photos.

She looks up at Louisa.

'Are you are saying that these two men found a sword and a chalice at Dryburgh dating from the twelfth century?'

Savitri nods.

'It's more amazing than that. If Ellie's right, they are two of the four items mentioned in the document her great-aunt gave her.'

Louisa comes to sit down with her.

'So whose sword is it…? And what's the…?'

She can't say the words.

Tears are rolling down Savitri's face.

CHAPTER 19

THE ABBEY

What happens over the next ninety minutes is difficult to comprehend afterwards.

We're on the side-lines, not watching – Ziggy hasn't managed to set up the multi-screened tracking system yet – but we are following the various race competitors as they all, we soon realise, head to the abbey.

Dryburgh.

It's a ruin.

So is this a buried treasure hunt?

I found a book about it on one of the shelves in the house.

I doubt it's been opened for some time, and it is an ancient book. Only black-and-white photos.

Walter Scott is buried there instead of at Abbotsford.

I visited the house after the lockdown was lifted last year. Jam-packed with Japanese and American tourists wandering about, listening to some actor playing Sir Walter.

It's also absolutely crammed with books, as well as having a whole room full of guns and swords. In fact the man was an obsessive collector of all sorts of things. Basically anything old. Even Roman stuff stolen from Hadrian's Wall.

Not sure why he's buried at Dryburgh. There was plenty of space in his own gardens.

Apparently, after he died, the funeral cortège meandered there from Abbotsford with a huge crowd following all the way up to Scott's View, which looks out at the Eildon Hills, and then they went back down to the abbey.

It's only afterwards that we learnt the first party to arrive were Louisa, Fletcher and a little Indian lady called Savitri.

I know. I'm not making it up.

What happened after that was a sort of slow-motion mayhem, which we could only follow via snatches of messages and dots on a screen.

⁓

Fletcher doesn't even get to go to the loo.

As he gets back from Berwick, Louisa hustles him into her other car, where Savitri is already ensconced in the front passenger seat.

Fletcher hates being in the back seat but Louisa is at her snappiest, so he's not up for a fight with her in that mood.

'Where are we going?' he asks, trying to sound as peevish as possible, knowing Louisa hates whining from the back seat.

'Back to the twelfth century,' she snaps.

He just stares at the back of her head. What can he say?

'I meant place, not time,' he manages.

'Dryburgh Abbey,' Savitri helpfully explains. Although she's not sure she's up for what might turn rather unpleasant, to say the least.

'Well, it's too rainy for a seance,' he mutters.

It only takes half an hour or so.

The abbey grounds are still closed to visitors, but the wall is easily scaled.

There are a few cars outside the hotel. Louisa thinks it's been open for people who need to be in the area and are permitted by the government.

They're quickly hidden beyond the fir trees as Louisa leads them to where Sir Walter is buried in one of the few buildings left standing.

Savitri shakes her head.

'If there was anything here, it would have been found years ago,' she says. 'Unless …'

Louisa shakes her head.

'Not necessarily. Burke and Hare were at their business not long after Scott was interred here, so it's possible.'

Fletcher is bemused.

'What are you on about?' he asks.

Louisa looks at Savitri, who shrugs her permission to relay what she's just revealed to her.

Fletcher tries hard to follow what Louisa and Savitri are trying to tell him, but he can't concentrate because he's getting desperate to empty his bladder.

They've just got to the point of explaining about Hugh de Morville when he puts up his hand and sets off to find a big enough tree to stand behind.

When he's sighing with relief he sees that the two women have gone to stand beside one of the few bits of the abbey that are still vertical.

He wanders over, not looking forward to another history lecture.

'This is Scott's grave,' says Louisa, 'and Erskine's is over there.'

'Who went first?' asks Fletcher, thinking he needs to get some order into this investigation, even if it is only for himself.

Louisa frowns at him, but Savitri puts her hand on her arm.

'Erskine died in 1823, then Scott followed in 1832,' she said.

Fletcher nods.

'So have they ever been dug up?' is his next question.

The two women look at each other.

Savitri shrugs.

'Not to my knowledge. Why do you ask?'

'Just wondering, that's all,' he says, and looks around.

It's quiet, just the odd crow cawing above them and a slight breeze rustling the branches. Deciduous trees? It's started raining again, only a light drizzle, but getting stronger.

But, as they stand still, there are few more birds beginning to chatter and call at one another.

'And why are we here again?' he asks, wondering why the two women aren't being very communicative.

Louisa sighs and looks at Savitri, who then quietly tells her story.

When she's finished Fletcher is left staring at her.

He looks again at the mausoleum.

'Are you seriously suggesting that the Holy Grail is in that tomb?'

She shrugs.

He shakes his head.

'You've been watching too many *Indiana Jones* films,' he mutters.

She smiles.

'Try telling your granddaughter that.'

He looks back at her, knowing she takes Ellie seriously, which then leads to wondering what's happened to her.

'But if that guy thinks she knows all this, why hasn't he brought her here?'

Louisa sighs.

'I think he's got it,' she intones.

He looks from one to the other of these two women. One tall and still elegant, the other small and neat.

'Only … he was last tracked taking her into the hills, in completely the opposite direction.'

'Yes, that is confusing. Maybe it's a diversion. To give himself time to "persuade" Ellie to tell him what she knows.'

Fletcher glares at her.

'If he—' is all he can manage. He looks away.

They stand in silence. Even the birds are quiet. Just a breath of cold wind to make them shiver … or is that something else?

'So what's your plan?' he asks looking at one and then the other.

'I think that's your department, Michael,' says Louisa huffily.

Thinking he's too old for this, he shakes his head.

Savitri shivers again. Louisa puts her arm around her.

Fletcher grunts.

'OK. Let's go back to the car, get out of this rain.'

～

Becket is putting her foot down.

Ziggy's figured out where the shoot-out is going to be.

Why does he have to act as though he's orchestrating a film set?

'How do you know he's going to take her there?' she asks.

'Because that's where the bodies are buried,' comes the reply.

'Which bodies?'

'Scott and Erskine, but more importantly Hugh de Morville.'

'Who?'

'I'll tell you later.'

She growls and tries to remember which way you get through Hawick now. Last time it was all being dug up, diversions all over the place.

The one thing that leaves her cold is digging up dead bodies. The stench always makes her retch. Still, the three he's mentioned have all been dead for hundreds of years already, so they should all be nice clean bones by now.

But that still makes her shiver again.

⌐

Ziggy's switching from one mobile to another.

He's just been talking to Becket, and now he's contacted Magda's brother and told him to get back to Dryburgh.

The conversation is brief, and we don't hear the other side of it.

I didn't even know he was in touch with him, and I wonder how Magda will be feeling about that.

Freya rolls her eyes at me.

I shrug.

It's out of our hands now, but it feels like it's going to end violently.

⌐

Fletcher is beginning to fret about what they ought to be doing. That's not normally his first instinct. But if there's going be shooting then he's terrified about what will happen to Ellie, who will be caught up in the middle of it.

He gets on his mobile to Ziggy.

The two women wait as he listens.

When the conversation stops he stares out of the window.

Louisa turns to stare at him.

'Well, what's happening?'

Fletcher sighs.

'Hook thinks they'll all be coming back here.'

He stares at the hotel.

'Do you know the people in there?' he asks.

Louisa sighs.

'I used to, but it's a big chain now. I only went once.'

Fletcher understands the wrinkled nose attachment, so tries a different tack.

'Is there somewhere we could hide out?'

Louisa frowns.

'I think there might be a groundsman's hut somewhere,' she says. 'Over the other side.'

He nods.

'Come on, then, let's go find it.'

~

Tomasz pulls up at the gates of the abbey and stops.

Imelda stares down the drive.

'Is this it?' she asks.

He nods, thinking of his childhood visits. He'd always found it quite exciting. The ruins were a great place for hide-and-seek, although you also had to look out for the gardeners. He remembered how frightened Magda used to be, especially in the ruins.

But this was no use to him now. He needs to be up above the scene.

He reverses the car and drives back along the access road, and then turns up the hillside.

The little car park has had an overhaul. New fences and a smart new sign telling you all about the Wallace statue, which is only a few hundred yards away through the trees.

Imelda gets out and goes to read it.

Tomasz gets his gun.

It's nothing special, but he knows the distance will be fine.

'Do you want to stay here?' he asks.

She stares at him, but then shakes her head.

'No, I'll come with you.'

Although he's heard they've cut all the foliage back from the statue, the vantage point he needs is off to the left.

So they only walk a few yards before he strides off down a farm track.

She follows.

It's also only a slightly longer distance to the cliff edge, where you can look down over the abbey. It's the only place where you can see how neatly it's positioned in a big bend in the river, which winds nearly three sides around the grounds.

He knows there's a big oak tree right on the edge.

It's still standing, if even nearer to the steep drop than he remembers.

He looks towards the ruined buildings.

The chapel where Scott's grave lies is clearly visible. Maybe two hundred metres. Relatively simple.

He's brought a length of rope as well, and now he winds it round the much slimmer beech tree to the left of the big tree. Puts the gun through a loop and turns it three times until it's held firmly. Sights up the shot and then loads the gun.

Imelda watches all this silently.

She's never seen him prepare for a shot before, although she's watched him practising up at old Tom's farm.

He doesn't speak. A quiet man doing a quiet job. Although that makes her shiver. He is, after all, a professional assassin.

It looks a long way away to her. But she knows that this is what he's good at, while reflecting how different this personality trait is to what he's like otherwise.

Satisfied, he sits down on a fallen log and stares into the distance.

It's only then that he notices a strip of police blue and white tape caught on a fence. What's that about?

Imelda goes to sit next to him.

He almost flinches, but then turns and smiles at her.

But not with his eyes.

They're the same blue as they always have been … but now they're different.

Somehow dead.

Time passes.

But slowly.

↬

The pain in Ellie's stomach has dulled, and although her cheek feels swollen the throbbing has stopped.

The monster who's driving the car is cursing and swearing at other drivers. This only stops when he's driving fast, so she's guessing that they're out of whichever town that was and are now powering along what seems quite a straight road.

The broken boot lid allows her to see the hedges and trees zooming past, but she's too afraid to move very much in case her chest hurts.

The only comfort is feeling the ring in the hem of her sweater.

He might think he's got what he needs, but he hasn't.

Whatever he plans to do – and now she's sure where he's heading, even if she can't see it – she knows this can only get worse.

What is she going to do?

If he knows what Savitri has worked out then he's going to come unstuck, because he's only got one of the four pieces … and even that might not work.

So how's he going to react when it doesn't work?

She shivers.

Tries not to cry.

Fails.

↬

DS Gatti is getting more and more worried.

He glances across at Magda.

She's staring out of the windscreen, but he knows she's not seeing what's ahead.

She's already at Dryburgh in her head, planning how they're going to play this.

They should have already called for backup. This mad stubbornness is going to end badly.

He coughs.

She glares at him.

'Not yet,' she almost snarls.

'The last thing we need is the cavalry coming over the hill. Especially led by General DCI Custer,' she adds, with a worryingly mad laugh.

They're not even armed, and the person they're chasing seems to have access to both guns and explosives.

He grits his teeth.

A brief flash of his wife's angry face makes him shiver.

～

There isn't any tumbleweed rolling down the drive, but Dryburgh Abbey car park is eerily silent.

There are four cars.

One of them is Louisa's.

But it's empty.

The three previous occupants are now huddled in the shed beside the groundsman's hut, which affords a slightly blocked view of the abbey ruins.

The birds seem to be aware of something about to happen, but there is the occasional fluttering of wings and a little chatter.

In the distance there's the sound of a car.

It arrives and pulls up in the car park, and the handbrake is applied.

Apart from the gentle patter of the rain, it's quiet.

The door opens quietly and a tall figure steps out.

Ex-DS Janet Becket stands up straight and looks around. She's wearing a jacket, so no one watching would be able to see the gun in its holster.

She looks at the silent hotel.

There's no one coming out to greet her.

She looks over at the abbey kiosk, which is clearly closed.

As she walks to the wall she can see the red stone ruins through the trees.

She takes out her phone and makes a call. It's brief.

She waits for a few minutes, gets another call back and looks towards the ruins again.

'Where's that, then?' she asks quietly.

She nods and pockets the phone. Then reaches into the car and finds a pair of binoculars before climbing the wall and making her way to the gardener's shed.

Having found the three people hiding there, she discusses what they should do.

Fletcher is relieved to have some backup but is still of a mind to call for the cavalry. Becket is a little surprised about this. Not Fletcher's style at all, and certainly not hers.

This debate is cut short with the gravel-spitting arrival of a white car with a damaged boot.

Through her binoculars Becket can see a figure sitting still in the driving seat.

She hasn't been given a description, so has no idea if this is the guy they're expecting.

They wait.

He gets out of the car.

Looks all around

Goes to the boot.

Unties the ropes keeping it shut.

Reaches inside and pulls a thin figure out and pushes her forward.

She stumbles, nearly falls, but manages to stagger to the wall. Her left face is badly bruised and she's holding her right side.

The man has produced a gun and now waggles it at the girl, who gingerly climbs the wall.

He leaps over after her and pushes her through the bushes.

From above Tomasz follows them through the fir trees. His target is hidden by some of the hotel chimneys and now by the trees.

He's hoping that when they get to the ruins he'll have a better view.

He's still not managed to get a close-up view of either of them yet, so isn't completely convinced of who he thinks they might be.

It's also just then that Imelda taps him on the shoulder and points to another car arriving down the drive.

It stops halfway to the house, and a man and a woman get out.

'What's he doing here?' thinks Tomasz, instantly recognising ex-Corporal Franks. Last time he saw him was in Iraq. Bit of a clever shyster. Made a lot of mullah on the side.

The woman also looks familiar, but he can't place her, although she's the sort of eye candy Franks would go for. Long black hair tied back. Short skirt. Long legs.

He turns back to see where the man and the girl have got to.

They're inside the ruins already.

The man, he's sure now, is Hollis. He's pushing the girl along. Now he's grabbed her and is shaking her this way and that. She falls to the ground. He kicks her.

Tomasz lines up a shot, but Hollis disappears behind a pillar.

He waits. Glances back toward the other couple, who are now making their way towards the ruins.

Is this a planned meeting? Do they know each other? He watches.

The new couple soon get to where Hollis sees them.

It's the woman who seems to know him.

They seem to be shouting at each other.

Franks has now produced a gun.

Tomasz doesn't know what to do and can't hear what they might be saying.

He curses in frustration.

At the gardener's shed, the three people are uncertain what to do.

Louisa points to the arrival of Jane and her companion.

'What are they doing here?' she rasps.

Fletcher frowns.

'Do you know her?'

'Yes,' she whispers. 'I was at school with her mother.'

'And?' he asks.

'She married some rich guy. Rumour has it that she's leeched him to the bone, although I've never met him.'

'And the man with her?'

'I don't know him. He's her latest dalliance, I presume. They called in yesterday.'

As Tomasz watches it becomes clear that the woman and the man are having an argument. He's frustrated because Hollis keeps moving in and out of view, which makes a definite hit uncertain. He can only wait until this falling-out is resolved one way or another.

In the event it's resolved by Ellie making a run for it. Not as fast as she could normally run, but quick enough to evade Hollis's first shots.

But then the woman goes up behind him and berates him. Hollis turns and points the gun at her, but then there's a stand-off as Franks is pointing a gun at him.

The woman carries on berating him and then slaps him.

But then they realise that Ellie is getting away, so they all go after her.

Tomasz can't follow them as they disappear into the trees.

Down at ground level Ellie is racing for her life. Despite the throbbing cheek and the aching chest she heads for a bank of rhododendron bushes, but is then startled to see someone coming through them towards her.

Afterwards she could only describe him as pale-faced and oddly dressed, because she turned to see if her assailants were still coming. She also said that she somehow knew this man was going to save her.

Which he did.

But what she swears happened next was unbelievable.

The man had now unsheathed a sword. Not long, but heavy, with a flat blade.

The three assailants came one after the other through the trees.

The blade flashed and glittered in the bright shafts of sunlight, which made her hide her eyes.

There were screams and yells of pain and one shot, but it was all over in a few seconds.

When she took her hands away, she gasped in horror at the carnage.

Three bodies still twitching, but unmistakably butchered.

She fell to her knees and hid her face.

A hand touched her shoulder.

She looked up at the man's face.

He was dark-haired with a moustache and a beard, but had a pale face and empty eyes.

But it was his expression she would never forget.

Was it a smile or a wince of pain?

He only said a few words.

In Occitan. Very old Occitan.

'The Lord keep you safe.'

Then he backed away and melted into the bushes.

CHAPTER 20

CARNAGE

The next day, when Gatti was writing up his report into what they found when they arrived at the murder scene, he looked up the words *carnage* and *slaughter*.

Of course he knows the Italian word for flesh or meat, but the only other place he'd seen anything like it was when he was in a team raiding an abattoir suspected of harbouring a gang of drug dealers.

They arrived at the hotel car park probably only a few minutes after it had happened.

They found Louisa and Savitri cowering in a gardener's shed, and then Fletcher holding on to the shuddering figure of his granddaughter.

Fletcher pointed off into the trees, where they went and found the bodies.

Or rather the parts of bodies. There were chunks of flesh and entrails splattered all around.

He only just managed to control his revulsion, but Magda staggered away and was violently sick.

He called for backup.

Who on earth did this?

Who could even do such a thing?

None of the immediate potential witnesses, for sure.

And what sort of weapon?

He decided that the hotel was the best place for them, so he quickly organised this.

Thankfully the backup arrived within ten minutes, and he was able to tell them what he'd seen … which was nothing other than the aftermath.

The whole of the hotel and the abbey grounds were all sealed off.

The staff were all questioned. Nothing.

Most of the potential witnesses hadn't seen the actual murders. And the two who had weren't speaking.

Ellie because she was in deep shock. Eyes staring or crying. Her mother and father were on their way.

The other person had gone home to his mother, taking the shocked Imelda with him. She'd only seen the flurry of activity at a distance, while he'd seen it in all its gory close-up. He'd obviously seen such things many times, but never someone wielding a sword like that.

The following day DCI Irvine organised a thorough search of the grounds.

The SOCO team carried out their meticulous examination of what was quite a large area, including the abandoned car belonging to the dead woman. They also took away the car with the damaged boot.

They were unable to find any weapon that could have accounted for such terrible wounds, but a weapons expert had been asked to come down from Edinburgh University to examine the bodies.

No one present at the events had been interviewed yet, but it was on that day's agenda.

After discussing it with the superintendent, DCI Irvine decided to start with Mrs Cunninghame, who seemed the one to be the least shocked.

Louisa knows that Magda doesn't rate this man, so gives him a stern look.

He's decided to be direct, having heard from other sources that she can be rather waspish with officials. He's also agreed to conduct this interview at her home, which he has to acknowledge is rather grand.

'Would you go over what happened yesterday at the abbey?' he asks.

She looks away.

He shuffles in his seat.

'Can I start with asking you why you were in the abbey grounds?'

The pale blue gaze held his for a few seconds.

'As I've already told your people,' she snaps, 'we thought the kidnapper might bring Eleanor back there. And we were right.'

'Why didn't you tell us that?'

Louisa sighs.

'Because finding a convoy of police vehicles there would have put him off or put Eleanor in more danger.'

He frowns.

'We are capable of being inconspicuous, madam,' he says quietly.

She merely raises her eyebrows.

He coughs.

'So you waited until the man arrived with her?'

She nods.

'Then what happened?'

'Well, we only saw them when they were well into the grounds.'

He waits.

'We didn't actually see the other man...'

He frowns.

'We just heard the screams...'

She looks away.

'Whose screams?' he asks.

'Eleanor's and the other woman's, I think. Maybe even a man's. Difficult to tell.'

He waits.

'Did you see the attacker?'

She shakes her head.

He hesitates.

She looks back at him.

'If and when Eleanor is able to talk to you, I'm pretty certain that she'll say it was a man who has been dead for over eight hundred years, so...'

He stares at her.

She stares back at him.

⁓

Magda looks at Tomasz.

He's just told her what he saw.

While she can believe him, it's still incomprehensible.

'This man who wielded this sword, how was he dressed?'

Tomasz frowns.

'It was only a brief flash. The lens only gives you a tiny window to see through, even though it's very enlarged. It's not much use for tracking something moving as fast as he was.'

She nods. She's looked through one at the rifle range.

'Grey cloth ... long hair and a beard, I think. A bit like those pictures of Robinson Crusoe...'

She waits. He shrugs and turns away.

'The sword?'

He puts out his hands to show a length of about two feet.

'As far as I can tell he was using it one-handed, slashing this way and thrusting the other ... like you see in the movies... I looked away.'

She stares at him. Eye to eye.

'Yes,' he nods. 'Even me. I've never seen anything like that. Blood and guts flying about.'

She waits again.

He puts his head in his hands.

She reaches out.

He flinches.

She goes to him and holds him.

⌒

It's now two weeks since the bloody massacre at the abbey.

The local newspapers have finally got other things to talk about.

Magda is back at work after a week of leave.

Tomasz and Imelda are ensconced upstairs. They rarely go out.

Magda has serious misgivings about them staying there, but she's knows the case against Tomasz is flimsy at best. And, even if he hands himself in, the powers that be down south have too much other trouble on their hands to bother unearthing potential further embarrassment for the embattled government.

Suffice to say, they've got nowhere trying to find the 'ghostly warrior', as Louisa has called him.

Ellie and Mali are now back at her mother's, down south.

She's been seen by a psychologist colleague of her father's, who has declared that she's not making things up, and she continues to insist that she saw a man dressed in grey clothes wielding a sword.

This has been confirmed by a specialist sword maker, who was consulted by the pathologist. In his report he wrote that the shock of the cutting and stabbing was as likely to have caused their deaths as the loss of blood. He reckoned that even the woman would have still been conscious for a short time before bleeding out. After all, no one reached their bodies until Fletcher forced himself to go and look.

And even that was only a quick glance or two, as he helped a wild-eyed Ellie away from the still twitching remains.

Despite what it means for Ellie's sanity, she is adamant now that it must have been the younger Hugh de Morville protecting the items that she still believes are buried there.

This doesn't sit well with the superintendent and his Presbyterian beliefs, but Magda can't do anything about that. Neither can he account for the complete lack of any evidence of the man the girl insists she saw, even though he must accept she couldn't have possibly carried out the savagery herself. And he has summarily dismissed silly talk about ghosts or opening up the graves of Scott and Erskine.

So she's at a loose end.

For no good reason she's parked her car at the Wallace monument car park and walked to stand next to the statue looking out at the Eildon Hills.

She doesn't hear the man approach, and so jumps when he appears to her left.

He gives her a watery smile and she nods.

They both stand there surveying the view.

He clears his throat.

'You're DS Steil?'

She freezes.

'I saw your photograph in the paper,' he continues.

She turns to look at him.

He's a bit skinny, so she fancies her chances if he tries anything.

'Have you got any further with those dreadful murders?' he asks.

She frowns.

'I'm not at liberty to talk about that,' she says. 'It's an unresolved case.'

He nods.

'Have you got any information that might help our enquiry?' she asks.

He shakes his head.

She stares at him.

He's looking at the view.

'Well, I need to be going,' she says, and goes to walk past him.

'No, but I do know something about the other body.'

She stops and looks back.

'Which body?'

He nods.

'It was me,' he says quietly.

Now she's really confused.

'You mean you were the man with the sword?'

He turns to look at her.

'A sword?'

She stares at him.

He frowns and looks away.

'All I wanted was to keep her ... love her, but...'

Magda frowns.

For a second she's stumped.

'Who?' she asks, then it dawns on her. But which one?

'There's rosemary. That's for remembrance,' he whispers.

A minute later she's on her mobile, whispering. Tells them where to come but not to use their sirens ... and to come via Scott's View. The irony is not lost on them, but is still a relief in one sense: that the two crimes aren't connected, except by proximity.

And, DCI Irvine, that's two cases closed on her watch.

~

He lived only two streets away from the art teacher's, same Edwardian mid terrace house with the same gloomy staircase and an attic, which is where he'd kept her.

Meticulously clean, no fingerprints of either himself or the girl, but that wasn't necessary as photographs of her covered every wall. One set documenting the slow lengthening of her hair and then another even creepier set of her lying in her grave, which became the stuff of Magda's nightmares for years to come, even worse than seeing the rotting corpse itself.

But the irony of his name being 'Geoffrey Steele', was not amusing to either Magda or Tomasz.

Sir George Alexander Steil's funeral was at the church in Melrose.

Magda and Tomasz's father was hardly a much-loved man but his family were expected to put on a good show, so they did. A limited list of guests, all smugly double-jabbed, despite most nearing the ends of their lives as well.

After all the them have left and the hired help are earning their money, the family gathers on the terrace.

'Family?'

Well, it includes a lot more people, which pleases Helena no end.

She can now look after both her children and their partners and a flock of grandchildren, although she doubts there will be any more … unless they are little dragons or snakes? She shouldn't think that she tells herself, but can't stop a fit of the giggles, which is what you get from drinking too much wine.

But then they all stop to watch the sunset.
When was the last time they saw that?
Red sky at night?
Or, as Amelia's only daughter cries,
'Look, Mummy, the sky is bleeding.'

FOR ANYONE INTRIGUED TO KNOW
MORE ABOUT THE REAL PEOPLE
FEATURED IN THIS NOVEL

Hugh de Morville, the elder, was given the tenure of the Abbey by King David of Scotland, became a monk, died and was buried there.

https://en.wikipedia.org/wiki/Hugh_de_Morville,_Lord_of_Westmorland

His son was one of the murderers of Thomas a Becket and was later a hostage for Richard the Lionheart.

https://en.wikipedia.org/wiki/Hugh_de_Morville,_Lord_of_Westmorland

Richard heart was recovered from the tomb in Rouen Cathedral and examined, but his body was desecrated and removed from Fontevraud Abbey during the French Revolution.

https://www.bbc.co.uk/news/science-environment- 21609783

Rosamund Clifford was Henry the Second's lover and was buried with flowers.

https://en.wikipedia.org/wiki/Rosamund_Clifford

Walter Scott and his friend David Erskine are buried at Dryburgh Abbey and were both complicit in 'romanticising' the ruins.

https://en.wikipedia.org/wiki/Walter_Scott#Financial_problems_and_death
https://en.wikipedia.org/wiki/David_Erskine,_11th_Earl_of_Buchan

The painting Savitri referred to does exist.

https://www.nationalgalleries.org/art-and-artists/8196/sir-walter-scott-and-his-friends-abbotsford

A 'rain of blood' is a recognised meteorological phenomenon

https://en.wikipedia.org/wiki/Blood_rain

Lightning Source UK Ltd.
Milton Keynes UK
UKHW011245221021
392644UK00002B/39